A Bag of Lucky Teeth

An almost true to life novel

VAL BRANDT

First Printing Edition, 2021

ISBN 979-8-48-440144-4

Cover design: Carolyn Patton

Edited by: Angela Jenkins

For Edelayne, who's still teaching me big words,

tricky moves and shocking facts.

A Bag of Lucky Teeth

1. The Bad Patch

I was standing at the window of the room I picked as mine for the week holding two long stockings up to the light and asking Jesus to make them match. When I opened my eyes and they still didn't I put the right hand one down and picked up another one from the pile on the bed. After I got through the whole pile I pushed the Left Hand No Match one as far as I could under the mattress and started over with a different stocking.

My sister Rosy yelled down to the restaurant "She's doing it again." Pretty soon after that I heard Mommy's high heels clicking up the stairs to the guestrooms and one second later she was down the hall and in my room and handing me a brand new pair of long stockings still in the package. She must have taken another twenty-five cents out of the Cash Jar and gone out to the store to buy them without telling Daddy and I felt bad about that but what could I do? "She's just going to put her snow pants on over them anyway" Rosy said but Mommy said "Hush darling, you know Posy's going through a bad patch."

We weren't even coming to Flatte Butte. We were moving to Edmonton so Rosy and me could have Opportunities but right after our restaurant in St. Hildegard sold Daddy heard that The Flatte Butte Hotel was going cheap and he said he could buy it and spruce it up and sell it for enough to give us a better start in Edmonton. "We'll be out of there in six months" he promised.

I came down with Chicken Pox on moving day so I had to stay behind with Grandma and Grandpa and by the time I got to Flatte Butte Daddy was busy tearing up floor boards and Mommy was going at the kitchen with bleach and Rosy was running from school to birthday party to skating rink making friends at every stop. "Poor little tyke" Daddy said when they found me hiding under a bed.

Mommy took time out from scraping grease off the back of the big stove to turn one of the guestrooms into a playroom and go out and find some other kids who weren't old enough for school yet that could come over to play. I was waiting in the hall when she brought three girls and two boys up the stairs and said "Posy meet Bunny, Bucky, Essie, Diddy and Eleanor." I said "Hello" but they just stood there looking around like they'd never been in a hotel before. Mommy said "Have fun" and left us in the playroom. By the time she finished clicking down the hall the kids started playing so rough all I could do was stand against the wall and hope I didn't lose an eye. I didn't dare move while Eleanor shook the money out of my piggy bank and Bucky dumped my toy box upside down and Essie laughed at my finger paintings but when Bunny and Diddy started fighting over my doll I knew I had to do whatever it took to save her. When I did what I had to do they yelled "NO FAIR" and said they weren't playing with me anymore and left. I wrapped Pansy Daisy up in her blanket and crawled back under the bed with her.

Next day Rosy got me started making a snowman at noon but as soon as she went back to school a bad boy came along and peed on it. When I ran inside to tell Mommy she gave me a five-cent package of Mackintosh Toffee partly to cheer me up and partly I heard her tell Daddy because it was the only thing that would keep me busy and out of her hair for an hour which I guess she needed since it looked like sprucing up The Hotel was going to take more work than Daddy figured.

All week I prayed that my Sunday School class would have well-behaved children and songs I knew the words to. When I got there it was just three of the toy breakers and me. The Sunday School teacher didn't know I was coming so she was short one little lamb Attendance Sticker and an I Love Jesus Valentine.

Monday, February 14, 1949,

Dear Grandma and Grandpa,

This is my first letter ever. I am telling Mommy what to say and she's writing it down and I get to take it to the Post Office myself.

Thank you for the nice Valentine and the one dollar you put in it. It is the only good thing that has ever happened to me in Flatte Butte.

I miss my friends in St. Hildegard who all play nice and I miss your cows especially Wee Teats and Strutter the rooster who likes only me and most of all I miss you.

Love,

Posy

Mommy always steps nice into places but she sort of marched into the Flatte Butte Skating Rink shack and told the Figure Skating teacher Miss Wilma Lutz in a voice that sounded like someone I didn't know that we had come to sign me up for Beginners. Miss Lutz said "I'm sorry but we don't take anyone new after November." Mommy's face must have changed her mind because she said "We might be able to fit her in but it's too late for her to be in the Ice Carnival." Mommy kept on lacing up my skates and said "Oh I'm sure you'll find a small part for Posy" and Miss Lutz said "Well I suppose she could be a Snowflake in the Big Finale but she's only got a week to learn the routine and she doesn't have a

3

costume." "She'll know the routine and she'll have a costume" Mommy said in that voice I never heard before.

"One-two-three skate forward, two-two-three turn, now hold hands and make an arch with your arms, and the back girls skate through." I missed my turn to skate through and when Miss Lutz blew her whistle and yelled that we had to start again I looked over at Mommy. She was standing away from the other mothers and holding the boards with both hands and watching with her eyes half shut the way she does when she's paying close attention. I didn't see the Intermediate Girls bunny hopping towards me until it was too late and when I jumped out of the way one of my blades hooked the skate of the first girl in the row and down they went one two three four five six seven eight.

When we got home Daddy was spraying water from a hose onto a skating rink he'd made out back of The Hotel. Mommy pulled a chair up to the prep table in the kitchen and started drawing lines and circles with a red crayon all over the Saskatoon Star-Phoenix and every minute or so she'd stand up and spin around or make half an arch with her arm or do a little hop and glide somewhere. I spent the rest of the day moving my things to a different room.

Mommy had us on the little rink almost before it was light out next morning. "When the music starts you skate straight over and stand beside the girl with no front teeth. Then you count to three and skate forward. Keep your eye on the tall dark-haired girl over here where I'm standing." "That's Eleanor" I said and Mommy said "Well she's got it right anyway. When she turns you turn. When she puts her arms up you put your arms up." Mommy borrowed the

Snowflake pattern from one of the other mothers and went out and bought the right amount of white cloth and tinsel.

The first thing I saw when I woke up Ice Carnival morning was my finished Snowflake costume hanging in the doorway. Rosy reached it down for me and slipped it over my head and I took one look at myself in the mirror and ran downstairs and spun around and around the table for Mommy and Daddy and then I ran back upstairs to the mirror and then back downstairs in case anyone in the kitchen had missed seeing me. Mommy said she guessed breakfast was out of the question and Daddy said maybe I'd better be a helper carpenter for a while to work off some of that energy.

My first job was holding Daddy's and my toast with jam while he ripped a rotten wood table out of one of the booths. He was carrying it over to the pile of scrap when I hop-hop-hopped on one leg into the empty booth. On the third hop my foot came down on a rusty nail sticking straight up out of the floor. By afternoon I had proud flesh.

It was while Mommy was putting a poultice on my foot which was in her lap and I was wrapping a flat piece of toffee around my back teeth with my tongue that I figured out I had turned into an unlucky girl and that's why the kids broke my toys and the Snowflakes were doing The Big Finale without me and my foot was going to turn black and fall off.

Mommy finally hung the last new guestroom curtain and Daddy finished stocking the kitchen and we all went outside and watched him put up the HOTEL FOR SALE sign. Then Rosy and me put on long evening gowns and high heels and lipstick from our dress-up box and we sat on the new stools at the new counter and I pretended I could read the new menu and whatever we ordered Daddy brought it out from the kitchen on a tray up over his head and when Mommy poured more cream soda in our glasses she said "Will there be anything else Ladies?" And then Daddy got the Wurlitzer going and we danced until my bedtime.

After that when I woke up Daddy was already in the kitchen cooking and he was still there when I went to bed and about all he ever said was "Watch out that's hot" and on top of Mommy serving breakfast, dinner and supper the travelling salesmen played cards in the restaurant at night and kept ordering coffee and pie until they turned in so it got to be my job to keep my own self busy.

Mommy said it wasn't good for Pansy Daisy and me to always be under the counter eating our way through the Mackintosh Toffees. Daddy said he might have an idea. When Mr. Alvarez the bachelor with one leg shorter than the other one that owns Alvarez's Photography and the Movie Hall behind it came in for his supper and I crawled out from under the counter and sat on the stool next to him so he could teach me another magic trick Daddy came out of the kitchen with a pot of coffee and said "So Albi, what would you say to me giving you a free supper every week in trade for you letting Posy into movies whenever she wants?" Mr. Alvarez said "Sounds like a fair deal to me. Tell me Posy what kind of movies would you like to see?" and I said "All of them." Daddy said "Now Posy" but Mr. Alvarez said "I think I might be able to arrange that."

On Wednesdays I went to the Ladies Matinee of Film Favourites From The Past which I watched two times through. I always sat a bit over from the middle on the front bench because smack in the middle is where Miss Paisley sat and you better never be in her spot when she got there. People said she wasn't quite right but Mommy said she was harmless. My favourites are the musicals and since I always pay close attention I know almost all the words to every song in Flying Down To Rio, The Gay Divorcee, Follow The Fleet, Gold Diggers Of 1933 and 1935, and Yankee Doodle Dandy which is the best one of them all. Fridays Rosy and me went together to the New Movie Of the Week plus cartoon two times through and Saturdays I went back by myself and saw it two more times while she did stuff with her friends. I'm pretty sure I've seen every movie ever made and most of them four times.

I heard Mommy say "Oh hi Albi, we don't often see you in here this time of day" and Mr. Alvarez said "Tuesday's my morning to walk up and down Main Street delivering Movie Flyers and my bum leg's acting up worse than usual. I need a coffee and a sit before going on." Mommy said "You should get someone to do that for you" and he said "Yeah but who'd want to work one hour a week for ten cents?" I squeezed myself out from under the counter and gave him my best smile.

When he was done his coffee Mr. Alvarez said "Alright Posy, let's go introduce the Flatte Butte business folk to my new Girl Friday." I said "It's Tuesday" and he said "My mistake, Girl Tuesday" and off we went.

Next Tuesday morning I went to The Flatte Butte Beat newspaper office where Mr. Alvarez gets his Movie Flyers printed up and the lady said "You must be Albi's little Girl Tuesday he told me about" and I said I was and she said "Howdy-doo, I'm Liddy Frisch, Editor In Chief and Head Flunky here at The Beat" and she put the Movie Flyers in a canvas bag and showed me how to hang it by my neck and I delivered them nice and polite to every business folk on Main Street. When I went to Alvarez's Photography to get my ten cents he said he was going to try something new for the next week and if he paid me another ten cents would I be willing to go back out on Thursday with a Special Flyer that says JOIN YOUR FRIENDS FOR SHIRLEY TEMPLE TUESDAY. 3 MOVIES FOR THE PRICE OF 2 and I said I would be willing. When Rosy came home at Noon I told her about the extra ten cents and I think she was a little bit jealous of me getting rich while she's at school.

On SHIRLEY TEMPLE TUESDAY Daddy packed me a boloney and mustard sandwich and a piece of gingerbread cake to eat while I watched Stand Up And Cheer!, Baby Take A Bow and Bright Eyes. Shirley was perfect in all of them. I wish I was her.

It finally got warm enough to make good mud pies out of the muck my skating rink left behind but then I got big heck for tracking half the yard into the kitchen so I was being mad under the counter when I heard such a racket at the front door I peeked out to see what was going on. A tall lady in an ugly coat was holding the door open with her foot and dragging things in after her. I slapped my toffee to the wall and wiggled out of my spot and ran over to help her or at least get a good look at what she was hauling in which turned out to be a big suitcase with lots of stickers on it and a long flat wood box with handles and a thing like the travelers' sample cases except it had a red cross on the lid. Mommy got there first and was holding the door open and saying "You mean no one helped you carry these from the station?" After the lady could breathe again she told Mommy in a strange way I found out later was an English Accent that she needed a room not just for sleeping

8

but to look after patients in. She said she's a Special Nurse, not exactly a Chiropractor but close.

The first thing The Nurse did after Daddy carried her stuff upstairs was walk around town putting up signs telling people to bring their aches and pains to The Hotel. She and me said "Hello" three times on Main Street because SHIRLEY TEMPLE TUESDAY worked so good that Mr. Alvarez had me delivering DON'T MISS TORCHY TUESDAY STARRING GLENDA FARRELL AS TORCHY BLANE, THE SNAPPY SNOOPY NEWS HOUND ON THE TRACK OF A HEADLINE. 3 MOVIES FOR THE PRICE OF 2. When I got back to The Hotel The Nurse had changed into a white uniform and was sitting in a booth waiting for people but nobody came so Mommy started chatting with her like she used to with people at our restaurant in St. Hildegard and pretty soon they were sitting in the booth together and getting along like a house on fire.

Four people showed up next day asking for The Nurse and more started coming after that but she was never too busy to come downstairs a few times a day for a pot of tea and she'd invite me to sit in the booth with her whenever I was nearby which was always. She told me stories about children who wear pinnies and bathing costumes and play in the garden instead of the yard. After her supper she'd stay for more tea and Mommy would pop over for a chat. Sometimes when they were laughing Daddy would come out and say "Sit-Sit" to Mommy and pour people's coffee and work the till until somebody ordered food and he had to go back to the kitchen.

My Flyers must have worked again because half the benches were full up for TORCHY TUESDAY. Torchy was so snappy and snoopy in Smart Blonde I couldn't believe it and then she caught a murderer and a counter fitter in Blondes At Work and Torchy Gets Her Man.

Even though she's a grown-up the Nurse told me that since we're friends I could call her by her first name Beryl which she said isn't spelled like a rain barrel.

Whenever Mommy came and sat in the booth with us I tried not to make a peep because Rosy had taught me if you stay quiet long enough around grown-ups they forget you're there and you hear all sorts of interesting things. That's how I found out Nurse Beryl met Her Jim in a hospital Over There and after The Army sent him back to Canada she came over too and they got married and she looked after him but he died anyway and there didn't seem much point in going back. She sounded so sad I said "Besides you're too brave to just give up and nail the windows shut like Rosalind Russell made Seth do in Morning Becomes Electric." That made her happier.

Nurse Beryl must have finally fixed every ache and pain in Flatte Butte because she waited in her booth until suppertime and nobody came. If you could have seen her and Mommy and me when she said she'd have to move along to another town next day you'd have guessed we'd been friends our whole life.

The bobby pins I asked Mommy to put in at bedtime had fallen out so I had no ringlets in the morning and I was worried I wouldn't have time to go through all my long stockings before Nurse Beryl left to catch her train so I had to take two matching ones out of the dirty wash and I'd accidentally eaten the package of Mackintosh Toffee I was going to give her so I was thinking that now she'd only always remember me as the selfish little girl with stick-out hair and baggy stockings but I made myself as pretty as I could and I quick hurried down the hall.

When I peeked in her door she was folding up a stretcher bed into that long box I wondered about back when she was just a lady in an ugly coat at the front door. "Posy, the very person I was hoping to see" she said "and my what lovely jewellery you're wearing." I said "I'm sorry I ate your goodbye present" but I don't think she heard because she was busy patting a chair in the middle of the room for me to sit down on and saying "Your Mum and Dad gave me fifty cents last night" and if I hadn't stopped to pull my stockings up I'd have gotten all the way there before she said "and they asked me to fix any aches or pains you might have before I go." I said "I'm fine thank you" and I started backing up but she took three steps with those long legs of hers and walked me by the hand to the chair and sat me down in it. "Let me see now" she said "what can I do for fifty cents?" "Please no needles" I asked Jesus in my head with my eyes open. "I could stretch your left leg a certain way and clear up any painful rheumatism you might have. Or I could squeeze your right elbow three times and fix your indigestion. Or I could do the neck crack which for scientific reasons makes you a lucky person, but perhaps I should let you decide." So I picked one. "Pardon?" she said. "The neck crack please."

She took my head very gently in her hands and moved it back and forth slowly and then she quick twisted it to the left and I heard a crack. Right away she patted my cheeks and said "Well that's that" and she let go of my head. "How long before I'm lucky?" "When you stand up it should happen right away" so I did and that exact second the sun came out from behind a cloud and the whole room was full of sunbeams. "Oh!" we both said at the same time.

I didn't feel very lucky standing on the running board saying goodbye to her through the truck window while she gave Mommy a card with her Post Office Box Number in Regina on it so they could keep in touch before Daddy took her to the station.

And I felt even unluckier when I found out the new sign on our front window next to the HOTEL FOR SALE one said FREE ICE CREAM AT 4 O'CLOCK TODAY FOR ALL CHILDREN WITH PARENTS which meant I wouldn't be able to leave my hiding spot from three-thirty until almost suppertime. But then the Power Station man fell off a ladder drunk and maybe broke his leg and the ice cream company delivered only chocolate by mistake and Daddy said I could go with him to haul garbage to the Nuisance Ground so I figured maybe Nurse Beryl's neck crack was working after all.

We were singing so loud when we got back I didn't hear a thing until I pushed open the swinging door from the kitchen into the restaurant and there was every single kid in Flatte Butte and for miles around. I couldn't back up because Daddy was behind me and I couldn't run to my spot under the counter because they'd all see me and next thing I knew Mommy put two chocolate ice cream cones in my hands and said "Take these to the front booth" and I had to walk the whole way in front of everybody but at least I was still wearing my jewellery. When I got to the front booth it was Bunny and Eleanor and they both said "Thank you Posy." For the next while all Rosy and me did was carry ice cream cones and say "You're welcome" and "Would you like another one?" until the mothers waiting by the door started saying to their kids "TIME TO GO. I HOPE YOU'RE HAPPY YOU'VE RUINED YOUR SUPPER" and they all were.

12

2. Thick Thieves

The morning after Nurse Beryl cracked my neck and left town the first two stockings I pulled out of my drawer matched perfect and when I got downstairs Mommy said to quick finish my breakfast because Bunny, Bucky, Essie, Diddy and Eleanor were all out back ready to play nice with me.

After we hadn't heard from Nurse Beryl for quite a long while she up and phoned to see how we were doing. Mommy said "How lovely to hear from you... Uh-huh... I know... Oh you're in Weyburn, that's nice. I lived down there for a while as a child... No it hasn't sold yet... Not even a sniff of interest and we have ads in six different papers... Yes there's always someone knocking at our back door wanting to play... she's so much happier... the six of them have been thick as thieves for weeks."

The day after school was let out for the summer and I got my sister back during the daytime a man came back again to look at The Hotel and after three pots of coffee he up and bought it. Mommy told Grandma on the phone that he is a Vulcher from Regina and she doesn't think we'll lose much money so long as she and Daddy don't count their time.

Bucky was waiting for me downstairs at their front door when I delivered my last ever Movie Flyer to Beddoes Funeral Home. I told him he better take off his Buffalo Bill holster but he said "You know I don't go anywhere without my guns." When we got to Alvarez's Photography Mr. Alvarez wasn't in his shop but he heard the bell tinkle and yelled "IS THAT MY GIRL TUESDAY?" and I yelled "YES IT'S HER" and he said "COME ON BACK TO MY OFFICE" where I'd never been before. After he gave me my ten cents I said

"Mr. Alvarez I have some very bad news for you. Our hotel sold and I'm leaving Flatte Butte for good." He said "Oh no, I'm really sorry to hear that." I said "This is my friend Bucky Beddoes. I could teach him how to be a Boy Tuesday if you like. He's six-and-a-half and he's lived in Flatte Butte his whole life so he knows his way up and down Main Street." Mr. Alvarez said "I've seen Bucky growing up. Hello son how are you?" Bucky didn't answer. I said "Mr. Alvarez is talking to you Bucky" but he just kept staring at a poster on the wall of a big boy in a cowboy suit standing on the back of a galloping horse with one hand holding a six-shooter and the other one waving a rope over his head. I said "BUCKY". He finally turned around and said "Did that used to be you?" Mr. Alvarez laughed and said "Yep that was me at nineteen. Ropin', Ridin', Sharp-shootin' Alberto. I was part of The Alvarez Family Rodeo Show. That is until the day I had a bad fall and shattered my left leg. After that I had to settle for being a photographer on the rodeo circuit" and then it was like I wasn't even standing there because it was just them saying "Where did you live?" "New Mexico but we were mostly on the road." "How old were you when you started?" "Oh four, maybe five." "Did you use real bullets?" "Not when I was firing in the air like that." "What about when you were sharp-shootin'?" "Well yes then I did." "Did you ever shoot an Indian?" "I never shot anyone, especially not an Indian. My Mom is half Navajo. She taught me to shoot." "You looked more like a cowboy than an Indian." "I was both." "Who taught you ropin'?" "My Dad." "What about ridin'?" "Both of them." I don't think they even knew when I left.

After all the supper people left Mommy and Daddy told Rosy and me the biggest and luckiest news we'd ever heard being that before we moved to Edmonton we were going to go off and SEE THE WORLD.

What Daddy was building for us to live in while we saw The World had half the men in town stopping by for a look. It was a little wood house that he said he was going to paint silver to look like aluminum on the back of our truck with room inside for mattresses to sleep on and shelves for our clothes and all our things and a place for his boxes of Stock. When Mr. Cohen who is Essie's Dad who works at his cousin's lumber yard since they got themselves out of Poland came to pick Essie up for supper he told Daddy he should build a cubbyhole for Rosy and me to sleep in that's up a ladder and right out over the cab and Daddy said "What a good idea." Mr. Cohen said now that he can speak English he's going to look for work in a big city like Toronto doing what he did back in Poland which was being an Architect which I knew what that was from Mr. Spider singing "Heigh-ho an Architect am I."

Mommy took us to the Dentist to get our teeth looked at before leaving town which didn't turn out good for Rosy because Dr. Spitzer said she had a cavity that needed filling right away. I asked Mommy if I could go to the Ladies Matinee of Film Favourites From The Past since it might be my last movie ever in Flatte Butte and she said I could.

It was called King Kong and it was so scary that Miss Paisley and me slid closer and closer along the bench until we were holding on to each other for dear life. I forgot all about my honey sandwich and she forgot about her Assorted Peak Freans so we sat and ate them together after the lights came back on. She told me that Fay Wray and her were both born in Cardston Alberta on exactly the same day being September Fifteenth only she was born ten years after Fay was and I told her I was going off to see The World and she told me she saw most of it while she was on Tour being a tap dancer and I told her I'm going to live in Edmonton Alberta and she told me she's moving to Hollywood like the ad promised and I asked her what ad and she said the one in The Winnipeg Free Press saying send a dollar-fifty plus twenty-five cents postage and handling for a booklet and I asked her what booklet and she said it's called Your Stairway To Stardom and I asked her when is she moving to Hollywood and she said as soon as the booklet comes and she finishes doing whatever the Six Easy Steps are and I asked her did she cut the ad out and she reached in her purse and up and gave it to me and I quick hugged her thank you and ran home to show Rosy because I sure wasn't going to stay and see King Kong for the second time. Or ever again.

What happened next was even scarier than King Kong. Mommy and Daddy told me that seven of my back teeth had to be pulled. "NO!" "Better Dr. Spitzer we trust than some stranger in Edmonton." "NO!" "He will nicely put you to sleep without needles and take them all out at the same time." "NO!" "You won't feel a thing." "NO!" "You and Daddy will go to the hospital." "THE HOSPITAL!" "Next Tuesday." "TUESDAY'S MY BIRTHDAY!" "It's the only time Dr. Spitzer could book the hospital before we leave town." "I MIGHT DIE!" "They're only baby teeth." "LET'S WAIT A WEEK!" "The new owner takes over the hotel that day." "OH! OH! OH!" "And then we'll head out to see The World!" "EXCEPT UNLESS I'M DEAD!"

I asked Rosy who was lying down would she please write a letter for me if I tell her what to say and she said "I geth tho but not until after the freething wearth off.

Nurse Beryl McKenna,
A Guest at The Imperial Hotel,
SWIFT CURRENT, Saskatchewan,
Canada.

Wednesday, July 20, 1949

Dear Nurse Beryl,

Lucky I always listen in on the upstairs Guests Telephone because when you called to tell Mommy you are over come with loneliness you told her where you are staying now in case she would like to chat again so Rosy and me knew where to write you fast.

Please answer me right away if you know of anything I can stretch or squeeze or crack that fixes back teeth. Otherwise I am going to be taken to The Hospital on my Birthday next Tuesday and put to sleep.

Your friend Posy

Everybody tried cheering me up. Rosy said "The Tooth Fairy only pays a nickel for front teeth but she pays a quarter for back ones." Daddy said "But not a quarter each for all seven" and Rosy said "Yes a quarter each which adds up to one dollar and seventy-five cents" and I said "That's exactly how much I need for a Your Stairway To Stardom booklet" and Mommy said "Well then that's a miracle isn't it." Daddy said "Maybe hold onto the teeth until we're settled in Edmonton in case the Tooth Fairy can't find you in the camper house." On Sunday night I told my family that cheering me up wasn't working because I was still not one bit happy about going to The Hospital on my Birthday morning and Mommy finally said "Oh alright I'll somehow rustle you up a party for after."

On Monday afternoon a package came Special Delivery for me from Swift Current. In it was a blue velvet jewellery bag with blue satin lining and matching blue drawstrings from Nurse Beryl and on the card she wrote "Happy Birthday Posy. Here is a bag to keep your lucky teeth in."

Mommy was so busy packing she had to order a boughten Birthday cake from The Bakery and when she got back from picking it up she said "When I tried to pay for it Ian Rolheiser said 'Oh no you don't! The Girl Tuesday's cake is on me'" and you could see he put more icing roses on it than he had to.

Dr. Spitzer said he couldn't figure how seven of my back teeth had got rotten so fast and Daddy said neither could he. Then the nurse pulled a bottle-dropper out of a glass thing and put a drop of something on a thing and handed it to Dr. Spitzer and just before he came at me with it I asked Jesus in my head to not let him kill me and then he held the thing over my nose and I don't remember anything else. After I came to and threw up twice I asked the nurse for my teeth and she wiped the blood off of them and put them in my blue velvet bag and Daddy drove us back to The Hotel.

By the time I had my ringlets fixed and my party dress and jewellery on the kids were there for my Birthday Party. I got a Jeanette MacDonald cut-out book, eight coloured pencils, two red satin hair ribbons, a set of water colours and a bag of Licorice All Sorts. Mommy saved a big piece of cake with one of the six candles on it so I could wait and make my wish later in case some bloody cotton batten came out when I blew.

18

I was watching my best friends play pig-in-the-middle on the other side of The Hotel and wishing I had goodbye presents for them when all of a sudden I knew exactly what to do. I yelled "I CAN MAKE YOU AS LUCKY AS ME." They all yelled back "WHAT?" maybe because of the cotton batten. I waited until they were all standing in a circle around me and I said in a voice all smart and brave like Yvonne de Carlo in Salome Where She Danced "I had my neck cracked to make me lucky for scientific reasons and I know how to do it." Essie said "How do you know it works?" and I smiled and let them all look at me and think about Edmonton and the camper house and how I was going off to see The World and pretty soon they were all lined up on the grass and I went to work.

I kneeled down behind Bucky who is bigger than me but no matter how hard I twisted nothing happened so I stood up and bent over and gave his neck a good yank and it finally cracked. Eleanor who was next in line stood up and looked like she was thinking about leaving so I grabbed ahold of her skirt and did my same Yvonne de Carlo voice only slower "You ... will ... be ... lucky ... for ... the ... rest ... of ... your ... life." She sat back down and I took her head in my hands and moved it back and forth and then quick as can be I twisted it to the left and sure enough there was a good crack. I got through Essie and Diddy and Bunny pretty fast after that so I was done everybody by the time their parents came to get them. When no one was looking I took Bucky behind the fence and kissed him on the lips and asked him if he still wanted to marry me and he said "Sure."

Everybody stayed to see us off. Daddy let each kid try out the ladder and·cubbyhole and Eleanor Privett's Dad said "This thing is going to work so good you two should take out a patent on it" and

Daddy and Mr. Cohen laughed. Then Mommy remembered she forgot party bags so she went back into The Hotel and got five Mackintosh Toffees from the Vulcher and I could see by my friends' faces they figured my neck cracking was already working for them.

Then we climbed into our washed red truck with the shiny silver camper house on the back and before we drove off to see The World Mommy rolled down her window and I waved goodbye out of it with one hand and held my bag of lucky teeth with the other one and my five best friends all stood there rubbing their necks and sucking their toffees and looking like there was nobody they would rather be than me.

3. Seeing The World

Wednesday, July 27, 1949

Dear Bunny,

Rosy is writing this postcard since I won't know how until first day of Grade 1. It took so long getting out of Flatte Butte because of my teeth and my party and packing up the camper house and then waiting at Petrov's filling station while Daddy traded him a pickle barrel and a Cuckoo Clock for a tank of gas and a real Russian Samovar that we haven't seen much of The World yet. Mommy says Alberta will be a whole new ball game.

Your friend Posy

Thursday, July 28, 1949

Dear Diddy,

Well Alberta is a whole new ball game. I was just standing beside our camper house in Alberta playing catch with Rosy who was still in Saskatchewan. Supposing you never get this far away from Flatte Butte in your whole life I will explain how we did that. In Lloydminster where we are today the Provincial Border goes smack dab down the middle of town. I will teach you something this interesting every time I send you a postcard.

Your friend Posy

Friday, July 29, 1949

Dear Essie,

This is The Alberta Badlands. The things with lids are Hoodoos and the rest is what's left after ice gets scraped off dead dinosaurs. Daddy traded a man a Flow Blue Chamber Pot for a bone longer than Rosy is tall. The man didn't know where the rest of the dinosaur was because a drunk traded the bone to him for Home Brew. A big kid in Drumheller said where we were standing used to be a big sea with turtles and sharks. Liar liar pants on fire.

Your friend Posy

Saturday, July 30, 1949

Dear Eleanor,

Daddy castrated a colt for free to get us into Medicine Hat Stampede. A mean bull bucked a bull rider off and stomped on him but a Rodeo Clown named Slim Pickens ran right up and teased it so it chased him and let some cowboys get the man who wasn't quite dead out of there toot sweet. We met Mr. Pickens after and he said he's off to Hollywood to be in a movie with Errol Flynn. Daddy said later maybe Slim had fallen on his head a few too many times.

Your friend Posy

Sunday, July 31, 1949

Dear Bucky,

I bet you think this is Buckingham Palace. Well you're wrong as usual. It's The Alberta Temple in Cardston Alberta. When you see it you can't blame the owners for calling it a Temple to show off instead of just The Mormon Church. Daddy says the main difference between Mormons and The United Church is that their God wrote on gold plates for them to have lots *of women and no wine and our God told us on stones to do the other way around.*

Your friend Posy

Mr. Alvarez,
Alvarez's Photography & Movie Hall,
FLATTE BUTTE, Saskatchewan,
Canada.

Sunday, July 31, 1949

Dear Mr. Alvarez,

How are you? I am fine. The other letter in this envelope is for you to give Miss Paisley when she comes in for the next Film Favourite From The Past. Please don't forget. Thank you.

Posy who used to be your Girl Tuesday

Dear Miss Paisley,

You'll never guess where I am so I will tell you. I'm in Cardston Alberta where you and Fay Wray were both born on September 15. People living here brag about 2 things being The Alberta Temple and Fay Wray. I told everybody we met they better get ready for another Cardston movie star by the name of Miss Paisley. I will write you again when we have a house in Edmonton so you can write back to say what Step you're up to on the Your Stairway To Stardom.

Posy from the front bench.

Monday, August 1, 1949

Dear Diddy,

Name any animal in The World and I saw it today even monkeys and baby lions and a new animal called an Armadillo. We were at The Calgary Zoo which we didn't know was there but it was near where we went to see the fancy world famous Bandstand but men were knocking it down to make something better. Daddy said they'll be sorry some day. A monkey threw his stinky poop at my head but it was almost dried so it bounced off except for a bit.

Your friend Posy

Tuesday, August 2, 1949

Dear Essie,

Before we took off to see The World I didn't know there were things that are so ENORMOUS even Rosy who just turned 9 but is going into Grade 5 because she skipped Grade 2 can't think of good enough words to describe them. They are The Rocky Mountains. We've already seen 4. There may be more. I drew a teeny elephant on the picture of Mount Rundle on the front of this postcard to show you how small an elephant is in Banff Alberta.

Your friend Posy

Wednesday, August 3, 1949

Dear Bunny,

When we were done Banff which is my favourite town in The World we crossed a nice bridge to see Banff Springs Hotel that's in this picture. They call it a hotel but you can see plain as day it's a castle. Everything inside it is either gold or marble or from Toronto. The servants are called Bell Hops and wear funny hats Mommy says are pill boxes. Ha-ha. After High School let's you and me come here and make 2 handsome princes dance with us.

Your friend Posy

Thursday, August 4, 1949

Dear Bucky,

Instead of you always wanting to shoot them here's a fun thing to do with animals. If a herd of elks are bent down eating grass and you pour water out your truck window onto the ground they perk their heads up and bug their eyes out and look around like crazy. Daddy says they think another male elk is peeing nearby. You can wait for them to settle down and do that over and over. Mommy says it's not fair to them but Daddy and me couldn't stop ourselves.

Your friend Posy

Friday, August 5, 1949

Dear Eleanor,

This is The Cave And Basin Hot Springs that reminded Mommy of when her and her best friend swam in the Mineral Pool at Watrous and then dressed to the nines to go to Dance Land where she first saw Daddy play a sax in a cream suit that looked so good on his wide shoulders. A Hot Springs is a hot swimming pool that smells like a fart but people stand in it anyway wearing ugly bathing suits you can rent except we had our own.

Your friend Posy

Saturday, August 6, 1949

Dear Essie,

This is the place in Yoho Park that keeps all the water in the world from running into one place and drowning every single person and animal. A little stream called The Great Divide splits into 3 parts here. One part goes to the Pacific Ocean and one part to the Atlantic Ocean and one part to the Arctic Ocean picking up all the rivers on their way. There should always be a policeman here. One bad boy with a shovel could ruin everything.

Your friend Posy

Sunday, August 7, 1949

Dear Diddy,

Well it looks like Alberta is just one castle after another. This one is called Chateau Lake Louise. Mommy said let's treat ourselves to a meal here but Daddy checked the prices and said now he knows why it's called High Tea. He took a real silver candlestick from his Stock in to the manager and we got taken to The Royal Parlour and given free party sandwiches and Skawns with Clotted Cream and strawberry jam and 4 Petty Forzes.

Your friend Posy

Monday, August 8, 1949

Dear Bucky,

Rosy and me held Daddy's hands and walked right out on a rock only 2 steps from falling into Athabasca Falls. Mommy stayed in the truck

26

because of her Verdago and to make sandwiches. When we turned around a Mama Bear and 2 cubs were walking right at us and we sure couldn't back up. Mommy got out of the truck and ran at the bears like Slim Pickens does with bulls. I'll say if we're still alive in my postcard to Eleanor.

Your friend Posy

Tuesday, August 9, 1949

Dear Eleanor,

DON'T READ THIS POSTCARD UNTIL BUCKY SHOWS YOU HIS. Lucky for Daddy and Rosy and me the bears decided not to eat us. Instead they turned around and headed for Mommy who stood perfectly still either because she was scared stiff or knowing her it was so the bears would eat her while we got away. But they walked right by her to the truck and ate our jam sandwiches and tonight's wieners and took off but left a bad stink.

Your friend Posy

Wednesday, August 10, 1949

Dear Bunny,

We found a camping spot in a prettier place than you'll ever see and Daddy was firing up the Coleman stove out on the nice grass when a man in a snazzy uniform rode up on a 2-wheeler with one hand on the handlebar and one holding a tray up high with a liquor bottle and fancy glasses on it. We tried not to laugh at how funny he looked but he up and stopped his bike and said Sir and Madam you can NOT camp inside the gates of Jasper Park Lodge.

Your friend Posy

Thursday, August 11, 1949

Dear Diddy,

A nice fat lady in the campground cook shack told us that only people with Untold Wealth can stay at Jasper Park Lodge being The King and Queen of England and Bing Crosby. A man rode up on a rusty motorcycle wearing a leather helmet with a guitar and played We'll Meet Again I think so the ladies would sing along and feed him and they did. He told us the glamour of life on the road isn't all it's cracked up to be. Mommy said Amen.

Your friend Posy

Friday, August 12, 1949

Dear Essie,

Well the glamour of life on the road isn't all it's cracked up to be. We were climbing Mount Edith Cavell up to Angel Glacier and got to a stream so icy cold Daddy went barefoot to carry Rosy across and Mommy piggy-backed me but she slipped and I shot over her head and landed on my face on the other side so we came back down. I have 5 bandages on my face. Mommy gave me marshmallows for the pain and snuck me a quarter for the Shock.

Your friend Posy

Saturday, August 13, 1949

Dear Eleanor,

We caught Rosy crying from worrying about starting another new school. Mommy said if you make a wish while swimming up a moonbeam it comes true. Rosy wished for nice new friends. Mommy wished for a house that isn't a hotel or a truck. Daddy said Brrrr I wish Pyramid Lake wasn't made of melted glacier. I wished for party shoes with bows and to meet BARBARA ANN SCOTT and I whispered Jesus please don't leave scars on my face.

Your friend Posy

Sunday, August 14, 1949

Dear Bunny,

We're almost done seeing The World. We just have Edson left and that's that. We'd be in Edmonton now but yesterday the motorcycle man with the guitar named Charlie Buckler whose stage name is Chuck The Buck asked Daddy to bring his sax to a gig in Jasper. I asked what's a gig and Mommy said a beer parlour. Daddy's resting today but a family with kids just drove here from Scotland and listening to them talk is almost the most fun so far.

Your friend Posy

Monday, August 15, 1949

Dear Bucky,

We quick did Edson today then Mommy said let's be sure to end our trip on a high note. We didn't stop in Entwistle or Stony Plain but at Spruce Grove she said let's pull over here for the night. I still don't know what a high note is. I start Grade 1 in 12 days so this is the last time Rosalind who used to be Rosy will ever have to write for me. It's also the last time you'll ever hear from your good friend Posy because my city name is Paulette.

Your friend Paulette

4. Edmonton, Alberta

You could put one hundred Flatte Buttes in Edmonton and still have room left over for St. Hildegard. You can keep driving straight ahead for fifteen minutes after you pass the WELCOME TO THE OIL CAPITAL OF CANADA sign and you'll still be in Edmonton if you don't drive too fast. The river which is called The North Saskatchewan by mistake has three bridges going across it and you are still in Edmonton on both sides of all of them.

Daddy picked the High Level Bridge which is so far up above the water Mommy had to close her eyes until we got over to the south side of the river which is called The South Side. Pretty soon after that the car behind us up and started making an awful howling sound. Daddy pulled over to let the idiot go by but instead he stopped in front of us and got out and it wasn't an idiot it was a Policeman and he said "Sir you just went through a red light." Daddy didn't say anything and the Policeman said "Sir I said you just went through a red light." Daddy still didn't say anything even though the Policeman's face was getting mad. Finally Daddy said "What's a red light?" and the Policeman pointed back at a green light on a pole and said "I won't give you a ticket this time but make sure it doesn't happen again eh?" and then he got back in his car and drove off. Daddy got out of the truck and stood there for a while looking around and not whistling. When he got back in he said "Are we sure we want to do this?" and Mommy said "We sure are sure" and she started looking for Queen Elizabeth Park that she'd heard about. We found it toot sweet by driving around in circles.

Queen Elizabeth Park has swings and teeter-totters and campfire pits and men's and ladies' outhouses and a swimming pool with a changing room where you can stand under warm water showers as long as you want. We did swimming and then showering and then swimming again and then showering again. Mommy left and came back with some dirty clothes and quick washed them under a shower when no one was looking which she said was a godsend after three weeks of heating wash water in the stew pot on the Coleman.

On our walk back Rosy read a sign saying NO OVERNIGHT CAMPING but Daddy said it just meant no tents allowed and then he drove the truck farther into the trees and parked it. Mommy made tomato dumplings and by the time we washed up our dishes over at the pump and Rosy and me had gotten into our nighties it was almost dark and everybody had left except us. Daddy lifted us up on top of a picnic table and pointed over to the north side of the river which is called The North Side and there were more lights twinkling along the top of the river bank than any of us had ever seen in one place in our whole life and right in the middle was another Alberta castle called a hotel that was shining like it was made of gold. Rosy said "It's Fairyland." Daddy got his sax out and started playing Gonna Take A Sentimental Journey and Mommy put her arms around Rosy and me and we swayed back and forth and sang along and kept on looking over at Fairyland all the way through Tangerine and I'll Be Seeing You before our bare feet got cold and Mommy and Daddy carried us to our ladder.

Daddy can do anything so he got hired right off the bat to make maybe a thousand drawers for airplane parts at The Edmonton Airport. Before he drove off to work in the morning Mommy took everything we'd need out of the camper house and then her and Rosy and me played City People On Vacation all day being mostly swimming and eating. When Daddy got home from work he said because his drawers all fit perfect he was put in charge of the other man which I wasn't surprised about because he always measures exactly right. We cooked wieners on sticks and then Daddy got a surprise bakery bag out of the truck and then it was bedtime.

"Dear Jesus. Thank you for this bless-ed day. Thank you for my nice one-day friend Jenny in the swimming pool whose three brothers tried to drown us with splashing. Thank you for the doughnuts. And I just remember I forgot to thank you for not leaving scars after I fell on my face going up Mount Edith Cavell. So thank you very much. My face is perfect. Well except for the mark you can only see when I'm flushed where Mrs. Fitz burned me on the cheek with a flat iron in St. Hildegard. I don't know why you let that happen. Just lucky for me she was on her way from the ironing board to the stove and not the other way around. Bless Mommy and Daddy and Rosy. Bless Grandma and Grandpa who must be missing me like crazy. Bless all the starving children in Africa and please try to figure out how you can feed them before they die. That's all for now. Amen."

Saturday, September 3, 1949

Dear Grandma,

The camper house got so cold last night Rosy and me put on socks and sweaters over our nighties and now it turns out the swimming pool is going to close after the long weekend. Mommy said moving can't happen a moment too soon and since it's already the Saturday before the Sunday before Labour Day Monday before Tuesday when school starts she and

Daddy are going off house-looking after they drop Rosy and me off at the Capital Theatre to watch I Remember Mama starring Irene Dunn who Rosy had never heard of but I already saw her in 2 Film Favourites From The Past being Magnificent Obsession and High Wide and Handsome.

We love us don't we Grandma.

Posy

Mommy said "Oops, we forgot Grandpa" and she told me that's what a P.S. is for and she wrote *P.S. Say hi and I love you to Grandpa* after my name at the bottom.

We were still crying from the end of I Remember Mama when Mommy and Daddy picked us up but they told us they found a nice house to rent and bought us ice cream cones to celebrate so we perked right up. Daddy dropped us off on Jasper Avenue at a store that sells nothing but children's shoes and on the way in I reached over and took a pair out of the window that were perfect for me. They were red leather with teeny holes in the shape of a heart on the toes and black patent bows at the back. Mommy said they might be a bit dressy for school but I couldn't let go of them even when the lady pulled. I put them on and Mommy said they seemed a bit tight and the lady said "Then why don't we step over to our brand new Fit-Rite Fluoroscope and see what the X-rays tell us." I limped over to the machine and the lady said "Now just slip your foot into the opening dear and I'll look through this eye-piece" and she said "Hmmm, at least a size and a half too small." She stepped aside for Mommy to look who said "Oh my goodness, it's a miracle machine. I'm just beside myself" which I never heard anyone say before. Then she looked at the lady and said "Are these the kind of shoes that come in just the one size?" and the lady said "Um, yes" and they took them off me and went to find a different pair. I put my foot back in and looked through the eye-piece. It had no skin, only bones like a Hallowe'en skeleton. I quick pulled it out but it seemed okay so I put it back in and looked again. Took it out. Put it back in. Out. In. Out. Innnnnn. Out. Other foot innnnnnnn. Out. Innnnnnnn. Out. Innnnnnnn. Out. The lady put another pair of shoes on me. Innnnnn. "See now? These are nice and roomy for her." Out. Innnnnn. The kid behind me hiss-whispered "Quit hogging the X-ray machine!" and we left. We were half way back to Queen Elizabeth Park before I took the box out of the bag and opened it up.

5. Grade One

I was very happy from the ankles up with my first day of school outfit. Rosy finally grew out of her navy blue jumper with red piping which looked perfect over my white blouse with puffed sleeves and red rose buttons and my new red socks and just before Daddy started the truck I quick put on my three best necklaces, two brooches and a bracelet. On our way there Rosy told me one more time how school works. Grade One-ers sit in the row near the door since they're always asking to go to the outhouse. Grade Five-ers like her get the row by the window because they've learned by now you get heck if you're caught staring outside. And the teacher stands in front of the blackboard and faces the row of whichever Grade she's talking to.

Well that all went right out the window when we saw Lord Strathcona Elementary School. It's made out of bricks and is two stories high or three counting the tall basement. Daddy walked us up the steps to the big front door and handed us our lunch boxes and gave Rosy her Grade Four Report Card from Flatte Butte and said to be good girls and he'd be back at three-thirty to get us.

Inside so many kids were going so fast Rosy and me just held hands and stood against a wall. After a while a lady came and asked our names and she looked through her papers and said we weren't Registered so we better come with her to The Office which was very busy. She told Rosy to sit and wait until they got to her and she told a big boy my name and said for him to take me to Class Room Number Five and that was the last I saw of Rosy.

The big boy told the pretty teacher "Her name is Patsy Something" and left. I tried to tell her it's Paulette but before I could we all had to stand for the playing of God Save The King on what's called the P.A. System which she said to sing along if we knew the words which I mostly do but I didn't sing anyway. After that she told us "When I say Good Morning or Good Afternoon boys and girls you must all say together GOOD MORNING OR GOOD AFTERNOON MISS SEMONICK back to me" and she gave us each an Exercise Book and a new pencil and showed us how the pencil sharpener on the window sill works. Then a bell went off for Recess time. She told us where the Little Girls Room and Little Boys Room are but I didn't know what they were for so I just went and tried to find Rosy in the schoolyard until the bell rang to come back in. One or two of us got lost getting back to Class Room Number Five and before there was time for class to start up again the man on the P.A. System said "Teachers prepare your students for the Fire Drill" and Miss Semonick said "Follow me boys and girls and remember you must return to this room after the Fire Drill and wait here for the Noon Bell." She walked us two by two with me holding a girl's hand named Rebecca up some stairs and down a hall to the Fire Escape Chute. When it was your turn each Grade One-er had to sit down on the floor in front of a Grade Six-er who held on to you with their arms and legs. I did not get a well-behaved Grade Six-er. She pushed off hard and yelled "YEEEE HAAAW" and leaned forward so we went faster and faster down and down and around and around the Chute until WHOOSH we were outside sitting on a pile of sand. She screamed "YUCK SHE PEED ON ME" and kids started laughing but I was already up and around the corner of the school and still running when somebody grabbed my hand. It turned out to be Rebecca and she said "I know how to get you out of here" and one second later we were past the swings and out a hole in the fence and through a lilac bush into a back alley. She said her house was two blocks over and she knew a short cut through yards.

There was no one home because her Mom is in the T.B. San in P.A. Saskatchewan and her Daddy drops the littler kids off at her Nonna's on his way to work. Rebecca said she's too young to have a key so she stood on a stump and squeezed in through the clothesline door and came back with an ugly skirt and clean underpants for me. She said not to feel bad because she has lots of experience helping with wet underpants so while I put on the dry ones and the skirt which I told her was pretty she washed my underpants and the back of my blue jumper in the rainwater barrel and hung them on the line. I gave her my second-best necklace and told her she could keep it. We figured there was no use going back to school just to get our lunch boxes so Rebecca squeezed back in the house and got two pieces of bread, two wieners and two apples and I rode standing at the back of her big three-wheeler down her road and across Ninety-Ninth Street which she told me will kill you if you don't obey the Crossing Guard who wasn't there and down a hill into a place called Mill Creek Ravine. After we ate our picnic she said "How long do you think an hour and a half is?" I said "Pretty long" so she showed me how to dig wet clay out of the creek bank and make cups and saucers and plates. She said now we're best friends I can call her Becca and I said she can call me Paulette. When I had gotten a whole tea set made and lined up on a log to dry for next day I said "We better get going or we'll miss out on learning how to read and print." On our way back to Becca's house I saw some grown-ups looking in bushes and under porches and calling "PATSY, PATSY." One of them yelled something at us but I don't know what because Becca had already pedalled us into the next block. When we got to her back yard my jumper was dry and my underpants almost were so I quick changed back into them.

A Policeman and two teachers caught us climbing back through the hole in the fence. The Policeman said "Where have you been?" One teacher said "Do you know how many people have been out looking for you?" and the other teacher said "Why did you leave the school yard?" I was afraid I'd have to tell them why but Becca put her head in her hands and said "The Fire Escape Chute was so dark and scary and we're so little that we ran away and cried." That answer seemed to work perfect because one of the teachers told Becca she could go back to her class room. I quick unpinned one of my brooches and snuck it into her hand and she said "Oww, thank you." Then the Policeman took me away.

We ended up in the Vice Principal's Office called Mrs. Ketchum who asked me "What is your name?" which I said "Paulette Kohler" and "How old are you?" and I said "Six." The Policeman said "Do you have any siblings at school?" and I said "No but it's only the first day." Mrs. Ketchum said "What is your Address?" and instead of asking her what's an Address I remembered what worked for Becca so I put my head in my hands as if to say I've had enough which I had had. Just then a bell rang for school to be over and Mrs. Ketchum took me out the front door to the top step and pointed up and down the street and said "Where is your house Paulette?" and just like that Daddy pulled up and I said "There it is now!"

6. Untold Wealth

We didn't know Daddy wasn't taking us back to Queen Elizabeth Park until we went through Ninety-Ninth Street which I told Rosy will kill you if you don't obey the Crossing Guard and next thing we knew he parked in front of a yard with a crabapple tree and said "Guess what this is?" and we guessed "OUR NEW HOUSE." When we jumped out Rosy pointed at some numbers over the door and said "I think that's our Address."

It turned out Daddy had already unloaded Mommy and all our stuff out of the camper house and gone out and bought a bunch of furniture that belonged to an old lady who had luckily died so one second after Mommy opened the front door and said "Welcome home darlings" we had a chesterfield and two arm chairs and beds and dressers and a blue kitchen table with five chairs even though we only needed four. Down in the cellar which has a cement floor instead of dirt so you call it a Basement there was a little room called a Bathroom with a huge white bathtub that had two taps hooked to it and when we turned them on one of them came out hot water and Mommy said "POOF! No more melting snow on the stove." Then she said "Now Posy let me show you something that was invented just for you." She pointed to a fancy white toilet and said "Watch" and she took a piece of toilet paper and dropped it inside and said "Now press down on that lever" which I did and the piece of toilet paper went around and around in some water and *WHOOSH* down a hole and then more clean water came up. Mommy said "It's called a Flush Toilet and you will never have to smell another slop pail or outhouse or honey wagon again." I dropped another piece of toilet paper in the Flush Toilet and pressed the lever and watched it go away and then I waited and did it again. I asked Mommy why was I crying and she said "Because you have never been this happy in your whole life."

Daddy was in the back yard trying to get the camper house off the truck by himself when the man next door saw him and came over to help. He said his name was Hank Beagle and his nice Schnauzer who came with him is called Wiggy. When they got the camper house on the ground Daddy said "How about I leave it back here as a playhouse for you girls?" and Rosy and me both did a "YIPPEE" and we took Wiggy inside of it to show him around.

Tuesday, September 6, 1949

Dear Bunny,

Nobody in Flatte Butte will believe it but tell them all anyway. One hour ago our family turned into people with Untold Wealth.

We have an Address and our own electric refrigerator and a telephone with our own private line not a party line and a big bathtub with a tap that hot water comes straight out of and the best thing ever invented which is a Flush Toilet that takes everything away for good lickety-split.

You know I am not a bragger. Everything is true.

Your friend Paulette who used to be Posy

P.S. These are mostly my words but Rosalind who used to be Rosy wrote them.

After we ate supper which was wieners and beans at our blue table with Pansy Daisy sitting up straight on the extra chair Rosy and me spent a whole hour in the bathtub turning the taps on and off and sending our little birchbark canoe back and forth to each other with the soap in it and lying back and watching our legs float up and holding our breath under water until it was my bedtime. We pulled up the plug and all the water ran out by itself down a drain and we got dried off and I put on my nightie and got kissed and sung to. Rosy was in the Living Room which we don't call the parlour now reading until eight o'clock which is a Grade Five-er's bedtime but I could see which side of the bed was hers because of the pile of books on the floor on that side so I put the blue velvet bag with my seven lucky teeth in it under my side's pillow and I prayed to Jesus to make sure The Tooth Fairy would find me at our Address and that she'd pay me all the money she owed me. Then just in case I ran to the Living Room and got Daddy to write a note to put in the bag saying *"Dear Tooth Fairy, don't forget these are 25-cent back teeth."*

The minute I woke up I checked under my pillow and the bag of teeth and the note were gone and instead there was a one-dollar bill and three quarters. I quick got out the ad for my Your Stairway To Stardom booklet from The Winnipeg Free Press and gave it and all the money to Mommy to mail off for me.

On our way to school Rosy and me met nice Mr. Street which I told him is a perfect name for a Crossing Guard and he said "Well my goodness aren't you clever. I never heard that before" and then he held his sign up for us to cross Ninety-Ninth Street without being killed. I had to wait in The Office to give Mrs. Ketchum the note from Mommy and I told her "Here is my Address and the telephone number for our private line but you should let it ring for a long time because Daddy might have poked his head into the electric refrigerator to get something and Mommy might be in the Basement flushing the toilet and my sister and I might have just turned on the hot water tap for our bath" and she said "I have no idea what you're talking about. Off you go."

The kids must have already said "GOOD MORNING OR GOOD AFTERNOON MISS SEMONICK" and I was too upset at Mrs. Ketchum to sing God Save the King and then Miss Semonick gave me my own desk at the very front of Row Three and said loud enough for everyone to hear "That way I can keep my eye on you" which wasn't fair because I would NEVER sneak out of the school yard again.

At recess my new best friend Becca and me played with a nice girl she's known all her life whose real name is Margaret but she gets called Peggy and by the time the bell went I had two best friends. I was just turned around in my desk asking Becca and Peggy if they'd like to come over to my Address after school to drink cold cream sodas out of our electric refrigerator and maybe float paper boats in our hot water bathtub when Miss Semonick said "If Paulette is finished talking I would like to teach you the letter A."

7. Cities Are Not Like Towns

After school Rosy doubled me on her two-wheeler to Mill Creek Ravine and we had just found my mostly dried clay tea set and wrapped it in newspaper and put it in her bike basket for bringing home and painting when a man in a dirty plaid coat and a cap with ear flaps and yellow rubber boots came out of the trees and said "Hi girls, what are your names?" I said "She's Rosalind and I'm Paulette" and he said "How did you two pretty little girls get such pretty names?" and I said "Mommy's father has a drop of French blood" and he said "I have something to show you" and he quick unzipped his pants and took his thingy out and shook it at us. Rosy picked me up and dumped me over the handlebars and jumped on and started pedalling as fast as she could away from him but we could hear him right behind us and then he banged on the back fender and the bike fell over and Rosy hit her head on a branch on the way down and she grabbed my hand and we ran our fastest up and up and up the hill and her head was bleeding but we didn't stop until we got all the way home. Daddy was just getting in from work so while Mommy fixed Rosy's forehead he drove straight out to get her bike and look for the Bad Man. When he got back he had her bike in the back of the truck and thank goodness my tea set was still in the basket. He said he found the Bad Man and told him off and he was pretty sure we'll never see him again anywhere near Mill Creek Ravine or even in Strathcona or maybe not even in Edmonton and Mommy said "Here let me get some iodine on those knuckles." After Rosy's head stopped hurting she helped me glue my tea set back together.

While I was eating breakfast at the blue table Mommy showed me how she'd written down what had to be written down to send away for my Your Stairway To Stardom booklet but I told her that I was worrying because right after the Tooth Fairy took my lucky teeth Mrs. Ketchum was mean to me and I got embarrassed by Miss Semonick and the Bad Man shook his thingy at Rosy and me and chased us and she cut her head and two of my clay tea cups were too broke to fix and so I was pretty sure my luck must have flown away with my teeth. I asked her "Do you think if we write Nurse Beryl she'll come to Edmonton and scientifically crack my neck again?" Mommy said "Hmm, why don't we try this first?" and she wrote a letter saying *"Dear Tooth Fairy, Posy doesn't blame you but it seems that her good luck accidentally disappeared with her teeth. Here is your money back. Could you please return her bag with her seven teeth in it at your earliest convenience. Thank you, Posy's Mom."* And we went and put it under my pillow before I even left for school.

Well the letter worked. In the morning there was my bag of lucky teeth back under my pillow as good as new. AND THE TOOTH FAIRY GAVE ME BACK THE WHOLE ONE DOLLAR AND SEVENTY-FIVE CENTS WHICH SHE DIDN'T HAVE TO. Mommy said as soon as she cleaned up the breakfast dishes she was going straight out to the Post Office with the envelope to The Winnipeg Free Press.

When she was out Mommy bought Rosy and me a pad of writing paper to share and a box of envelopes and she showed us the drawer where she put two-dollars' worth of three-cent stamps so anybody in the family who ever needed one would always have it. Rosy used our new supplies and I told her what to write in my four important letters.

Sunday, September 11, 1949

Dear Eleanor,

I doubt if they've heard of it yet in small towns so you should talk to your teacher about getting Girls Tumbling started at Flatte Butte Elementary because it's the very best thing in Grade 1 at Lord Strathcona School. We do it in P.T. which stands for Physical Training and is taught by a very strong lady who doesn't put up with any nonsense whose name is Miss Callaghan. So far she's only taught us somersaults and cartwheels which I already knew how to do way back in St. Hildegard when Mommy got us doing them for limberness and grace but Miss Callaghan says there's lots trickier stuff coming up. I would never ever say this out loud but I am better at tumbling than any of the other girls.

You shouldn't brag.

That was Rosy who just said that not me. I am not a bragger. Now here is the really big news. I am going to start a tumbling club called The Lucky Tumbling Club with me as the head tumbler and the other members will be my best friends Peggy and Becca.

Your friend Paulette who used to be Posy

P.S. When I just called Peggy and Becca my best friends I meant in Edmonton so don't start thinking I like them better than you.

P.P.S. Too bad Rosy and your big sister Darlene still have to read and write for us. Won't it be nice when we can do our own letters? Yes it sure will be! That last bit was Rosy again.

Sunday, September 11, 1949

Dear Essie,

Right this minute tell your Dad to quick quit his job at his cousin's lumber yard so he can stop wasting himself in a small town like your Mom says he is doing and move to Edmonton while people are still coming here from everywhere else to dig up oil and sell it or he'll be too late to architect all the new houses they're building. Besides if he waits any longer you'll be 7 years old and you will have used up another whole year seeing nothing interesting in Flatte Butte. Since we got here I have already seen a taxi cab, a pair of girl twins, another Alberta castle called The Ledge, a French poodle, a 50-foot-high milk bottle, a bad man's thingy and I have eaten a Tamale.

You're probably wondering what a Tamale is. Well it's very-very good mashed food from Mexico tied up inside a corn husk that you don't eat at The Siesta Cafe which is the restaurant Daddy took us to for a big treat.

You see Essie those are the kinds of things that happen every day in a big city.

Your friend Paulette who used to be Posy

P.S. Tell your Mom and Dad that Edmonton is just like Poland and Toronto and probably New York.

An interesting thing happened while we were eating at The Siesta Cafe being that POOF in the door walked our friend Charlie Buckler the guitar player whose stage name is Chuck The Buck who up and sat down at our table and said "Well it sure is a small world eh?" and ate our last Tamale. He invited Daddy to play at a wedding gig at Highlands Hall that night which he said he can't pay him for but it'll be a good time because his buddy Gilliland wrote some new songs for it and then he told us he's going to Hollywood to try his luck at being a Singing Cowboy in the movies like Gene Autry and Tex Ritter just as soon as he finishes his gigs at the Vermilion Curling Club, Frenchman Butte Legion and The Flatte Butte Hotel and we all said "THE FLATTE BUTTE HOTEL?" and Daddy said "And the world just got even smaller."

I walked him to the door when he left and told him I knew a tap dancer in Flatte Butte who was going to Hollywood soon and maybe he could take her with him on the back of his motorcycle and he said "Tell her why doesn't she pop by the hotel so we can get to know each other."

Mr. Alvarez,
Alvarez's Photography & Movie Hall
FLATTE BUTTE, Saskatchewan,
Canada.

Sunday, September 11, 1949

Dear Mr. Alvarez,

How are you? I am fine. Please give Miss Paisley the letter that I am putting in its own licked shut envelope that says FOR MISS PAISLEY that's inside this envelope.

Thank you,

Paulette who used to be Posy

P.S. If she's already moved to Hollywood then please send it to her Address there at your earliest convenience.

Dear Miss Paisley,

Well it sure is a small world isn't it? We had supper at The Siesta Cafe in Edmonton where you probably ate Tamales from Mexico when you and your Tour tap danced here and POOF in the door walked our friend Charlie Buckler whose stage name is Chuck The Buck who is on his way to Hollywood to be a Singing Cowboy and I told him about you moving there to tap dance in the movies. You should pack just the things you really need in a carpet bag and go see him at his gig coming up soon in The Flatte Butte Hotel. I'm pretty sure if you're nice to him he'll take you with him on the back of his motorcycle.

Yours truly,

Posy from the front bench

P.S. My sister is putting our Address on this letter so you can write back and tell me if you're finished all of the Six Easy Steps on the Your Stairway To Stardom. If not you better hurry up because Chuck The Buck is on his way.

P.P.S. Happy Birthday to you coming up on September 15.

8. Big Trouble

Well I was told I was lying by Miss Semonick. And I got sent to Mr. Rasmussen our Principal's Office for having a temper. And I got in big trouble for leaving school for the second time without permission. And I got called a stealer by Robbie Beagle. And I got talked to by Mr. Beagle for not locking their door. And Mommy who should have been on my side wasn't. And when Rosy found me hopping mad under the bed and I told her everything that happened all she said was "You... left... school... without... permission.... again?" And then when Daddy got home and heard why I was called a liar he just laughed until he couldn't stop. And none of it was my fault.

It started when Miss Semonick was teaching us Animals Of The World which the Animal Of The Day was the Camel that is the Ship Of The Desert who spits at you when you make it mad. Then came the surprise when she said whoever has seen the most unusual animal wins a box of Animal Crackers which are my favourites. I was sure I'd win because of being to the Calgary Zoo but it turned out some other kid must have been there too because by the time I got my hand up to say "Monkey" it was already taken and she didn't pick my hand when I was ready to say "Baby Lion" but just before she was going to give the Animal Crackers to Ricky who had been to a circus for "Elephant" I quick yelled "A CALF WITH TWO HEADS." Miss Semonick said "Now Paulette you know that's not true" and I stood up without permission and said "Yes it is" and she told me to please sit down and stop making up stories but I stayed up and said "I saw it running around the pasture and the farmer thought it was sent by The Devil so he shot it dead and

Daddy cut its heads off which were born hooked together and we have them in a box in our Basement." She said "Now Paulette" and I said "It's true" and she said "PAULETTE" and I said "IT'S TRUE" and she wrote something down on a piece of paper and said "Take this note to the Principal's Office." When Mr. Rasmussen read it he said "I see you're having trouble telling the truth" and I said "No I'm not. It's just that Miss Semonick is having trouble believing me" and he said "Young lady I think you'd better stand out in the hall until you change your tune." As soon as I got out in the hall I thought of how I could prove I wasn't a liar and maybe still win the Animal Crackers so I quick left the school and ran all the way home except for walking carefully across Ninety-Ninth Street but Mommy wasn't there so I got the key from under the mat and let myself in and got the box out of the Basement but it was too heavy to carry very far so I went next door to borrow Robbie Beagle's wagon but nobody was home so I got their key from under their mat and opened the door to their verandah and took his red wagon and put the box in it and pulled it all the way back to school. I got there just when the End Of Day Bell went and Miss Semonick and Mr. Rasmussen were standing on the front steps looking at me with mad faces. Before they could start yelling I quick opened the box and lifted out our stuffed two-headed calf head stuck to the nice piece of wood Daddy glued it to and held it up in front of my face so they could look right at its four eyes and two mouths and I waited for them to say they were sorry for calling me a liar WHICH THEY DIDN'T. Instead Mr. Rasmussen told me to go home and take the wagon and the heads with me. When I got there he had already called Mommy and told her HIS side of the story which it's always better to be the first person to tell what happened not the last one especially if the last one is a kid.

I am not going to talk to Miss Semonick or Mr. Rasmussen or any of the Beagles or anyone in my family for the rest of the year even if they beg.

Thursday, September 15, 1949

Dear Bunny,

Thank you for your letter I got today. I was very sad to hear about little Dennis. He died so young. Eleanor and her family will never be as happy as they were before.

Bunny stop feeling bad that your Mom had to write every word of your letter for you. IT IS NOT YOUR FAULT that you are a slow learner. You started school 3 days late because of Chicken Pox and now you're stuck at home with nobody wanting to get near you and your Pink Eye.

Even though I'm printing 4 of the words in this letter all by myself Rosy still has to write most of it so I'm probably not that much smarter than you. Cheer up you'll be printing to beat the band sooner or later.

Your friend Paulette who used to be Posy

P.S. Put honey and a pinch of salt in warm water and wash your eye out with it once a day or every hour.

Friday, September 16, 1949

Dear Eleanor,

I wanted you to know how very very very very very sorry I am that sweet little Dennis died so I bought the Sympathy Card that this letter is in with my own money instead of just drawing and colouring one. I bet you cry every time you look at his empty little bed or walk to school by yourself. Here is my very good advice. As soon as your family gets over thinking every day about how the coyotes got Dennis you should quick get another dog. You should try to get a German Wirehaired Pointer which I found out is the kind that the dog named Promise was in the movie The Biscuit Eater that the Dad thought was useless but Billy and his friend Text trained him in secret.

Your good friend Paulette

P.S. I won't tell you if Promise becomes the Champion or if he gets shot and dies at the end so I don't ruin the movie for you if it ever comes back to Flatte Butte.

9. STEP 1

Most people I bet won't know for sure what the luckiest day of their life was until just before they die but not me. When I ran to the door to hug Daddy home he said "For you" and handed me a thick envelope with three stamps on it and even I could tell it was from The Winnipeg Free Press.

MY YOUR STAIRWAY TO STARDOM BOOKLET HAD COME AT LAST.

My family knew how much I couldn't wait so at supper Daddy and Rosy took turns eating and reading my letter out loud to me and explaining the big words.

Dear **Paulette Kohler,**

CONGRATULATIONS! You are about to start Your Stairway To Stardom, our proven method for turning dreams of fame into exciting careers in the world of entertainment. People of all ages have completed these Six Easy Steps and gone on to make a big name for themselves in a wide variety of artistic pursuits.

We won't lie to you **Paulette Kohler** *not everyone who sets out on the Your Stairway To Stardom program will achieve success. In order to do so, you must approach each and every one of the six steps with enthusiasm and determination and follow the instructions of our experts to the letter. That takes willingness, discipline and strength of character.*

But let's not get ahead of ourselves. As you know, every trip up a stairway begins with the first step. So **Paulette Kohler** *open the enclosed booklet now and let's get started!*

Sincerely,

B. S. Archibald (Archie) Stromberg, Esq.,
Program Developer & Master Coach,
Your Stairway To Stardom Enterprise,
McCreary, Manitoba, Canada.

If it hadn't been Chicken and Dumplings my favourite I would have forgotten to even keep eating my supper I was so excited about finally getting going on my Your Stairway To Stardom that I'd been waiting and praying to do since King Kong in Flatte Butte.

STEP 1

Be Careful What You Wish For. Here's How.

All talented **Hopefuls** like yourself believe they will somehow turn their dreams of fame into reality. Sadly, almost all of them don't. Why not? (This will come as a shock.) Because they don't know **EXACTLY what they want**!

And so, your climb up **Your Stairway To Stardom** will begin with our **proven technique** for replacing the wish you merely **THINK** you want with the deep-down, **unbridled desire** beneath. This will involve voicing your hopes and dreams – **OUT LOUD, IN WORDS** – so that slowly, carefully, gradually, you will hear yourself express – possibly to your shock and amazement – your **ultimate wish** and **true destiny**.

We are about to guide you up that important first Step. Yes, a moment from now, we will demonstrate our patented method for revealing the **unspoken longing** that has been secretly **festering inside** of you. Armed with that crucial knowledge you will, at long last, be heading in the right direction – straight **UP** – toward the **CAREER OF YOUR DREAMS!**

NOTE: The following is an Example only. Be sure to substitute the Terms and Achievements that apply to your personal Specialty or area

54

of interest (e.g. **Hollywood** Movies, **Your Own Radio Show**, The **Rockettes**, Grand **Ole Opry**, **Nobel Award for Literature**, etc., etc., etc.)

N.B. Do not attempt this procedure until you are: (a) Alone; (b) Situated in a safe, comfortable setting; (c) Well-rested; (d) In a hopeful state of mind; and (e) Standing up straight. When you feel you are ready, proceed as follows:

I. Say out loud to yourself, "**I want to be on Broadway**." (Repeat.)

II. Then be a little braver and say, "**I want to sing in a HIT SHOW on Broadway**." (Don't be afraid. Just let it out.)

III. Attempt to sound sure of yourself as you say, "**I am GOING to sing in a hit show on Broadway.**" (Repeat as needed.)

IV. When you feel you can, try stating with confidence, "**I am going to be the STAR in a hit show on Broadway**." (Remember, nobody's listening!)

V. And again louder, "**I AM GOING TO BE THE STAR IN A HIT SHOW ON BROADWAY**!" (Dream on!)

VI. Feel free to switch to a different Specialty at any time and begin again.

Now that you know **EXACTLY** what you want, make it **your motto**. Repeat it and keep repeating it, over and over and over again, until you firmly believe **you can achieve your true dream**.

Only then, and not before, will you be ready for **STEP 2**.

When Mommy brought the rice pudding I asked if I could take mine out to the playhouse so I could work on my Step 1 and she said yes. It took quite a while to get it exactly right.

"I want to be in a Hollywood movie."

"I want to be a GIRL TUMBLER in a Hollywood movie."

"I am GOING to be the girl tumbling STAR in a big Hollywood MUSICAL."

"I am going to be the FAMOUS girl tumbling star like Esther Williams is with swimming in the BIGGEST HOLLYWOOD TUMBLING MUSICAL EVER."

"I AM GOING TO BE THE MOST WORLD FAMOUS GIRL TUM—" There was a knock on the playhouse door and Mommy said "Posy, I mean it, come inside right now, it's past your bedtime."

10. STEP 2

There was an explosion when something blew up at Rosy's Science Club after school next day and they all had to stay and clean up the mess even though it was two Grade Six boys who did it she's positive on purpose and then Daddy got home late because The Edmonton Airport was showing him a new job they needed doing now that the drawers were all made so I'd been waiting at the table with my booklet for HOURS before they were both washed up and ready to take turns eating and reading Step 2.

STEP 2

Be An Original. Be One-Of-A-Kind. BE YOURSELF.

But be warned: There are a lot of other **Hopefuls** out there. Some of them may be just as talented as you. To be a star, **you need pizzazz** so you'll stand out from the crowd. Whatever your talent is, you should **develop a specialty**, a unique or **daring trademark**, something you do better than anybody else.

It's also important to **LOOK** like an original. Put your own personal stamp on your appearance. Try for a **knockout walk**, attention-getting clothing, a hairstyle with *oomph*.

Whatever you do, don't copy your idol's style and techniques. That's already been done. **BE YOURSELF**. But do consider choosing a **stage name** if your own lacks glamour or is difficult to pronounce.

Rosy and me were lucky because Mommy loved Rosalind Russell and Paulette Goddard and she knew she could get away with giving us fancy names in Saskatchewan because even though she's mostly English and Scottish her father has a drop of French blood so I decided to stick with Paulette but I told my family I'd have to think about Kohler.

Before bed time I thought up and drew and coloured an attention-getting costume and Mommy thumb-tacked it to the wall over her sewing machine and promised she will make it exactly to a T when the time comes. It is going to be made out of red satin and shiny beads and bare legs like Esther's except mine will also have feathers because I will be performing dry.

Miss Semonick started the week off printing "See Dick run" on the blackboard. When she turned around and asked "Who can read that back to me?" she stared right at me and said "Paulette, you look like those words come as a complete surprise to you." I said "No Miss Semonick I only look surprised because my eyebrows are up" and she said "Then maybe you should put them down" and I said "I can't" and she said "Why?" and I said "Mommy's not too good at fancy braids but in Saskatchewan Daddy used to be a veterinarian on-the-side for extra money because the real one was always drunk so he showed Daddy how to do everything and one of the things he got really good at was braiding horses' tails." Miss Semonick said "I see" but I could tell she didn't so I said "Well he did such a nice job this morning of doing my hair in braids and wrapping them around the top of my head like Esther Williams in the movie Bathing Beauty that I didn't want to hurt his feelings and say they were too tight." Miss Semonick got a coughing fit just then and had to leave the room so I'm still not sure how *oomphing* my hair went except for Becca saying she loved it to bits and a headache.

It had been four whole days since I started Step 2 and I still didn't have a daring trademark but then a lucky thing happened at afternoon recess. The Dad of a Grade Five boy in Rosy's class walked by the schoolyard wearing his soldier's uniform while The Lucky Tumbling Club was practising our routines and he pointed one of his crutches at me and said "Why don't you try standing on your head. Germans should be good at it since they have square heads" which I didn't think was true for half-Germans like me especially since Daddy was born in Manitoba but I tried doing it just in case and even though Miss Callaghan hadn't even started us on head standing yet I balanced on my head for ages with my feet straight up in the air. I quick changed most of our routines to either start or end with me standing on my head while Peggy and Becca do somersaults around and around and around me to prove how long I can stay up. So that was pizzazz taken care of.

I'd been trying different ways but I still hadn't come up with a good stamp for my walk I think because of wearing brown leather shoes with buckles and rubber soles. I bet I could have knockout walked in those red ones with the teeny holes in the shape of a heart on the toes and black patent bows at the back.

11. The Rules For Madam

Saturday was blowy with sideways sleet outside so I telephoned Peggy and Becca on the Private Line and asked do they want to come over to our Address and play a perfect new game Rosy just invented for us called Madam that can only be played in our Basement because that's where Daddy keeps his Stock of antiques which he said we could use if we were very careful. They came right over and we told them all the rules for how to play it but then nobody wanted to be Madam because she has to just sit on the pink brocade Victorian Petticoat Chair the whole time while everybody else gets to be the servants but then Rosy said "Oh alright I'll be Madam if I have to" which was perfect since she knows all about old history and the way book people talk. Before we even got started a lady Browser showed up and liked the pink Petticoat Chair so much she bought it but after she left Daddy said he'd allow Rosy to recline which is half sitting and half lying down on the blue velvet Louie The Fortieth Shezz Lounge instead. We put two antique bells and a Chinese Gong with its wood hammer on the Turn-Of-The-Century Parlour Table and as soon as Rosy was reclined and us three had put our aprons on we got started. First Madam tinkled the Crystal bell so Becca had to run into Madam's Drawing Room behind the two bedspreads Mommy had hung on the indoors clothesline for us and say "You rang Madam?" and Madam said in a snooty voice "You forgot to curtsy you impudent wench. No gruel for you today. Bring me my antique Japanese Silk Kimono this instant" and Becca said "Yes Madam" and ran upstairs and got Mommy's housecoat and put it on her. Then Madam ping-pinged the little Chinese Temple Bell and Peggy ran in but she curtsied so low she tipped over and Madam said "You clumsy scullery maid see if you're capable of getting me my Ming Dynasty Dragon Cushion with the sequin eyes" and Peggy said "Yes Madam" and she went and got it. Then Madam held the wood hammer way up high and BONGED the Gong so loud I was all the way into the Drawing Room and finished curtsying and I still hardly heard her say "You unlettered strumpet go to the East Wing and get my book Pride and Prejudice from the window sill of my celebrated boudoir" which I did and then she said "Turn on my priceless Repro Tiffany Lamp" which I said "Yes Madam" and did and then she said "Now take your leave" which I curtsied and said "Yes Madam" and did but I was barely through the bedspreads when we heard tinkle-ping-ping-BONG, tinkle-ping-ping-BONG and Becca and Peggy and me had to all run in at the same time and curtsy. "Yes Madam" we said and Madam sat up and said "You lazy drudges do not deserve the pittance I pay you. I demand that you go to every corner of the Mansion and pick up every sock and book and toy and crayon and put them exactly where they belong and then go out and tidy the Ancestral Playhouse and scrub it until it shines." Then she picked up her book and stretched out on the Shezz Lounge with her feet on the Ming Dynasty Dragon Cushion and said "Begone with you" and Peggy and Becca and me got to have fun being scullery maids and impudent strumpets all morning.

12. My Very Good Advice

Wednesday, September 28, 1949

Dear Eleanor,

Thank you for your letter telling me about Bunny's very bad trike accident on Main Street where she should not have been riding.

It's lucky you also told me you're worried about Diddy because I have some very good advice. You and Essie should take turns walking him home after school or even half way since it's a long way out to The Slaughterhouse so other kids will see that he has good friends even if he can't talk English that good. Bunny can take turns later if she ever walks again.

I wish I could tell you what my Your Stairway To Stardom is all about and how good and fast I'm going up it but Rosy says it's too much writing to ask of her.

Instead I will tell you what Allowances are so you can get them started right away in Flatte Butte. An Allowance is money you get every Saturday morning for doing things you have to do anyway like help my sister make the bed and tidy our toys and stuff away and dry dishes. I get 15-cents a week and Rosy gets 25-cents which I suppose is fair since that's what my friend Peggy and her big sister Joy get so ask for the same for you and Darlene.

Anyway it turns out that 15-cents buys such a big bag of candy you will be sick and sorry if you eat it all in one go. Daddy said from now on I should spread the money out over the week to make the good times last.

Your friend Paulette

P.S. YIPPEE I'm happy for you that the Flatte Butte Elementary Teacher Miss Talbot already had you doing Grade 1 Tumbling.

P.P.S. Too bad our big sisters still have to write and read us our letters even though we've been in Grade 1 for 3 whole weeks. School is not all it's cracked up to be.

Wednesday, September 28, 1949

Dear Bunny,

It is very horrible that a car crashed into you on Main Street where you weren't supposed to be crossing by yourself and you fell off your trike and broke your leg.

If your cast is too tight you will get Gang Green so tell your Mom to tell the doctor right away if your foot turns black

It's too bad you probably have to use crutches from now on especially since Eleanor says you were getting almost as good as her at tumbling once you got back to school after the Pink Eye.

Your friend Paulette

P. S. Lucky that the car was parked or you would be dead.

Mommy told me that the reason Diddy looks sad sometimes is because he and his parents were in a terrible car accident on their way from Montreal to his Dad's new job playing a cello in the Regina Symphony Orchestra and he flew out the window that was open and hardly got hurt but his Mommy and Daddy died which made him an Orphan and he got taken in by his Daddy's sister Veronique and her husband Wally Wolff who already had four boys and a baby on the way. She said "So you can see how fitting into a big family you barely know and struggling to speak English and living behind a slaughterhouse would not be an easy new start for a grieving child."

Diddy Desjardins,
The House Behind The Slaughterhouse,
FLATTE BUTTE, Saskatchewan,
Canada.

Thursday, Sept. 29, 1949

Dear Diddy,

I am writing you to cheer you up because living behind The Slaughterhouse is not an easy start for an Orphan.

I saw you at lots of the same musicals as me in Flatte Butte so I am going to tell you what it's like to go to a movie in Edmonton. Here is the shock. There's more than one movie theatre. I have already been to 3 of them being The Capitol, The Garneau and The Princess. And you don't sit on wood benches. Oh no. You sit on soft seats with soft backs and soft arms. And the movie screen is so big you almost don't know where to look.

Every second Saturday Mommy gives Rosy and me each 50-cents being 5-cents each way for the bus, 15-cents for a cream soda and Cracker Jacks and 25-cents for the movie plus cartoon and then we stay in our seats and watch them both all over again. And movies get here when they're only 1 year old instead of 2 years old or 10 like in Flatte Butte.

Your friend Paulette who used to be Posy

P.S. If you write me back all about a musical you liked I'll write you back all about one I liked and we can keep doing that until you're happy.

13. What Would Torchy Blane Do?

When Daddy brought the mail in he said "Hmm, there's a letter for Mommy and me from Albi Alvarez. I wonder what on earth he's…" and then one minute after opening it they called Rosy and me into the kitchen and read it to us.

Monday, September 26, 1949

Dear Max and Isobel,

Posy sent me another one of her letters for Miss Paisley a while back which I passed along to her at the next Wednesday Ladies Matinee. Course I didn't read it because a person's mail is a person's mail but Posy did say an odd thing in her note to me that if Miss Paisley has already moved to Hollywood would I please send it to her there. Well Miss Paisley's been living in Flatte Butte for maybe half a year now and I see her at every Wednesday Matinee but that was the first I heard about her moving anywheres let alone Hollywood. And now it seems she's up and gone missing.

Did you ever meet Mrs. Cruickshank that nice-looking war widow who takes in boarders? Well she put the word out around town has anybody seen Miss Paisley because the last time she showed up for her supper or slept in her bed was this past Friday night the 23rd of September although she was seen the next night at some sort of hillbilly music do at the hotel but that's two days ago now. Right away I locked up my shop and popped over to Mrs. Cruickshank's to tell her about Posy's Hollywood note. She said she doesn't want to bring the RCMP into this in case it's nothing but that what's worrisome is #1. Miss Paisley left most of her things behind including all her warm clothes and it's coming up October. #2. We all know she's not quite right in that she barely talks or even looks at you although she's harmless enough. And #3. What if she's gotten some crazy notion in her head and is headed for trouble?

What's more, her weekly room and board was due the day she disappeared which left Mrs. Cruickshank in the lurch which is too bad because she seems to be a very nice person.

Well today I dropped by Connie Cruickshank's again with half a dozen bakery doughnuts and she said her heart is in her throat thinking of how Miss Paisley might be lying dead somewheres and she didn't do anything to stop it. So I promised her I'd write and ask if Posy knows any more about what she might have been up to – Miss Paisley that is.

I hope you and the girls are settling in nicely in Edmonton.

Yours sincerely,

Albi Alvarez

I said "MISS PAISLEY'S LYING DEAD SOMEWHERES?"

Rosy said "It's somewhere not somewheres" and Mommy said "What on earth were you two doing writing Miss Paisley?" and Rosy said "Ask Posy. I'm the writer not the writer" and Daddy said "So Posy what was your letter about?" and I said "Mostly just tap dancing and eating Mexican Tamales at The Siesta Cafe and asking did she finish doing all her Your Stairway To Stardom Steps yet." Daddy said maybe I should pull back a bit on my letter writing from now on and Rosy said "That's a very excellent suggestion" and Mommy said "There's bound to be a good explanation for where Miss Paisley is" but still I could barely eat my Macaroni Surprise and Crabapple Betty with strawberry ice cream for worrying.

When we were doing dishes Rosy waggled her soapy finger in front of my face and hiss-whispered "You should have told Mommy and Daddy you got Chuck The Buck to maybe take Miss Paisley to Hollywood on his motorcycle. What if they hit a bump and they're covered in blood in a ditch?"

"MISS PAISLEY'S COVERED IN BLOOD LYING IN A DITCH UNDER A MOTORCYCLE SOMEWHERES?" Rosy said "Somewhere."

Rosy had been asleep for quite a while and I could already hear the end of The Jack Benny Show on the radio. I finally made myself brave enough and I tiptoed out of the bedroom and into the Living Room and said "I might have told Miss Paisley to go to Chuck The Buck's gig at The Hotel and see if he'll take her to Hollywood with him on the back of his motorcycle" and then I quick tiptoed back to bed.

Saturday, October 1, 1949

Dear Essie,

I put 2 letters in this envelope. One is this one and the really long one is for Bunny but I can't send it to her because her Mom would have to read it to her. So when your big brother David finishes reading this to you ask him to read the other one right away to Bunny but first make him swear he won't tell another person except you what it says or hope to die.

Your friend Posy

P.S. You can tell Eleanor what it says but you both have to swear to die too.

Saturday, October 1, 1949

Dear Bunny,

Since your name is Bunny Cruickshank and since you don't remember your Dad because he died the first week he went Over There with The Army then your Mom must be Mrs. Connie Cruickshank the nice-looking War Widow who takes in boarders and if she is then Miss Paisley lives at your house or at least she did until she up and went missing.

You might already know some of this because Daddy tattled Long Distance to Mr. Alvarez about me writing Miss Paisley that if she goes to Chuck The Buck's gig at The Hotel maybe he'll take her to Hollywood with him and now your Mom is in The Lurch and Miss Paisley might be lying dead in a ditch under his motorcycle covered in blood somewhere and since her being disappeared might be a little tiny bit partly my fault and since your Mom doesn't want to bring the RCMP into this I'm going to have to find her all by myself.

I have seen 3 Torchy Blane movies and I'm pretty sure Torchy would take your Mom's key ring and sneak into Miss Paisley's room and snoop through every drawer and pocket and under the mattress and the rug looking for clues. And Rosy who read every Nancy Drew book before she out-grew them says be sure to steam open any letters that come looking like clues could be in them and also check if there's a loose floor board because there's always something shocking under it.

Your friend Posy

P.S. If you find a diary under her pillow Rosy says get David Cohen to see what she was up to on September 23rd – Miss Paisley that is.

Sunday, October 2, 1949

Mr. Vulcher,
The Owner,
The Flatte Butte Hotel,
FLATTE BUTTE, Saskatchewan,
Canada.

Dear Mr. Vulcher,

I am Mr. and Mrs. Kohler's youngest daughter who you bought The Flatte Butte Hotel from writing you from Edmonton, Alberta.

Do you know where Charlie Buckler whose stage name is Chuck The Buck was heading to after he finished doing his gig at The Flatte Butte Hotel? Only tell me where he is and nobody else in order to keep the RCMP out of it. Now here is the important part. Put in the letter if you saw a tap dancer named Miss Paisley take off with him.

Since my heart is inside my mouth about where she might have gotten to because she's not quite right although she's harmless enough would you please write me back the MINUTE you finish reading this letter so I can use the clue to find out if she is lying dead in a ditch under his motorcycle somewhere and I can stop worrying about where she is.

Yours truly,

Paulette Kohler

P.S. Please write PRIVATE in big letters on the envelope.

I told Daddy that since I've started being the person in the family getting all the letters that I don't mind taking on his job of bringing in the mail every day from now on and he said "Well thank you Posy, that's very kind of you."

14. STEP 3

I decided to skip to Step 3 and go back to stamping my walk a little later. Daddy says that is a sensible decision. Besides I started praying again for those red shoes with the black patent bows so you never know.

STEP 3

Work Harder Than Anyone Else In Your Chosen Field.

I.   **Picture this**. Two equally talented **Hopefuls** walk into a casting company's office. They **can act**, they **can sing**, they **can dance**. They're told to go to an audition in one week's time. One calls up friends and says "This could be my big break, let's celebrate!" The other one makes a list of five things to do before the audition that reads "1. **Practise**. 2. **Practise**. 3. **Practise**. 4. **Practise**. 5. **Practise**."

II. Can you guess who got the role? **BINGO! The one who worked the hardest.**

III. We made up a saying here at **World Headquarters of Your Stairway To Stardom Enterprise** and we've seen it drive people on to **Fame** and **Big Money** time and time again. It is *"The harder you work, the luckier you get."*

The first thing I did to Work Harder Than Anyone Else In Your Chosen Field was ask Daddy if he would help me clear out a place in the Basement and lend me one of his antique rugs from The Salvation Army Thrift Shop that's big enough for three people to tumble on.

Ever since then if anybody in my family doesn't know where I am all they have to do is head down to the Basement because that's where I'll be on my tumbling rug doing five things being practising, practising, practising, practising and practising. I also made sure that The Lucky Tumbling Club practises our routines almost every recess in the Girls' Playroom and Friday after school in our Basement.

Something happened Saturday that was NOT FAIR. We played Madam again and Rosy thought up the best thing ever for us to do. Right off the bat she did the tinkle-ping-ping-BONG, tinkle-ping-ping-BONG so we all went running through the bedspreads together and curtsied and said "Yes Madam" and she said "I demand a feast. Prepare me a groaning board of sweetmeats and trifle and black pudding and a spit-roasted joint. And to drink I shall have a Flagon of Champagne and an Imperial Pint of Elderflower Cordial." We quick ran upstairs and asked Mommy what we were allowed to have. She gave us four crackers with jam, a sliced apple and a little box of raisins plus a bottle of cream soda for the Champagne and an Orange Crush for the Elderberry Cordial and she cut up a wiener into pieces and said "Here's Madam's spit-roasted joint" and gave us a tray for the groaning board. We carried it very carefully down the stairs hardly spilling anything and served Madam her feast. She took some bites and sips out of everything and then she made an ugly face and yelled "FIRE THE COOK AND FEED THIS VILE GARBAGE TO THE MURDERERS AND SCOUNDRELS IN THE DUNGEON" but instead Becca and Peggy and me took all of it behind the furnace and had a little party eating and drinking everything until Madam BONGED the Gong and demanded me to go get her another book. I was just running down the stairs with it when I slipped on some Champagne on the bottom step and fell into the Victorian Tea Table and over it went and the Ruby Glass Girandle sitting on top of it went down with it and cracked into four red pieces with broken prisms everywhere.

Someone must have told Daddy where I was hiding because I could see out between the bedspread and the floor his shoes walk into our bedroom. His voice said "Running around my stock isn't being careful like you promised. No more playing Madam in the basement. Ever." Which if you ask me was pretty big punishing for one used Girandle.

15. **Where Are Their Whereabouts?**

PRIVATE & CONFIDENTIAL

Friday, October 7, 1949

Dear Miss Kohler,

There seems to be some confusion about my name, but I am, in fact, the person who bought The Flatte Butte Hotel from your parents in June of this year.

As requested, I am replying within a MINUTE of reading your intriguing letter. To answer your question about the possible whereabouts of Charlie Buckler whose stage name is Chuck the Buck, I distinctly recall him saying "When I picked up my mail at Lloydminster Post Office I got a boffo offer for four weekend gigs in a row at a lively saloon in a ghost town just over the Montana border." He did not mention the dates of his engagements, nor did he reveal the name of the town. I did not see him leave the hotel on the morning of Sunday the 25th of September as I was at church.

In response to your important request that I put in the letter if I saw "a tap dancer named Miss Paisley take off with him", Charlie did introduce me to a woman on the night of the 24th of September whose name was Patsy or Polly or possibly Penny Paisley. There was no mention of tap dancing.

I sincerely hope these clues will prove helpful in your urgent quest to find Miss Paisley and put you out of your misery.

Kindest regards,

Cyril Pankhurst

P.S. Please be assured that I will not discuss our correspondence with the RCMP.

PRIVATE & CONFIDENTIAL

Thursday, October 13, 1949

Dear Mr. Pankhurst,

I am very sorry about getting your name wrong. I don't know how that happened since Vulcher doesn't sound anything like Pankhurst.

Thank you for writing me back right away with those 2 very good clues. My sister Rosy is going to go to the School Library tomorrow to look up Lively Montana Ghost Towns. I don't know what Miss Paisley's first name is but I bet that was her.

Too bad you had to go to Church because now we don't know did Chuck The Buck pick Miss Paisley up from somewhere on his way out of town or did she maybe take off somehow all by herself the night before. If this was in a movie called Torchy Blane And The Mystery Of The Disappeared Tap Dancer I bet Torchy would be asking people on the street #1. Where were Miss Paisley's whereabouts after the gig on the night of the 24th of September because she sure wasn't in her bed at Mrs. Cruickshank's? #2. Is she with Chuck The Buck now? And #3. Or isn't she?

Yours truly,

Paulette Kohler

P.S. I think she might be headed to some place warm like oh Hollywood or somewhere because she didn't take her winter clothes with her.

Rosy had no luck finding a Lively Montana Ghost Town at the School Library.

16. STEP 4

<u>STEP 4</u>

<u>**Invest In Yourself. Big Dreams Seldom Come True For Free**</u>.

Don't let a lack of financial resources keep you from achieving <u>**fame**</u> and the <u>**Big Money**</u> it brings. Allocate a portion of your current earnings to cover all the expected (and unexpected!) expenses. If that's not enough, borrow money, sell valuable possessions, or do <u>**whatever it takes**</u> so that you're able to:

I.   <u>**Take special classes**</u> with the best teachers you can find.
II. Pay for <u>**costumes**</u>, buses, taxis etc., etc., etc., when performing.
III. Have a professional <u>**headshot**</u> taken and get as many <u>**8x10's**</u> printed as you can afford.
IV. Set aside an <u>**Emergency Reserve**</u> for last minute costs like travelling to out-of-town auditions.

When your <u>**Big Break**</u> comes calling, you'll be saying "<u>**PHEW, I'm sure glad I paid attention to Step 4**</u>!"

I asked Daddy if he would raise my Allowance from fifteen cents to five dollars until I start making the Big Money. He put one eyebrow up and stopped whistling so I knew I'd have to sell valuable possessions. I said "Where do you think is the best place to sell good used jewellery?" and Rosy who l didn't even know was listening looked up from her book and said "Instead of going to tomorrow's movie why don't you use the fifty cents to sign up for a table at next Saturday's Fall Rummage Sale in the Community Centre?" and then she went back to reading.

I went through my jewellery boxes and showed Daddy the things I wouldn't mind selling. He said "As lovely as they are, three things might not be enough to get your money back from the cost of a table" but he said he had a good idea and boy-oh-boy did he ever. We headed straight for The Sally Ann which is what he calls The Salvation Army Thrift Shop where he finds hidden treasures that can become Stock and there was a whole counter of nothing but jewellery at my best prices ever although really I get most of my jewellery free from Mommy and my real and pretend Aunties. Necklaces were ten-cents each, bracelets and brooches five-cents and rings started at two for five-cents depending on if they were real or not. Then Daddy read me the sign EVERYTHING HALF PRICE FOR ONE DAY ONLY. I was just beside myself.

I was finding so many perfect things that Daddy let me use his Stetson to hold them all while he went off looking for Stock. When it came time to pay the lady she told me my jewellery would have cost three dollars and twenty cents but with the HALF PRICE FOR ONE DAY ONLY miracle it came to one dollar and sixty cents for the whole hat full. Trouble was I only had my going-away silver dollar gift from Liddy Frisch at The Beat and my fifteen-cents Allowance. Lucky for me Daddy gave me what's called an Advance of forty-five cents and said he'd take five cents off my allowance for the next nine weeks which didn't sound too bad since most of my life I didn't get anything. On our way out I saw an almost new beautiful blue leather jewellery box with its own lock and little gold key for twenty-five cents that would be perfect to put all the money I'm going to make in. I asked Daddy about another Advance but he said that would be pushing it.

When we got home I hid a nice heart-shape locket that opens for Rosy's Christmas present and kept a diamond ring for myself in case it turns out to be real but everything else was Stock. Daddy glued a piece of real brown leather Nogga-hide onto a tin box with a lid that works and hooked a padlock on it and said "Presto, an official strongbox to keep your resources under lock and key." Then he helped me make everything look good as new. If I'd known how long it would take us to fix chains and add hooks and glue on beads I'd have been more careful what I bought. When we were finally done fixing everything he said "Now what you need to sell your jewellery for more than you paid for it is Presentation. So it's over to Mommy to show you how to make your table sing."

Well it turned out that meant I had to perfectly cut out forty-one different size pieces of orange lining satin for Mommy to sew up on her sewing machine into jewellery bags for necklaces, bracelets, brooches and teeny ones for rings. Then I had to cut out forty-one little price tags and figure out with Daddy what to charge for everything and then get Rosy to help print the prices on them and then I had to pin them with forty-one itty-bitty safety pins to their proper bags. Two hours past my Friday night bedtime I finally got to bed with no song, no story and no prayer.

When we got to the Community Centre and found the table with my name on it Mommy covered it with gold coloured lining satin and I sprinkled real autumn leaves all over it and lined up all my Stock on top of their proper size orange bags and set up my official brown Nogga-hide strongbox. Everything was the perfect colours for the Autumn Theme of this year's Fall Rummage Sale. I asked Mommy "Does it sing?" and she stood back to look and said "Like lily ponds!" whatever that meant. They let people in at nine-thirty sharp and by three o'clock I was sold out. When we got home and emptied out my official strongbox I had seven dollars and eighty-five-cents which Daddy said was almost a five hundred percent profit.

Now that I had resources the first thing I did was ask Mommy how much special tumbling lessons would cost and she promised she'd ask around. When I got home from school she said "Well I phoned every tumbling expert in Edmonton and they all said that nobody anywhere is as good as Miss Callaghan and she's free if by ANY chance you HAPPEN to go to Lord Strathcona Elementary so it looks like you landed on your feet." PHEW that was a godsend.

As soon as we found out what a headshot is Mommy said "Who did we say just last week takes the best pictures of anyone we know?" I said "Uncle Otto" and she said "Well I'll give Fern a call and see if they'd like to pop over tomorrow night for supper and a professional photo shoot."

Daddy braided my hair up like Esther's again only not as tight and as soon as Uncle Otto showed up with his camera he shot my head before we ate supper so I'd still be tidy. He said "No charge for the film or my time but Auntie Fern and I expect an invitation to your first Premiere in Hollywood" and I promised. Another PHEW.

Next I asked Daddy how much it would cost me to take a train to Hollywood for an audition and he said no need because he'd be happy to drive me there and even back for free so that's three free PHEWS so far but he said I should put five dollars in an Emergency Reserve to cover hotels and meals. So five dollars was back under lock and key and I still had two dollars and eighty-five-cents left over for Other Expenses.

17. Lacing Up

A kid at school said the radio said the ice had frozen hard enough on all Edmonton Community Skating Rinks for them to open up so when the End Of Day bell rang Rosy and me ran home for our skates and headed straight to Strathcona Rink. Every kid we knew and some we didn't were pushing into the skating shack and lacing up.

I knew the words to mostly all the songs they played over the loudspeaker because of paying close attention to the radio being Buttons and Bows, Baby It's Cold Outside, Man-yanna is Soon Enough for Me, I'm Looking Over a Four Leaf Clover and Woody Wood Pecker so I sang along while my friends and me tried spins, bunny-hops, jump turns, spirals and flat irons like the big girls which none of them are anywhere near as easy as they look. Once every hour the loudspeaker played The Skater's Waltz and you're supposed to stop what you're doing and hold hands with someone and skate nicely 'round and 'round the rink in time to the music. Of course the boys – even the ones who are nice as pie everywhere else – don't care how good the music is they only do rough things like crack-the-whip and hockey fighting and passing people fast and sometimes knocking them down I bet on purpose.

Rosy read out loud the Notice in the shack that said GIRLS FIGURE SKATING LESSONS 12 WEEKS FOR $3.00 so us and all our friends ran home after skating to ask our parents to please-please let us sign up and PHEW Mommy and Daddy said we could.

Daddy painted Rosy's old tube skates silver to make them snazzy for me. I didn't tell him how bad a girl needs picks for bunny-hops and stopping. But it turned out there was some hope because Mommy told me in secret it looked like we might be almost out of the woods with Daddy maybe getting a better job where he'd be a Foreman and if that happened she was going to talk to him about me getting figure skates.

Wednesday, October 19, 1949

Dear Diddy,

Eleanor says you're even unhappier now because the dumb Flatte Butte Rink Figure Skating rules won't let boys into the classes and you told her you want to be a famous figure skater like Eugene Turner who she's never heard of but I saw him starring in Silver Skates at the same Ladies Matinee of Film Favourites From The Past that you did.

My very good advice is that Miss Lutz can't stop you watching the classes from outside the boards and then coming back at Free Skate times to practise and practise the moves. In case you think that won't work my Mother who never took a Figure Skating lesson in her life memorized a whole routine in one go just by standing there and paying close attention.

Your friend,

Posy

P.S. This is the last time you will ever hear from me if you don't write back after this.

The thing about flat irons is that you can either do them or you can't. Some girls that you would never ever think they could do one by looking at them just up and bend their knees until their bum is almost touching the ice and then they quick stick one leg out straight in front of them and away they go on one skate until they finally glide to a stop or they decide to come back up. While other girls who are just as good skaters or maybe even better get right down to where their bum is almost touching the ice and they very carefully stick their one leg out in front of them and then they tip over. Sometimes they even tip over while they're still just trying to get their one leg out from under them. I have tried over one hundred or maybe two hundred times to do a flat iron and I have never got it going for more than one second. I don't think it's fair to be born wanting to do something so bad but no matter how hard you try to do that thing in your life you just keep tipping over.

18. What Would Edith Head Do?

I had been so busy doing Presentation and headshots and solving The Mystery Of The Disappeared Tap Dancer and running The Lucky Tumbling Club and taking Figure Skating lessons and writing letters and going to school all at the same time that I almost didn't remember to come up with an idea for my Hallowe'en costume.

You never want to be something every other kid you know is going as. And your costume's got to be so good that grown-ups will say "Honey come quick there's a scary monster at the door" or "You're such a good clown I'm going to give you a Dubble Bubble AND a Cadbury Caramilk." What you don't ever want to hear is "Aww how cute, are you a hobo or a chipmunk?" And then Miss Semonick went and made it harder when she said "Be sure to wear a costume to school on Monday because I'm going to give prizes for Best Girl's Costume and Best Boy's Costume." So now I needed one perfect costume to fit UNDER my snowsuit to wear all day at school and another perfect one to wear OVER my snowsuit for going out Hallowe'ening that night and I only had three days to come up with them. I was sick about what if I never got two good ideas or even one. Then what?

When Mommy found me lying down sad on top of our dress-up box she said "Why don't we put our two heads together and think of what Edith Head who makes the best costumes for all the movie stars would do for Hallowe'en if it was cold in Hollywood?" I said "That's THREE Heads all together" and after we rolled around on the floor laughing at how funny that was of me to say we got busy coming up with a perfect idea.

Hallowe'en morning Mommy put a long shiny skirt and her flower blouse on me and tied a sash around my waist that she'd sewed little bells on and wrapped a fancy scarf around my head with the fringe hanging down the back and put red lipstick and rouge on my face and told me "Now go empty out all your jewellery boxes and put on anything that sparkles" and just like that I was a beautiful Gypsy Dancing Girl. It all fit under my snowsuit if I pulled the skirt up inside until I got to school. No one was surprised when I won Best Girl's Costume. The prize was a pink Dresser Set which I am saving for my Hope Chest. When I got home I took everything off but my underwear and long stockings and ate some mushroom soup with crackers and then Mommy put it all back on OVER TOP of my snowsuit and she drew wrinkles on my face with her eyebrow pencil and tied a deck of cards around my neck and PRESTO I was a fat old Gypsy Fortune Teller.

Mommy and me headed out to get Peggy and Becca at five-thirty so we wouldn't miss a single house in the neighbourhood. Peggy was a perfect Raggedy Ann Doll and when we got to Becca's I said to her "You're a very good devil." She said "I'm supposed to be a puppy. Daddy does his best." I quick said "Boy am I ever dumb" and Peggy said "Anyone can see you're a puppy" and Mommy said "Just look at that waggy tail" and off we all went.

In Saskatchewan you yell "Trick or Treat" but Becca and Peggy said in Edmonton you yell "Hallowe'en Apples" even though they're the last thing you want to get given. So we did "HALLOWE'EN APPLES" on the first porch and it worked. Lickety-split a lady and man opened the door with a bowl of stuff. I knew she knew right off the bat what I was because she said "You have to tell me my fortune first" so I made her pick a card and I looked at it and said "Someone will die and leave you a big fortune and you'll marry a handsome Duke and live happily ever after." The man said "Uh-oh" and they gave us peanuts and black licorice pipes and away we went to the next house. By seven-thirty when Mommy said we better call it a night she had to help carry my pillowcase home it was so full of Hallowe'en kisses and chocolate bars and caramels and licorice and bags of peanuts and raisin boxes and bubble gum and thank goodness hardly any apples. It took me more than an hour on the floor to organize and count everything. While I was doing that I ate all six of my little chocolate bars and accidentally ate three more that turned out to be Rosy's. She was hopping mad at me and Mommy and Daddy stood up for her and not one single person in my whole family cared one bit that I got sick with the flu before I went to bed.

19. STEP 5

I made the good decision to invent some new routines for The Lucky Tumbling Club with my parts being harder than the ones I'd gotten too good for. Rosy helped me come up with some perfect ones with me performing moves she says are called Show Stoppers while Peggy and Becca do their regular things behind me. I knew they weren't going to mind because Peggy's just going to be a Christian Missionary in Africa anyway and Becca goes along with anything because she likes to wear costumes out of our dress-up box and decorate cookies and dance to the radio and other stuff she can't do at home with her Mom being away with T.B. in the San in P.A.

Then at supper time while we were waiting for dessert which was Saskatoon pie my favourite I went and got my Your Stairway To Stardom booklet which I'd been too busy to do for quite a while.

STEP 5

Be Nice, Be Respectful, Be Versatile, Be Confident and Be Patient.

You may read about vain, selfish and demanding stars, but let me tell you, they didn't get away with that sort of behavior when they were starting out. Yes, **believe in yourself**, but be friendly and kind too because, well, here's a saying I personally made up: "**You meet the same people on the way down that you met on the way up**!" So before you snub somebody in show business, don't forget that you might need them some day.

And here's another **exclusive Your Stairway To Stardom tip**. Play the odds! The more of these things you can do, the more chances you'll have to **get hired**: act, sing, dance, juggle, play an instrument, speak another language, ride a horse, swim, dive, do gymnastics, fencing, archery and magic tricks.

AND be **willing to perform** anytime, for anyone who'll have you, for money or not. The **exposure** will be good for **your career**.

Now this might be the most **important tip** of all. No matter how many times you get rejected – and you will be rejected many, many times – **don't ever give up**! Keep on climbing (and re-climbing if need be!) every step until you reach the top of **Your Stairway To Stardom**!

Daddy said he thought I'd pretty much got Step 5 licked and after he explained all the big words I said I agreed with him. I'm nice, I'm respectful, I'm versatile, I'm confident, I'm patient, I'm friendly and I'm kind. I am not vain or selfish. I'm not demanding and I would never be a snubber. I could already play the odds with five things being sing, dance, swim, do gymnastics and magic tricks and I still had some time to learn the other eight ones. And nobody had to worry about me with the most important tip because I would never give up.

Thursday, November 3, 1949

Dear Eleanor,

That is NOT FAIR about your Dad's job. A President should not be allowed to cheat and do a mean thing like that to a nice man and his family.

Tell your Dad that everybody in Edmonton is going to be rich soon because of Oil Money and they'll all want to go curling and have banquets. You and your family could stay with us until he gets a job and finds a house and YOU CAN JOIN THE LUCKY TUMBLING CLUB.

Your friend Posy

P.S. Rosy says you and Darlene made a good decision not to ask for Allowances yet. She says 25-cents plus 15-cents equals 40-cents a week which can buy a lot of bread and milk for a starving family.

P.P.S. I had my second Figure Skating lesson today. It looks like it's going to take a few more Thursdays to get really good at it.

"You've been awfully quiet today Posy" Mommy said. "Most Saturdays I can barely keep up with your comings and goings. What's up?" "Nothing." "Where is everybody?" "Around" Then she said "Since Rosy's out and Daddy's arguing with Foster Hewitt on the radio why don't you go get the Pick-Up Sticks and I'll make some hot chocolate and we can have our own little party in the kitchen?" After Mommy lost six games in a row she said "You're just too good for me" and she started putting everything away. "Mommy" I said "supposing you THOUGHT two people were your best friends and then another girl in your class told you she heard them telling the new girl Marji who moved here from The States last month that you are bossy. Would you ever talk to either one of them again?" "Well" Mommy said "if it were me I'd probably want to think about why they called me bossy just in case there's one chance in a hundred there might be some truth to it." "There isn't" I said. "And they said I always make up tumbling routines where I get to be the big star and do all the Show Stoppers while I make them pose behind me or just do somersaults around and around my head stands and that the reason I won't let Marji be in The Lucky Tumbling Club is because she can do the splits." "Hmm" Mommy said, "is any of that partly right?" "The only thing Peggy and Becca are pretty good at is the crab walk and you know Rosy teaches me hard things the Grade Five-ers do in P.T. and I practise, practise, practise, practise and practise them. The daring stuff is what the audience comes to see. That's why I have to be in front. And I made up the routines for three people not for four so Marji would just get in the way." Mommy said "Just out of curiosity, have you managed to do the splits yet?" "No but I'm doing stretching every day so pretty soon I think."

I walked home from school by myself again and told Mommy "Well today Marji did a HAND STAND without any help and without even being up against a wall and do you know why she can? Because it turns out she took Tiny Tots Gymnastics in Great Falls since she was three years old which she says is harder and fancier than Grade 1 Tumbling. I bet that's why she can also do the splits any old time she wants. For her it's just drop and splits, drop and splits, drop and splits." Mommy said "Why don't you and I sit down with some fresh peanut butter cookies and think about this whole tumbling situation. I bet together we can come up with some give-and-take ideas that will make everybody happy." I could tell what was coming next so I said "I just remember I forgot to bring the mail in so I better just take two cookies and go out and get it" but I could see she wasn't going to let go of the cookie tin so I sat back down.

Well it turns out that give-and-take is mostly all give.

I told Marji she could join The Lucky Tumbling Club and do practising with Peggy and Becca and me at recess and in my Basement. I told all three of them that Mommy was going to make us four red-and-white striped tumbling rompers so everyone in The Lucky Tumbling Club would match. I told them I changed every one of our routines to be for four people instead of three and that one of the routines now starts with the rest of us posing behind

Marji while she does a hand stand instead of me doing one of my head stands. And I said I was going to make up a whole new routine of Marji and me mostly just doing cartwheels behind Peggy and Becca while they do the crab walk back and forth and back and forth and back and forth in front of us. And that I would even come up with a routine where Marji does the splits while Peggy and Becca do jumping jacks behind her and I juggle two oranges.

I don't know what else anybody thinks anybody is supposed to do to make everybody happy.

At supper time I told my family I didn't feel much like starting Step 6 right away. Mommy said she believed I was far enough up my Stairway that it wouldn't hurt my career if I took a break for a little while and got right back on it later when I was feeling up to it.

20. All Without The RCMP

A letter came for me from Essie that her brother David wrote for her saying an envelope came to Bunny's house TO MRS. CONNIE CRUICKSHANK that Bunny figured was a clue because she was pretty sure it said it was FROM MISS PENNY PAISLEY. She quick took it to Essie and David's house after picking Eleanor and Darlene up on the way and Darlene said "Yes it says FROM MISS PENNY PAISLEY all right" so they steamed it open over the kettle when Mr. and Mrs. Cohen went out but she said they must have steamed it too much because when they got the letter out the ink had run so bad David and Darlene could only read six words being "without telling", "warm", and "to this address" which didn't mean anything so they didn't know what to do with the five-dollar bill and five one-dollar bills that were folded inside. So Bunny took the money home to hide and David put the letter in the back of one of his stamp collecting albums.

I said "I'm not sure what Torchy would do about all that. What do you think?" and Rosy said "I don't know" but I was pretty sure if I left her alone for a while she wouldn't be able to stop herself thinking about it and I was right.

Tuesday, November 8, 1949

Dear Essie and everybody else,

Rosy says if the Post Mark beside the stamp on the envelope wasn't ruined by that big steaming mistake you all made it will say where it was mailed from and when. And she got a book called Detecting For Amateurs at the School Library with a Procedure For Reading Faded Or Water Damaged Handwritten Materials in it which she copied down what it said being

"Try experimenting with alternate light sources, various eye glasses, as well as different angles and distances."

Your friend Posy.

P.S. Rosy remembers David from school in Flatte Butte and says he's very smart so he should be the person to try that.

Thursday, November 10, 1949

Dear Mrs. Kohler,

The drilling company my husband Gil worked for in Great Falls transferred him here to run the Alberta office and we moved in down the street from you a few weeks ago. Our daughter Marji found it really tough changing schools six weeks into the year especially in a new country. She missed her friends and had trouble fitting in and came home in tears almost every day. But then your sweet daughter Posy invited her to join a little tumbling club which is right up Marji's alley being such an active kid and now she has several little friends and gets invited over to their homes to play and we have our happy-go-lucky Marji back!

We'd like to thank Posy for her kindness by inviting her to join us for dinner next Saturday at The Seven Seas which we've heard is quite an exciting restaurant. Please let me know if that's okay with you. We would pick her up at 5:45.

Marji says that next to me you are the best Mommy she has ever known in her whole life! I hope we can have coffee and a gab together someday soon.

Sincerely,

Jean Gilroy

Mommy was right that Marji would gasp when she saw my pink Dotted Swiss party dress she'd whipped up for me in two days with puff sleeves and a shirred bodice that looked perfect with my pink and green jewellery because she did gasp. Then Marji spun around to show me her sparkly blouse and blue velvet skirt and said "My Grandma embroidered all the jewel flowers and silk leaves on it and gave it to me when we left Montana." I gasped. "I thought you said you were from Great Falls." She said "Silly you, that's in Montana." I quick asked her if she'd ever been to a saloon in a lively ghost town there and she said "I don't know. You better ask my parents."

The minute the man pulled our chairs out for us nicely and we were sitting down I asked her Mom and she said "Hmmm, it sounds familiar. Honey?" and Mr. Gilroy put down the big menu and said "Yes dear?" and Mrs. Gilroy said "You know that rundown hotel and bar made up to look like a ghost town next to Joe Something's filling station on Highway 91 where we stopped for gas and cokes on the way up to Canada?" He said "Yeah, vaguely, somewhere between Coutts and Shelby" and she said "Do you remember the name of it?" and he said "Wasn't it a take-off on Fort Whoop-up? Like Fort Lively Saloon maybe? Camp Lively Cantina? Lively Something or other."

The Owner,
Fort Lively Saloon OR maybe Camp Lively Cantina,
Somewhere between Coutts and Shelby,
On Highway 91,
MONTANA,
United States Of America.

92

Sunday, November 13, 1949

PRIVATE & CONFIDENTIAL

Dear To Who Might Be Concerned,

I am writing this intriguing letter to find out if this is where Charlie Buckler whose stage name is Chuck The Buck did gigs 4 weekends in a row starting Friday the 30th of September or maybe the week after that or the one after that. If it is then here are 3 important questions. #1. Do you know where his whereabouts are now? #2. Did he say where else after that? And #3. Was a tap dancer named Patsy or Polly or Penny Paisley with him?

If they didn't get there I'm worried sick they're lying under his motorcycle in a ditch beside Highway 91. Would you please take a look and write me back the MINUTE you know if it's them so I can be put out of my misery.

Thank you,

Miss Paulette Kohler

P.S. I would have put a stamp in the envelope for you to use but I only have Canada ones and they don't work going the other way.

Sunday, November 13, 1949

Dear Essie and everybody else,

I wrote Fort Lively Saloon or maybe Camp Lively Cantina in Montana to see if Miss Paisley and Chuck The Buck are there or lying beside Highway 91 under his motorcycle. I'll let you know as soon as I hear which.

Your friend Posy

P.S. I didn't know Essie was short for ESTHER. I thought Rosy and me were lucky to be named after Rosalind Russell and Paulette Goddard but you were named after ESTHER WILLIAMS.

P.P.S. It might take him a while to check all the ditches.

Sunday, November 13, 1949

Dear Bunny,

It's too bad about the awful rash your cast left but at least you didn't get Gang Green. If it gets itchy my good advice is that you should rub wet oatmeal on it or maybe porridge would work but without the brown sugar.

Your friend Posy

P.S. Is Bunny your real name?

P.P.S. Don't scratch it or it makes it worse.

"THERE'S A LETTER FOR YOU FROM YOUR BOYFRIEND." Rosy grabbed it and said "Stop being stupid" and walked straight out of the kitchen to our room and shut the door. Mommy said "That wasn't very nice of you" but I could tell she was trying not to smile and Daddy winked at me.

I waited until I could make myself go in and say "I'm sorry" without laughing. Rosy said "If you must know, David Cohen said the letter to Mrs. Cruickshank was mailed from the tiny Post Office in Hill Spring Alberta which he said is a Hamlet in the mixed agricultural area between Cardston and Pincher Creek." I said "Thank you very much Rosy" and asked her politely if she'd please read the rest of David's letter to me which she did.

"By experimenting with my science kit magnifying glass and using an alternate light bulb and an angle from a closer distance I could read eleven more words and parts of some other ones which I added to the six we already had plus I deduced the possible words of Dear Mrs. Cruickshank and Sincerely Penny Paisley. Then I wrote them all out on another piece of paper so here's what we have now."

She unfolded the paper and read me what it probably said.

"Dear Mrs. Cruickshank... I'm sor...   without telling... not nice of... eek's... nd board... longings behin... warm cl...posta to mai... uld be so kind... to this address... Sincerely, Penny Paisley"

Then she went back to reading his letter:

"It still doesn't make any sense so I'm pretty sure it's written in code. I'll write you again as soon as I break the code. I remember you too from—"

That's when she stopped reading and she was blushing. Ha-ha.

Thursday, November 17, 1949

Dear Posy,

Yes it's me Chuck the Buck writing you from Fort Lively Hotel & Saloon. Aren't you and Rosy the smart little kids for finding me all the way down here in Montana!

I sure was glad you wrote Penny about my gig in Flatte Butte. She came to the hotel and we hit it off right away. Talk got around to Hollywood and I told her she could ride there with me and she popped home to pack a bag. Since I had almost 3 weeks to get to my next gig we took our time along the way sightseeing and camping under the stars and — I'm going to be honest with you kids — before we even made it to Lethbridge we were head over heels in love. Then right out of the blue she told me she had to go to

Cardston for a little while and could I please drop her off there. She wouldn't say why. She promised she'd get herself down to Montana as soon as she could and to please wait for her there.

That was over 4 weeks ago and she's still not here. But she did send a telegram 2 weeks ago saying *Need More Time STOP Will Come When I Can STOP Go Ahead I Will Find You in Hollywood STOP.*

I've been packing them in at Fort Lively Saloon 3 nights a week. Old Curly Watling the owner wants me to stay on permanent. I've even got my own free room upstairs. But I know Pen's got her heart set on Hollywood. Trouble is we're starting to get a bit of snow here and I'm afraid if she doesn't show up soon, old Trusty Rusty my motorcycle won't make it over the mountains before winter. In the meantime I'm staying put. A woman like Penny Paisley is worth waiting for.

Thank you for worrying about us. Say hi to your Mom and Dad for me.

Yours truly,

Charlie

Tuesday, November 22, 1949

Dear Bunny, Essie, Eleanor, Darlene and David,

Well I found Chuck The Buck. Rosy copied out every word of his letter on the other piece of paper in this envelope so stop reading this and read that and then come back to this.

NOW READ THIS. So nobody knows what Miss Paisley's been up to or if she might have been murdered after she sent the telegram. Rosy looked everywhere in the School Library but she only found one chapter on Cardston Alberta. It said almost only Mormons live there. She says the hard books she reads now about places of the world always say if the local people are warlike or are cannibals but this chapter didn't. We were in Cardston for an hour last summer and everybody seemed nice enough but Rosy is going to go to the big Strathcona Library tomorrow and ask the real Librarian if there's a book on Mormons In Cardston And What You Should Watch Out For.

Your friend Posy.

P.S. It's the next day now and here is the shock. THE REAL LIBRARIAN IS A MORMON FROM CARDSTON. She said if Miss Paisley is still in Cardston she doubts anybody will kill her or cook her.

P.P.S. FOR ESSIE ONLY. Too bad you're just named after Esther from the Old Testament. Still you can pretend it's after Esther Williams. It's not really lying.

P.P.P.S. FOR BUNNY ONLY. So how did your Mom pick the name Bernice for you since there aren't any movie stars named that?

P.P.P.P.S. FOR BUNNY ONLY AGAIN. Does your Mom give Mr. Alvarez free suppers in trades-ies like my Dad did so that's why you get movies free now?

Tuesday, November 22, 1949

PRIVATE & CONFIDENTIAL

Dear Mr. Pankhurst,

I am almost done snooping out The Mystery Of The Disappeared Tap Dancer. Your clues helped quite a bit but I got an even better one from my friend's parents who used to live in Montana. I found Chuck The Buck at Fort Lively Hotel & Saloon somewhere between Coutts and Shelby on

Highway 91 in Montana. He and Penny Paisley are going to Hollywood together because of being head over heels except she needed to go to Cardston first but she wouldn't say why. She hasn't showed up in Fort Lively for over 4 weeks but she sent him a telegram 2 weeks ago saying to go to Hollywood without her so we know she was still alive then. PHEW.

Do you know anyone in Cardston you could maybe get clues from in a sneaky way? If not I guess I'll just have to finish solving this myself.

Yours truly,

Paulette Kohler (but my friends call me Posy)

P.S. My sister Rosy told our parents about my first letter to you and now our whole family is very sorry about that Mr. Vulcher name accident.

P.P.S. I just found out you gave Mommy those 5 Mackintosh Toffees for free at my Birthday party. Thank you very much.

P.P.P.S. I don't think we need to tell the RCMP yet.

21. Sometimes Good News Isn't

Wednesday, November 23, 1949

Dear Bunny, Essie and Eleanor,

YIPPEE Mommy just told me one minute ago that now Daddy is a Foreman we are going out tomorrow to buy me figure skates which I already have picked out at The Hudson's Bay where I try them on every time we go there looking for something else and I happen to find myself in the Skates Department.

More good news is that the weather has got so cold that the streets finally iced over and Peggy's big sister Joy who has lived here all her life says now we can skate all the way to the rink and back as long as we're careful to walk not skate across Ninety-Ninth Street so no more wasting time in the skating shack because I never have to take them off.

Your friend Posy

P.S. They are white with picks and black heels and long white laces.

Thursday, November 24, 1949

Dear Eleanor,

Today is the day after I mailed my letter telling you about me getting new figure skates and I just this MINUTE got your letter saying the only skates that fitted you at the Flatte Butte Annual Used Skates Exchange were boys' hockey skates so I might have sounded like a bragger which you know I'm not but if it did sound like that I'm sorry honest.

I wrapped up my old skates and Mommy is going to mail them to you tomorrow so at least you will have girls' tube skates instead of boys' ones to wear for when you're in this year's Ice Carnival.

Your friend Posy

P.S. What you don't know is that Daddy painted them silver so they look snazzier than plain ones.

First thing after we finished singing God Save The King Mr. Rasmussen our Principal came on the P.A. and said "Good morning boys and girls this is Mr. Rasmussen your Principal. I know you've all been looking forward to hearing about the Lord Strathcona Elementary Annual Christmas Concert. I'm pleased to announce that this year's theme chosen by the Concert Committee is BETHLEHEM ON THE PRAIRIES. If we all work very hard we can make this our best Christmas Concert ever. Now please listen carefully to Mrs. Ketchum as she gives you all the details." And then Mrs. Ketchum came on and said "Every boy and girl in Grades One and Two will be assigned a musical instrument and together will form a Combined Rhythm Band. All Grade Three and Four boys and girls will be singing in our Special Christmas Choir conducted again this year by Mrs. Octavia Hammond who is well known in Edmonton and beyond. Anyone in Grades Five and Six wishing to act in the BETHLEHEM ON THE PRAIRIES Nativity Scene that's being written and directed by Miss Scrimm may audition right after school this coming Thursday in the Assembly Hall. She will be looking for one Mary, one Joseph, three Rich Dairy Farmers, two Hired Men, three girls to be Angels and four boys to be Cows – two fronts and two backs. All Grades Five and Six students not acting in the Nativity Scene will be performing as The

Northern Lights which I'm told by Miss Scrimm is going to be a dazzling spectacle for the audience. Any Grade Six boys willing to help Mr. McNabb build the stable are asked to sign up during Shop Class. Your teachers can answer any other questions."

Monday, November 28, 1949

Dear Bunny, Essie and Eleanor,

Well skating with picks isn't all it's cracked up to be. My best front tooth is loose and I came this close to breaking my nose. One of my eyes was swelled shut this morning so Mommy kept me home from school.

Rosy says she is tired and she has a Social Studies test tomorrow so she is going off to bed right this minute.

I am stil up. Mi nose herts. I wil rite mor abut wut I am gong throo latr.

Yor frend Posy

Then I did something to try and make myself happier while I was at home suffering. I came up with new words to a Christmas song I know and then I invented a tumbling routine in my head to go with it. I think it helped me feel a teeny bit less in pain.

Becca told me that when I wasn't at school the Grade One-ers joined up with Mr. Gilliland's Grade Two-ers for the first Combined Rhythm Band practice and most kids got the instrument they asked for out of the big box of bells, tambourines, maracas, rhythm sticks, triangles and two pairs of cymbals. Then Mr. Gilliland taught them the proper way to hold their instrument and how to ring, jangle, rattle, click, tinkle or clang it. When I got there the day after I was hoping for cymbals but there was only one instrument left in the box. I said "Miss Semonick?" but she said "No Paulette" and that was that. Mr. Gilliland played us three tunes on the piano which he's way better at playing than Miss Semonick and he said we're going to practise one each week and when we've got them all memorized we'll join them together into a rousing Medley of Christmas Favourites. I already know them all by heart because a triangle only plays one note.

22. Tumbling For Jesus

The minute Thursday's End Of School bell went Becca, Peggy, Marji and me quick changed into our matching red-and-white striped rompers in the Little Girls Room and snuck into the Assembly Hall before Miss Scrimm or any of the Grade Five and Six Nativity Scene try-outers got there. The exact second Miss Scrimm walked in the door and before she could say "What in good heaven's name are you Grade Ones doing here and why are you wearing—?" I said "Miss Scrimm what do you think about the very good idea of having four prairie dogs on stage singing a song I wrote to the tune of I Saw Three Ships Come Sailing In while they tumble with joy about Jesus being born?" She said "What in good heaven's name—" and I quick whispered "One two three GO" and we started singing and doing our routine.

As soon as we finished our Big Finale I said "Well what do you think?" and Miss Scrimm said "I'm speechless" which I didn't know if that was good or bad so I said "It'll be even better when we're wearing fuzzy costumes and prairie dog make-up." Miss Scrimm got her speech back and said "Only Grades Five and Six students can be in the Nativity Scene" and I said "But we've been practising for two days" and she said "It's too bad you've gone to all that trouble but you should have asked first" and I said "But" and she said "I'm afraid you'd just get in everyone else's way" and I said "We could start before them and be all done and crouching quietly in the hay before Mary and Joseph even get there." She said "I'm sorry but there won't be enough room on the stage what with the stable and all The Northern Lights" and I said "Then what about if we come in from the hall and just tumble in the aisles?" She said

"No and that's final" and she started walking away. I ran up to her and whispered "How about just one prairie dog?" She said "It is not in the script" and I said "But Miss Scrimm if you're still writing it" and that's when Rosy saw us and walked me and the rest of The Lucky Tumbling Club not very nicely out the door.

When Daddy found me sitting half mad and half sad in the Basement he said "I know you're heartbroken but—" "Don't try to cheer me up" I told him "because it won't work." But he tried anyway. "When a person is headed up the Stairway To Stardom and the tumbling rug gets pulled out from under her, she doesn't give up. She knows that her Big Break might be just around the next corner." I didn't believe him for one second.

23. Paisleys, Privetts and Puppies

An envelope that said SOMETHING-SOMETHING FOR MISS PAULETTE KOHLER came in the mail so I was watching out the window for Rosy to get home from her Young Bookworms Club at Strathcona Library to read it to me but the second she came in the door she whispered "I have news" so we went straight down to the Basement and I said "What?" and she said "The Mormon Librarian just told me that when her Mom called about Christmas plans Long Distance from Cardston last night she asked her has anyone called Penny Paisley shown up in town and her Mom said not that she's heard but she does know a Percy and Prizzie Paisley who farm nearby but just to say hello to because they're not Latter Day Saints and also Prizzie's Auntie by blood Pearly who never married so she's still a Pitt not a Paisley who used to own Pearly's Clip & Curl but not for years albeit she still lives behind her old shop." I said "all-be-it?" and Rosy said "That's what she said. Go get my Dictionary."

So now we knew there are two Paisleys on a farm near Cardston and one sort-of Paisley living on Main Street in Cardston. Albeit they might not be the right Paisleys.

Then I handed her the FOR MISS PAULETTE KOHLER envelope and it turned out the SOMETHING-SOMETHING said SPECIAL DELIVERY.

Wednesday, November 30, 1949

PRIVATE & CONFIDENTIAL

Dear Posy,

Thank you for your well-written letter updating me regarding the splendid progress you've made toward solving The Mystery of The Disappeared Tap Dancer. I must apologize for not answering you the MINUTE I received it. Travelling back and forth between Flatte Butte and Regina to manage both my hotels keeps me busy enough, but this past week I had to make an extra trip to bring my two dogs to Flatte Butte so that I can be with Margaret Rose ("Maggie") when she has her puppies. They are a fairly rare breed in Canada, in fact, they're perhaps the only German Wirehaired Pointers in Saskatchewan. Three families in Regina are anxiously awaiting the arrival of the puppies I've promised them.

Now, to answer your question, I don't know anyone in Cardston, however, when I moved here from Shrewsbury, Shropshire, England, my best mate Nigel Oswald from Oswestry, Shropshire, England came over as well and he works at the Prince of Wales Hotel in Waterton Lakes. I'm sure he would be as gripped as I am by The Mystery and would happily make the short drive to Cardston and sneakily snoop around for clues. I would suggest that he ask the townsfolk #1. Do you know a Penny Paisley? #2. Has she been seen in town recently? And #3. Has a tap dancer going by another name (I'd be suspicious) recently arrived in Cardston?

I will telephone Nigel the MINUTE you say I can share your confidential information with him and that it's okay to send him off to Cardston.

Your friend,

Cyril Pankhurst

P.S. I can't imagine what the RCMP could do that you haven't already done.

Friday, December 2, 1949
PRIVATE & CONFIDENTIAL

Dear Mr. Pankhurst,

My friend Eleanor Privett and her family are still heartbroken that their little Dennis died not long after school started which was bad enough but now the President of Flatte Butte Curling Club & Banquet Hall's sister just moved to town flat broke so HE GAVE MR. PRIVETT'S JOB TO HER HUSBAND BILLY. The whole town is UP IN ARMS because Mr. Privett has been a perfect manager of the Curling Rink and Banquet Hall for 6 years so I was thinking that a German Wirehaired Pointer puppy is exactly what Eleanor's very sad family needs to make them happy again – if you happen to have one left over that is.

Now, to answer your question, yes it's very okay with me for you to tell your friend Nigel Oswald from Oswestry, Shropshire, England everything. Those would have been good questions for him to ask townsfolk in Cardston but Rosy got a clue one hour ago from the Librarian at Strathcona Library who turns out to be a Mormon from Cardston whose Mom who still lives there told her that she says hello to a farmer named Percy Paisley and his wife Prizzie and her Auntie Miss Pearly Pitt by blood who lives behind her old shop Pearly's Clip 'N' Curl on Main Street. Albeit they might not be the right Paisleys. So I think that might be all the snooping Nigel has to do.

Your friend Posy

P.S. Did you know a German Wirehaired Pointer is what the dog named Promise was in the movie The Biscuit Eater? Maybe don't go see it if it ever comes back to Flatte Butte. It's so sad at the end you can't believe it.

P.P.S Thank you for paying extra for SPECIAL DELIVERY.

24. I Am Responsible For A Lot

First I covered up the antique tumbling rug with newspapers and spread out all my crayons and paints and coloured chalk and scissors and craft paper and glue and felt pieces and scotch tape and string and sequins and beads and pine cones and ribbons and then I went upstairs to my bottom drawer and got out the bags of barrettes and candy and bubble gum and noisemakers and little glass angels I bought at Woolworth's with the five dollars Mommy gave me and told me I'm old enough now to be responsible for buying my own Christmas presents for people and I went to work making the cards and fancy decorations Rosy had helped me invent for giving to my friends from what she learned in Fun With Fine Art at the Community Centre.

At Noon Mommy brought me a tomato and pickle sandwich and milk and a Christmas Baking butter tart and then I got right back to work at putting together my perfect cards and gifts for Becca, Peggy and Marji and my Flatte Butte friends being Bunny, Eleanor and Essie with a different card saying Merry Hanukkah for Essie which must be how you say Christmas in Poland.

Diddy and Bucky weren't getting anything because of not ever writing me back but then I started worrying what if the Reindeers are too scared to land on a roof behind The Slaughterhouse. So even though Diddy's not polite enough to ever answer me I found some left over stuff on the tumbling rug and made a thing for him that's sort of half card, half present and half decoration.

MERRY CHRISTMAS DIDDY

If you cut out the star on this card I made and poke a hole at the top and hang it by the red ribbon that I put in the envelope it turns into a Christmas tree decoration. I glued silver sequins on it to make it shiny.

Your friend Posy

I still couldn't think of one good reason why Bucky should get anything.

I carried everything upstairs and laid out my six beautiful gifts and Diddy's thing on the table for Mommy to see while I looked around to find if maybe she hadn't put the Christmas butter tarts away yet but she had. She said "My oh my, what a wonderful big job you've done. And I'm sure you also made something extra-EXTRA special for Rosy since she's been so kindly writing up a storm for you day after day after day for all these months."

Well Daddy was right as usual. It had only been four days around the corner from Miss Scrimm ruining everything by not allowing prairie dogs in Bethlehem and already a Big Break happened for me. Just before the end of the day's Combined Rhythm Band practice Miss Semonick and Mr. Gilliland took turns playing the piano while the other one walked up and down the rows of us musicians and leaned over to hear us each play our instrument. At the end of all five verses of We Three Kings of Orientar Miss Semonick and Mr. Gilliland whispered to each other for a minute and then Miss Semonick said "Paulette please come up to the front" and I did. She touched me on the shoulder with the end of her silver baton and said "You have an excellent sense of rhythm so Mr. Gilliland and I have chosen you to conduct the Combined Rhythm Band at the Christmas Concert."

Then Mr. Gilliland handed out short red cotton capes to every kid that last year's mothers had made for us to take home and get ironed and also red cotton pill box hats that stay on with elastic under your chin. While Miss Semonick was busy collecting our instruments at the door I asked her if my Mother could make me a different cape and pill box than the other kids and she said "What? Jimmy where's your other rhythm stick? I guess so." and I ran home and told Mommy exactly what I needed.

Next day I didn't go to the skating rink with everybody after school because I had to sit in the Basement and think hard about something. When Daddy got home I whispered to him to come downstairs with me and as soon as we were sitting on the tumbling rug where no one could hear I told him my secret plan. He said it was one of the best plans he's ever heard. Then he said would I mind if he made one tiny suggestion and I said I wouldn't. He said it might involve some elbow grease and I asked what's that and he told me and I said elbow grease would be okay. Then he told me how instead of going to The Hudson's Bay there might be a way to make my idea turn out bigger and better for the same money.

The phone rang after supper and Mommy answered it and then she looked at me and made a big "OH!" with her mouth and said "The Operator says she has a Long Distance call for a Miss Paulette Kohler" which was the first telephone call ever in The World where the Operator said "I have a Long Distance call for a Miss Paulette Kohler" and she handed me the phone. I said "This is a Miss Paulette Kohler speaking" and the Operator said "Go ahead please" and a girl said "Hello? Posy?" and I knew right away it was Eleanor Privett calling me LONG DISTANCE FROM FLATTE BUTTE SASKATCHEWAN. I said "Hi Eleanor" and she said "Hi Posy" and

I said "How are you?" and she said "I'M GETTING A PUPPY!" and I said "IS IT A GERMAN WIREHAIRED POINTER PUPPY?" and she said "YES!" and I said "MAGGIE HAD FOUR PUPPIES?" and she said "YES!" and then she told me Mr. Pankhurst from The Hotel called her Dad that day and asked him to drop by for a chat and a while later her Dad called her Mom and said they should all fix up and hurry over to The Hotel because Mr. Pankhurst had invited them for Dinner – which was how I found out that people in both Great Falls and Shrewsbury, Shropshire, England call supper Dinner – and she said the first thing he did when they got there was take them to a little room off the kitchen which I knew very well what room she meant and in it were two dogs and A BOX OF PUPPIES. And Mr. Pankhurst told Eleanor and Darlene they could pick the one they wanted but they couldn't take it home until it was ready to leave its Mother and Father whose name was Disraeli but they call him Dizzy. She said they picked the cutest and smartest one and Mr. Pankhurst told them that the name of the puppy they picked is Promise. And then she told me that when they got home after Dinner she said "Wait'll Posy hears we got the exact kind of puppy she said we should get" and her Dad said "Imagine that eh?" and then he said "Why don't you just call her Long Distance and tell her. Talk as long as you like." So she did and we did. She thanked me for my silver skates and told me Miss Lutz had picked her for a solo in the Ice Carnival and she said she was pretty sure she wouldn't have done that if she'd still been wearing boys' hockey skates.

Saturday morning I unlocked my official strongbox and took out the whole five dollars Emergency Reserve for Hotels and Meals and Daddy and me headed to The Sally Ann. When he pointed at a thing and said "That's exactly what we're looking for" I said I wasn't so sure but he said "Just wait 'til you get finished with it." When he carried it to the counter he said to the lady "What would you say to three dollars?" and she up and said "Sounds good to me" so at least I saved two dollars. When we got home Daddy covered the thing with gunny sacks and hid it in the back corner of the Basement. I put two dollars back in my official strongbox and then I went off to a movie with Rosy like nothing happened. It was called So Dear To My Heart and I learned the words to its best song being Lavender Blue Dilly-Dilly all in one go.

25. We Found Her But We Don't Know Where She Is

I knew that the date was exactly Monday, December 12 when I got another SPECIAL DELIVERY envelope because that morning Rosy said we should check the kitchen calendar every day from now on so we'd know how long it was until Christmas. I quick went and got the two-cent Cadbury Caramilk that I'd kept for myself from my gift making supplies and gave it to Rosy and asked her nicely if she would please read it to me.

Friday, December 9, 1949

PRIVATE & CONFIDENTIAL

Dear Posy,

I have RIVETING news! Therefore, I won't waste time telling you that Eleanor and Darlene Privett take turns helping me to look after Maggie, Dizzy and the four puppies or that Mr. Privett is settling in nicely to his new job as Manager of the Flatte Butte Hotel. I will get right to it.

Thurs., Dec. 8

9:45 am:	*Receive your startling clue in the morning post.*
10:00 am:	*Call Nigel. Share confidential details of The Mystery. He says Thursday is his only day off. It's either TODAY or wait a whole week.*
11:00 am:	*Nigel leaves for Cardston.*
11:25 am:	*Nigel arrives Main Street, Cardston.*
11:30 am:	*He spots faded sign "Pea---'s Cli- -N' Cur-". Knocks on door in alley behind shop. Neighbour says "You missed*

her. She's at Percy's service. It's at St. Andrew's United, they're not LDS you know."

11:45 am: Nigel arrives St. Andrew's. Finds Chapel empty. Townsfolk on street say "They've all gone to the burial. They're putting him in the family plot out on the farm with supper after." Nigel opts not to intrude.

12:15 pm: Nigel calls from News Agent's where he purchased this week's Cardston News. Says he can't talk or he'll miss his tee time at Waterton Lakes Golf Course.

12:16 pm: Nigel hangs up. Last I hear from him that day.

Fri., Dec. 9

10:00 am: Nigel phones. Apologizes for not reporting back yesterday. Says he played 18 holes, joined friends in clubhouse, lost all track of time and reason. Dictates Obit to me from Cardston News.

10:15 am: Nigel says 2 tour buses just arrived. He must rush off to escort 60 ladies to High Tea. Hangs up giving no further details.

Here is an excerpt from Percy Paisley's Obituary. (I've underlined the astonishing bits.)

"On Friday, December 2, 1949, Peter Percival "Percy" Paisley, born June 2, 1882 in Prestonpans, Scotland, passed away at home after a long illness. He is survived by his loving wife Priscilla "Prizzie", eldest daughter Pauline "Polly" (Perry) Pullman of Ponoka, son Paul (Patricia "Patty") of Pincher Creek, daughter Penelope "Penny" Paisley, in transit, aunt-in-law Pearl "Pearly" Pitt, grandchildren Poppy, Primrose, Parker and Patrick. All visited his bedside during his final days. Funeral service etc., etc., etc."

114

CONGRATULATIONS! The Mystery of The Disappeared Tap Dancer has been solved. Hats off to you for sniffing out a long and difficult trail of clues and for your quick thinking in sending Nigel off to Pearly's Clip 'N' Curl. We now know exactly where Miss Paisley has been and that she was still alive on December 8. PHEW.

Your friend,

Cyril Pankhurst

P.S. I bet the RCMP couldn't have managed any of that.

P.P.S. My COMPLIMENTS to Rosy for nosing out that startling bit of news at the library and for all her BRILLIANT letter editing.

P.P.P.S I took the liberty of giving a carbon copy of this letter to Eleanor who seemed to know all about The Mystery. She's gone off to pick up Darlene and then Bunny and take it to Essie and David's for a group reading.

I quick went and got the Dubble-Bubble-With-Free-Comic-And-Fortune that I had also kept for myself and gave it to Rosy and asked her would she mind if we wrote a letter right away. She bit off half the Dubble-Bubble and gave me the other half and we got started.

Mr. Charlie Buckler,
Fort Lively Hotel & Saloon,
Somewhere between Coutts and Shelby,
On Highway 91,
MONTANA,
United States Of America.

Monday, December 12, 1949

Dear Charlie "Chuck The Buck" Buckler,

Well I found Miss Penelope "Penny" Paisley for you without a lick of help from the Royal Canadian Mounted "RCMP" Police. Her father Peter Percival "Percy" Paisley died on December 2 and she was at his bedside on the farm so she's probably been too sad to write you and I bet that's why she didn't show up at Fort Lively Hotel & Saloon either.

I don't know exactly where she is now but I bet her Mom's Auntie by blood Miss Pearl "Pearly" Pitt will know if you knock on her door in the alley behind the sign "Pea---'s Cli- -N' Cur-" on Main Street in Cardston, Alberta.

Yours truly and Merry Christmas,

Paulette "Posy" Kohler

P.S. Don't tell her it was me who told you if I wasn't supposed to.

But then Rosy counted the days of how long it would take the letter to get to The States and she said it wouldn't be fair to make him wait that long to know where his Penny is. So we added

P.P.S. I paid extra for SPECIAL DELIVERY so you could know faster.

It cost fifty cents and left me one-dollar-and-fifty cents in my Emergency Reserve for Hotels and Meals.

And then Rosy without me even asking said "Don't you think we should write a letter to Mr. Pankhurst and thank him for everything he did to help?" and she was right so we did.

116

Monday, December 12, 1949

Dear Mr. Pankhurst,

Thank you very much for your RIVETING letter saying we found Miss Paisley but we don't know where she is. And thank you for the phoning and writing you did and for copying down the Obituary.

Your friend Posy

P.S. The CONGRATULATIONS for me and COMPLIMENTS for Rosy were very nice.

26. I Am Beside Myself

Tuesday, December 13. I kept my ear on Mommy's face when she phoned Nurse Beryl and asked what was she doing for Christmas and Nurse Beryl said "Treatments always wind down about the twentieth and I'm not checking into The Queen's Court Rooming House in Battleford until the day after Boxing Day so I'll probably just stay where I am in Maidstone and enjoy a few days of nice quiet time." Mommy said "You said you have a car now so why don't you get yourself to Edmonton and enjoy a few days of nice NOISY time with us instead?" and she said "Oh I don't know" and Mommy said "I'd love it if you came and Posy would be over the moon" and she said "It would be so much extra trouble for you" and I grabbed the phone and said "If you don't come you'll miss seeing me conduct The Combined Rhythm Band Of Grade One-ers and Two-ers in Lord Strathcona Elementary School's Annual Christmas Concert" and she said "Oh my goodness, then I guess I'll have to come won't I?"

NURSE BERYL WAS COMING FOR CHRISTMAS.

Wednesday, December 14. My hands were sore from Prepping which is really just sanding, sanding, sanding, sanding and sanding down in the Basement. Daddy said it's the price a professional has to pay for doing a thing better than anybody else.

I could barely finish my open-face hot beef sandwich with gravy and peas after we heard the radio say "Canadian skating star BARBARA ANN SCOTT who skyrocketed to international fame after winning the Olympic Gold Medal will be performing at The Edmonton Gardens early in the new year as the headliner of The Hollywood Ice Revue." Then later Pansy Daisy and me were behind the chesterfield listening when Mommy said "It would be a nice treat if we all went to see Barbara Ann" and Daddy said "As long as tickets aren't through the roof why not?" so it looked good WE MIGHT BE GOING TO SEE BARBARA ANN SCOTT.

Thursday, December 15. Almost no skating got done at Figure Skating class because all any of us girls could do was talk about the big news of BARBARA ANN SCOTT coming to Edmonton. Jackie our Instructor who is nineteen and can spin like crazy told us she just missed getting on the National Team by this much but if they hadn't played favourites with you-know-who, except none of us kids knew who-that-was, she might have been the next one winning the Gold Medal for Canada and skyrocketing to international fame like BARBARA ANN. She said what she thought she'd probably do instead is just turn Pro right away and work her way up to be a head liner in a big ice show as soon as she saves up enough money to fly out to wherever the auditions are.

When I got home Daddy gave me a new piece of sandpaper called Very Fine so I could sand everything I'd already sanded all over again plus some corners and curlicues I missed. Then when that was done he showed me how to do brushing off and wiping down.

Friday, December 16. I learned something that is a good lesson for any kid or even grown-up being that if you ever say something mean in a letter don't mail it.

Didier Desjardins,
c/o Miss Helen Talbot,
Flatte Butte Elementary School,
FLATTE BUTTE, Saskatchewan,
Canada.

Friday, December 16, 1949

Dear Didier, which I never knew that's what Diddy was short for!

Thank you for your letter I got today. I was not being a good friend at all when I said I wouldn't write you ever again if you didn't write me back. I didn't know your Tante Veronique and Uncle Wally are too busy to help you read or write a letter and that your oldest cousin Howie could help you but he won't. But I shouldn't have said that anyway. I'm sorry.

It was a very good idea of yours to take all my postcards and letters to your teacher who read them to you and then wrote the nice things you told her to say to me. I like you too and cross my heart I will never be mean to you again.

I am sad for you that your Grand-mère lives in Montreal where her Ballet Studio is and she is the only person left in the world that you know for sure loves you since your Mom and Dad died and your Tante and Uncle took you in as a chore. I don't know how lighting a candle can make you happier but if you think it could then you might as well try it.

Yours very truly,

Paulette

P.S. Paulette is a French name too because Mommy's father has a drop of French blood.

P.P.S. Pretty soon I won't need Rosy to help me and you won't need Miss Talbot and then boy-oh-boy you and me will write each other letters up a storm.

I thanked Rosy for helping me write such a nice and perfect letter to Diddy and offered to give her the pink barrette which was the last thing I kept for myself out of my gift making supplies but she said no that pink is my prettiest colour and I should keep it. PHEW.

Just before I went to bed I had one of my best ideas ever. When I told it to Mommy she said "YOU WANT ME TO DO WHAT? NEXT WEEK OF ALL TIMES?" But after a while of me begging she said "Alright but you really do take the cake sometimes."

Saturday, December 17. Mommy and me were out front of Silk-O-Lina before it even opened and when it did we went straight to the Remnants Table and found a four-yards-and-a-bit piece of brown corduroy that Mommy said was the very thing. It was one-dollar-and-forty-nine cents which I paid for with the one-dollar-and-fifty-cents left in my Emergency Reserve for Hotels and Meals and got a penny back.

Daddy was waiting for me with a can of something and he said "Lucky you, it's Primer Day!" which sounded like fun especially since it came with a paint brush but it made the secret thing look kind-of ugly after all my good sanding. But Daddy said it has to be done if you want to knock somebody's socks off when you're finished which I do.

Sunday, December 18. Sunday School was good because we got walked over to an Old Peoples Home to sing Christmas carols to them which they loved like crazy and clapped for us after every song and a lady passed around a plate of cookies in the shape of bells with very hard icing which was okay because my front tooth had tightened up again.

Monday, December 19. It was finally Paint Day and except for a spill that we caught before it made too big of a mess it turned out perfect so I figured I was done but Daddy said "Now if we let that dry overnight and you do one more careful thin coat tomorrow it will be a thing of beauty." I don't think I want to be a professional when I grow up.

Tuesday, December 20. Rosy moved her books from the window sill and the floor of our bedroom to a big box in the basement. I put my toys in a pile behind the furnace. Mommy took some of our clothes out of the closet and drawers and fixed our room up pretty for Nurse Beryl and on his way home from work Daddy picked up the Guest Room mattress that Mommy's new best friend Mrs. Gilroy said we could borrow and he put it on the tumbling rug for Rosy and me to sleep on while Nurse Beryl was here.

After Dinner Rosy went back to school for Nativity Rehearsal for Speaking Roles Only and Mommy started cooking company food for Nurse Beryl's visit and I went down to the Basement with Daddy and did my last very careful thin coat of paint. Even while it was still wet you could see it was already a thing of beauty.

Wednesday, December 21. Nurse Beryl phoned early in the morning to say she was on her way. She told Mommy she was just going to stop off in Lloydminster to do a bit of a shop on their High Street and she'd be arriving at our house about the time the girls got home from school.

Rosy had her last Nativity Rehearsal for Full Cast after school but I ran home as fast as I could except for Mr. Street saying "Whoa, slow down Posy" and then I saw a car with Saskatchewan license plates parked in front of our house and I ran inside and there was Nurse Beryl. I knew right away it was her because she hadn't changed one bit since last time I saw her in Flatte Butte which she said was over six months ago. I sat beside her on the chesterfield when Mommy brought in tea and mincemeat tarts and said "In honour of Beryl being here I've brought a cup of tea for you Posy." My first. She'd put lots of milk and sugar in it and it was a bit better than I thought it would be after trying Daddy's coffee once. The three of us sipped our tea and ate daintily and talked just like we were still in the booth in Flatte Butte. Then I sat on the bed and watched Nurse Beryl unpack and I showed her I still had my blue velvet bag with my lucky teeth in it and I let her read my Your Stairway To Stardom booklet and I asked her if she'd like to see some of my tumbling routines but Mommy came in and said "Beryl's been driving all day and I bet she'd love a little lie down before dinner." I sat outside the bedroom door so I'd know when she came out.

Dinner was pork chops with mint jelly and scalloped potatoes with Nurse Beryl sitting on Pansy Daisy's chair in a beautiful green velveteen dress she just got at The High Street in Lloydminster looking so young and pretty Rosy and me couldn't believe it when she told Mommy she'd just turned THIRTY.

27. Bethlehem On The Prairies

Thursday, December 22. Rosy and the other Nativity Cast-ers were already at school for Miss Scrimm's six o'clock sharp Costume Call when Mommy and Daddy and Nurse Beryl dropped me off. The hall was full of Northern Lights getting stapled into their bright pink for girls and bright green for boys crêpe paper capes. I peeked into the room where the Grade Three-ers and Four-ers were doing Mrs. Hammond's throat looseners and there were red ribbons around all the girls' heads and red bow-ties clipped to the boys' necks. When I got to the room where us Combined Rhythm Band-ers were told to come in our capes and pill boxes Mr. Gilliland said "Since you'll be entering with Miss Semonick you should probably go wait with her instead of with the musicians." I don't know why Mr. Rasmussen picked her to play the piano for us tonight instead of Mr. Gilliland who's way better.

I found Miss Semonick in the Music Room warming up playing Let It Snow Let It Snow on the piano. She had a cigarette in her mouth so when I asked where I should wait I couldn't quite tell if she said "Wait here 'til we go to the stage" or "Wait for me by the door to the stage" or "Wait for me right on the stage" so I picked one. When I was leaving the Music Room I nearly bumped into Mr. Rasmussen poking his head in the door and saying "Good luck Emmy. See you later tonight."

Back out in the hall the Hired Men were chasing the Cows, Mary was punching a Rich Dairy Farmer for un-swaddling her doll and not one Northern Light was behaving themselves. When Miss Scrimm stood on a chair and whisper-yelled "QUIET. QUIET

EVERYONE. THE HOUSE IS IN" I quick squeezed through the door to the stage before it closed behind Mr. Rasmussen.

I ducked behind a cardboard tree just as Mr. Rasmussen said into the microphone "Testing-testing. Good evening Ladies and Gentlemen, boys and girls." I peeked through the cut-out branches "Welcome to The Lord Strathcona Elementary School Annual Chris—" and started looking for Mommy and Daddy and Nurse Beryl. "In my role as Principal of—" I found them! "—understand the importance of introducing young children to The Arts, so not only will our students be singing, acting and playing musical instru—" They were half way back "—also made the posters, costumes and trees—" sitting all three together in a row "—even helped Mr. McNabb build this magnificent stable and manger—" I waved at them through some paper leaves "—in keeping with our theme will be called the Livery Barn and Feed Trough" but I guess they couldn't tell it was my hand. When the audience finished clapping for the magnificent Livery Barn Miss Scrimm out in the hall whispered "WE KNOW OUR BLOCKING. WE KNOW OUR LINES" and Mr. Rasmussen quick said "Now without further ado here are the students of Grades Five and Six performing BETHLEHEM ON THE PRAIRIES."

Mrs. Octavia Hammond who is well known in Edmonton and beyond started playing and singing O Little Town of Bethlehem which she couldn't have picked a more perfect song because it let the audience know right off the bat where they were. When she switched to singing really quiet for "How silently, how silently" Miss Scrimm whispered "PLACES EVERYONE!" and Mrs. Hammond jumped and missed "wondrous gift" but most people in the audience wouldn't know all the words like I do. She was halfway through her last word "Eee-maaan-ew-elllll" when Miss Scrimm whispered "AAAAND, YOU'RE ON." The stage door WHOOSHED and I quick switched trees so the Cows could get by me and then WHOOSH it was Mary and Joseph who went and stood beside the magnificent Livery Barn pretending to be tired and lost but mostly looking scared.

Joseph said "It was a long hard wagon ride here from Nazareth." Mary said "All because we have to pay our unfair taxes." Joseph said "Too bad the Log Cabin Inn was full Mary." Mary said "Yes. You're right Joseph. Now what will we do if the baby's born tonight?" Joseph said "Here's a Livery Barn we could bed down in." Mary said "And we could use this Feed Trough for a cradle." Then Mr. Gilliland out in the hall played the first line of Hark The Herald Angels Sing perfect on his trumpet. Joseph said "HARK! Was that a heralding trumpet?" Mary said "Here come two Hired Men. Let's ask them." But nothing happened. Miss Scrimm whispered "FOR GOD'S SAKE GO!" and WHOOSH two boys in overalls ran by me and one of them quick pointed to the silver star nailed to the Livery Barn roof and said "Look over there in the prairie sky" and Mr. May aimed a light right at it. The other Hired Man pretended to be shocked and said "I've never seen such a bright star before" and the first one said "BEHOLD! What are all those coloured lights?" and WHOOOOOOOOOOOOOSH, I was nearly run over by forty Northern Lights rushing by me to the top risers. Then Mr. Gilliland played the second line of Hark The Herald Angels Sing on his trumpet, Miss Scrimm whispered "ANGELS GO!" and WHOOSH the Angels APPEARED. Rosy who was Angel Number One said "Don't be afraid. The bright star and the Northern Lights are just the glory of the Lord shining 'round about you." She had tried out

126

for Mary which she would have been perfect as but it always goes to a Grade Six-er. Rosy looked so beautiful in her long white gown with a tinsel halo wired to her hair that anyone could see she outdid Mary and I was even a little sorry for the other two Angels. Then the Hired Men looked into the Livery Barn and one of them said "Hey! There's a little baby in the Feed Trough. Well I'll be, he has a halo" and the other one said "Here come those Three Rich Dairy Farmers from a few miles East of here." WHOOSH. The First Rich Dairy Farmer said "We saw a new star and followed it here." The Second one said "Let's open our saddlebags and get out the gifts we brought." And the Third one said "Why don't we kneel down and worship this baby who is obviously the Son of God."

Then The Northern Lights started swaying and singing "Away in a manger, No crib for a bed" which was EXACTLY what was happening in the Livery Barn. You could hear parents going "Ooooh" and "Aaaah" and even "Sniff-sniff" when they got to the "Bless all the dear children" and "Take us to heaven" parts near the end. Then Miss Scrimm whispered "KILL THE LIGHTS" and in the pitch dark Mrs. Hammond pounded a loud chord which was Mr. May's Cue to start swinging his light back and forth across The Northern Lights' bright pink and green capes and every single Grade Five-er and Six-er said all together "GLORY TO GOD IN THE HIGHEST AND ON EARTH PEACE, GOOD WILL TOWARD MEN" and the audience didn't know what to do with themselves.

They clapped and cheered and stamped their feet to make the Nativity Cast-ers take a bow but Miss Scrimm had told them "Don't bow. If you FREEZE where you are and stay there it will be wildly effective" and she was right. When the audience finally gave up waiting for them to bow and stopped clapping Mr. Rasmussen said "Wasn't that something?" and they started up all over again.

When it was almost quiet he said "Now the Grade Threes and Fours will sing The Twelve Days of Christmas with very clever lyrics and actions by Mrs. Octavia Hammond in keeping with our BETHLEHEM ON THE PRAIRIES theme." They came out carrying skis and brooms and horns and what else they needed and they sang on and on and on and on and on and on and on and on and on and on until they finally ended with "Twelve farmers seeding, Eleven riggers drilling, Ten skaters freezing, Nine skiers jumping, Eight curlers sweeping, Seven coyotes howling (YOW-OOOO), Six chipmunks chirping (chirp, chirp), FIVE... OY-ILL WELLS (GUSHHHHH), Four chickadees (CHICK-A-DEE-DEE-DEE-DEE), Three brant geese (HONK HONK), Two noisy crows (CAW CAW) AND... A... MAGPIE... IN... A... PINE... TREE."

When they were done bowing and leaving the stage Mr. Rasmussen said "And now, the Combined Rhythm Band of Grades One and Two students will close our Concert with a rousing Medley of Christmas Favourites with the very talented Miss Emmy Semonick on piano and Paulette Kohler conducting" and the shortest musicians marched by me and onto the lowest riser.

I re-tied the silver ribbon bow on my turquoise satin cape. I straightened my turquoise satin pill box with the rhinestones in the shape of a star glued on it. I squeezed my bag of lucky teeth in my skirt pocket and I waited for the medium and taller musicians to finish taking their places in front of The Northern Lights. And then *WHOOSH* Miss Semonick came up behind me puff-puffing and hiss-whispered "I have been looking everywhere for you. I can't believe I didn't try the stage!" Then she put on a smile and walked over to the piano. When everybody was where they were supposed to be I walked slowly out from behind my tree, past the magnificent Livery Barn, past the Three Rich Dairy Farmers, past the Cows, the Hired Men, the Angels and The Holy Family and I smiled at the audience. Then I turned and smiled for two more whole seconds straight at Nurse Beryl and then I swung around just fast enough to let my satin cape sparkle in Mr. May's light. I nodded to shush the musicians, I looked at Miss Semonick for my cue and I raised my silver baton.

After our big Jingle Bells Finale with everyone stopping exactly on time to my baton the musicians all bowed their red cotton pill boxes and the audience clapped for so long Mr. Gilliland had to run out from the hall and tell them to bow again. I waited until the clapping was just about finished and then I twirled around to give the audience one last look at my cape and I did a long low curtsy. When I looked up again everybody was smiling and clapping just for me and I could tell it was plain to everyone that I had been wasting myself in small towns.

28. It's CHRISTMAS!

Friday, December 23. Just before Mr. Rasmussen let us out an hour early to start Christmas Holidays Miss Semonick handed out our first ever Report Cards which were licked shut for our parents to open.

I got an H for Honours in Reading, an H in Printing, A-pluses in Physical Training, Music and Art, an A in Social Studies, a B in Science and a C in Arithmetic. At the bottom after the marks was a place for Teacher's Comments. Miss Semonick WHO THE DAY BEFORE I HAD EMPTIED THE PENCIL SHARPENER FOR WITHOUT EVEN BEING ASKED wrote "Clever, cheerful, can be willful, talks entirely too much." Rosy got all H's and "What a joy she is to have in class." Mommy said she was very proud of both of us and she promised not to tell Nurse Beryl about Miss Semonick's mean Comment.

Saturday, December 24. Daddy carried the secret thing upstairs to his and Mommy's bedroom and we shut the door behind us and he took out a little bottle of paint with real gold in it and gave me a teeny-tiny brush and showed me how to very carefully paint the ends of the curlicues pure gold. When I was done it was the most beautiful thing I'd ever seen in my whole life and I did it all myself.

For Dinner we had roast beef, mashed potatoes, candied carrots which I wish she always made them that way and something called Yorkshire Pudding that sure wasn't pudding but Nurse Beryl had two helpings of it with gravy and told Mommy "Bless you, I could cry." There was no dessert and I KNEW WHY. After doing dishes Rosy and me snuck downstairs to change and exactly at seven o'clock there was a knock on the front door and we heard Mommy tell Nurse Beryl to please go to the bedroom and shut the door and wait there for a surprise. Rosy and me passed Daddy on the stairs as he was coming down to get the antique French Empire Armchair that I had tied bows on and we got to the top just as Mommy was answering the door. It was Mr. and Mrs. Gilroy and Marji and one minute later it was Mr. and Mrs. Upright with Peggy and her sister Joy who is Rosy's best friend and after we waited a bit Becca got there with her Dad and her little brother Nico and little sister Nina. Mommy invited them all into the living room and Peggy, Becca, Marji and Rosy and me ran and hid in the kitchen with the door shut and the light off. Then we heard Mommy knock on the bedroom door and I poked my head out and yelled "OKAY NURSE BERYL YOU CAN COME OUT NOW" and I ducked back in. We heard Mommy introducing her to everybody and then Daddy said "Beryl, may I show you to the Chair Of Honour" and she gasped and said "My goodness, is this for me?" and then Daddy said in an important voice "Please take your seats everyone. The show is about to begin. And now, Ladies and Gentlemen, I would like to present the Premiere Performance of an all new, completely original production called BETHLEHEM NEAR EDMONTON." Then he walked over and KILLED THE LIVING ROOM LIGHT and I reached over and opened the kitchen door just wide enough for Rosy to get through and out she went in her beautiful Angel costume and halo walking very slow in the dark and carrying the Lead Crystal Candelabra from Daddy's Stock with all five candles lit. Then Daddy helped her step up nicely onto a kitchen chair he'd brought out and she looked down as if she was floating up in the sky and said:

"BEHOLD! While Oil-men watched their rigs by night, all seated on the ground, the Angel of the Lord came down, saying Look at what I found. Four rodents with no oil or gold, or myrrh or anything, What could they bring the newborn king? They'll do some TUMBLE-ING."

Then Daddy switched the light back on, I pushed the door open wide with my head and Peggy, Becca, Marji and me crawled out of the kitchen on our hands and knees wearing brown corduroy rompers and matching hoods with little ears sewn on them and the ends of our noses rubbed with brown shoe polish. I whispered "ONE, TWO, THREE, GO" and Marji and me started doing difficult moves into the centre of the room and Peggy and Becca followed us doing ordinary somersaults while we all sang my new words to I Saw Three Ships Come Sailing In:

"Two prairie dogs did straddle rolls
On Christmas Day, on Christmas Day,
Two somersaulted all the way
On Christmas Day in the morning.

One stood upon its head and said
I'll stay this way all day for you
And one can do the splits for you
On Christmas Day in the morning.

Two others crab-walked all the way
To Bethlehem, to Bethlehem,
Two cartwheeled up to welcome them
On Christmas Day in the morning.

Three prairie dogs do jumping jacks
While one does scary shoulder rolls"

Then we all bent over and put the tops of our heads on the floor to pretend we were going down underground, Daddy KILLED THE LIGHT and we sang in the dark:

"Then disappear back down our holes
On Christmas day in the morning."

I thought everybody would never stop clapping and cheering. All of us took bows together and then one of us at a time and then back all together until Mommy said "Fruit punch anyone?" and everybody went and got a glass of punch and a plate to put on all they wanted of butter tarts, mincemeat tarts, decorated gingerbread men, Christmas cake with marzipan icing and pieces of divinity fudge. Nurse Beryl hugged me three times and told me every time it was the biggest surprise and the finest Christmas gift she ever got.

When Mommy was kissing us goodnight on our mattress in the Basement I said "This was the best Christmas Eve in all my life and just think the whole perfect time only cost one-dollar-and-forty-nine-cents for corduroy" and she said "It was a Christmas miracle."

Sunday, December 25. It was still dark out on Christmas morning when Rosy woke up because of me jumping on the Gilroy's mattress and she raced me up the stairs. We woke Mommy and Daddy up and knocked on Nurse Beryl's door and then everything happened exactly like I'd been wishing and praying for it to. We got to the living room and Rosy stopped. And she looked. And she went closer. And she stared hard at the tall, beautiful, pure white, four-shelf-high bookcase with real gold on its curlicues and she read the card I made that said "To Rosy From Posy" and she jumped up and down and thanked me and she jumped up and down again and hugged me and she hugged the bookcase and she touched each one of the gold curlicues and she said it was the most exquisite thing she's ever owned and she thanked me again and hugged me again and then we sat down under the tree and got busy with the rest of our presents.

I had only badly wanted one thing for Christmas being a BARBARA ANN SCOTT Doll in her little lace skating costume with real marabou trim and a teeny pair of real figure skates so I asked Santa and Jesus both for it and then I didn't do one thing bad for two whole months except for a broken Girandle and a bit of candy borrowing at Hallowe'en. I was SHOCKED when I didn't get it. Mommy said Santa must have given it to a poor little girl in Africa since I had just got figure skates a month ago which I guess was fair. But then it turned out I hardly even minded because I looked and saw my own Pansy Daisy in a white lace wedding gown with a train and a long net veil hooked to her hair and she was leaning against a little wood dresser painted silver with four drawers that all work perfect and in them was a whole trousseau being a pink wool going-away suit with matching hat, a blue chiffon nightgown and bed jacket set, a knitted winter coat with a real fur collar, and a ball gown that was a miracle because Mrs. Santa had made it out of the exact same turquoise satin as my Combined Rhythm Band conducting cape. From Mommy and Daddy I got a pink angora skating hat and matching scarf that Mommy knitted and the almost whole set of Bobbsey Twins books I'd wanted so bad at The Sally Ann. From Rosy I got a bow and arrow set with suction cups on the arrows to practise getting good at Archery.

Rosy got a fountain pen and a bottle of ink from Santa and from Mommy and Daddy a Flash Brownie Camera and a skating hat and scarf like mine only blue. And we each got a card from Grandma and Grandpa with five one-dollars in it.

Then Nurse Beryl gave Rosy and me wrapped boxes to open at the same time. Mine was a long-to-the-floor pale pink nightgown with lace trim and a satin bow that looked more like an evening gown than a nightie. Rosy's was the same only blue. We ran and changed into them and everyone said we looked exactly like movie stars and I don't think they were kidding.

Then Daddy made us all Open Face Denver Sandwiches that he's famous for and that's when the phone rang.

29. The Last Thing To Leave Us Is Hope

Mommy said "Who'd call us at six-thirty on Christmas morning?" and she said "Hello... Yes this is Isobel Kohler." She whispered to us "It's Long Distance." "Yes?... Oh hi Dottie" She kept listening and her face got worried and she said "Just a moment, I'll ask her. Posy it's Mrs. Privett, Eleanor's Mom. Diddy Desjardins ran away last night. His Aunt's been calling his friends to see if they know where he might have gone. Has he said anything to you in a letter?" I said "Not about running away but he really misses his Grand-mère in Montreal so maybe he went there." Mommy said "No Dottie nothing that will help... Oh dear... that's bitter cold... The hotel? Good idea... I know... that poor little boy's been through so much. Please call us when you hear anything... Yes... No... The last thing to leave us is hope" and she hung up.

Mommy said "Dottie told me Veronique Wolff got up around eleven-thirty last night to see to the baby and when she walked by the boys' room Diddy's bed was empty. She looked through the house and Wally searched outside, then they called the neighbours and everybody headed out with flashlights to find him but a blizzard came up and pretty soon they couldn't see a foot in front of them. They all just barely found their way home. Dottie said thankfully Diddy's parka and snow pants and boots were gone – but it's thirty below. It quit blowing before dawn and now half the town's out looking for him. They're using the hotel as the check-in point. Dottie's handling calls. George Privett's organizing search routes. Mr. Pankhurst asked his cook to come in and keep the searchers in food and hot drinks when they come inside to warm up and he went out looking with the others. Diddy's been gone at least seven hours now. That poor sweet little boy."

Nobody felt Christmassy after that. Mommy said "I might as well get the bird ready. We have to eat." Nurse Beryl said "I'll help." Daddy shoveled the sidewalk and listened to CBC News. Rosy started me up reading the first Bobbsey Twins book but neither of us felt like finishing it. I changed Pansy Daisy into her going-away suit and Rosy went down to the Basement to get a book out of the box but one minute later I heard her running up the stairs two at a time yelling "QUICK GO GET YOUR LETTER FROM DIDDY" and I did and she said "EVERYBODY COME HERE" and everybody did and she read out loud "I tried and tried to make myself happy again but nothing helped. Not letters from Grand-mère, not musical movies, not even your lucky neck crack. But if I can go and light a candle on Christmas Eve maybe that will work." Mommy said "I don't know what to make of that but it's worth a call."

"Dottie it's Isobel. This might be nothing but Diddy said in a letter to Posy that if he could go and light a candle on Christmas Eve it might make him happy again. I wonder, does that mean anything to anyone? Yes please do." Mommy said to us "Some of the searchers are there warming up, she's asking them... Who?... And?.... Yes... Oh dear... Wally Wolff will blame himself... It's sure worth a look... By now they'll have tried everywhere else. Call me when you hear" and she hung up.

Mommy said "Miss Helen Talbot was there." Rosy and me both said "She's the Elementary teacher." "Right, and she said to them 'OH-GOOD-GOD-HOW-DID-I-NOT-PUT-IT-TOGETHER? I even

137

helped him write that letter to his little friend Posy!' Dottie said apparently Diddy told Miss Talbot he had asked if he could go to Midnight Mass on Christmas Eve and his Uncle Wally said 'No you can not! How would that look with me being an Elder in the Baptist Church?' and Dottie said Mr. Pankhurst said 'Let's go. We'll take my car' and off he and Miss Talbot went to search the Catholic Church."

We all stayed in the kitchen. Mommy and Nurse Beryl fixed things for dinner. Rosy and me played Pick-Up-Sticks and drank hot chocolate Daddy made us. When he sat down with his coffee he said "Hmm, so Diddy's uncle is Wally Wolff." Mommy said "You know him?" and Daddy said "No but about ten years back he was a whiz kid on the Melville team. People thought he'd follow Sid Abel into the NHL – he even had a try-out in Montreal – but then he dropped out of sight." Mommy said "Montreal eh? Maybe that's when he met Veronique" and Daddy said "Could be." But mostly we all just waited and waited for the phone to ring. And then it did.

Mommy answered and after a minute she said "Oh thank God." When she finished listening and hanging up she told us "When Mr. Pankhurst and Miss Talbot got to the Catholic Church and were making their way through the snow past the Christmas Crèche they saw that Mary and Joseph's robes were blown off and gone and the Baby Jesus was half buried in a snowdrift in front of the manger and then they saw a big notice on the front door that said ATTENTION: MIDNIGHT MASS CANCELLED DUE TO BLIZZARD. They tried the door handle but it was locked and they walked all the way around the church trying doors and windows to see if Diddy could have got inside, but no, everything was locked up tight. Then on their way back to the car, all heartsick about not finding him, Miss Talbot thought she saw what could be two small boots sticking out of one end of the manger and when they got closer a little wisp of steam came up out of the snow and straw. They lifted up the straw and the boots were attached to a bundle that filled the little manger. It was Diddy curled up in Mary and Joseph's robes with no room left to tuck his feet in. They spoke to him but he was unconscious. They scooped him up and drove straight to The Hotel because it was closer than the hospital or the Wolffs' house. Ian Rolheiser saw them through the window and shouted 'They got him!' and held the door open. Connie Cruickshank said 'Is he—?' and Miss Talbot said 'He's alive.' Mr. Pankhurst called out 'Get the Doctor' and headed for the stairs with his precious bundle and Dr. Demchuk said 'I'm right here' and followed Mr. Pankhurst up the stairs and Mrs. Cohen ran after them with a feather tick she'd brought from home just in case. Dottie Privett said she immediately called Veronique who sobbed so loud when she heard the news that she woke her baby. Dottie's husband George had just come back to warm up and he turned right around and went back out to call off the search. And while Dottie and I were talking Wally Wolff burst in the door saying 'I just heard. Where is he?' and Dottie said 'Upstairs but you better wait until—' but she said he was off up the stairs."

The phone rang again and this time it was Joy asking Rosy if she and me could go skating with her and Peggy. Mommy said she thought it was a good idea and I asked Nurse Beryl would she like to come and watch us do figure skating moves and she said she'd love to and off the three of us went and picked up Peggy and Joy on the way. At first Rosy and me just held hands and skated 'round and 'round to show off our new skating hats and matching scarves and Peggy and Joy did the same to show off their new red snow pants and matching mitts. But then another Christmas miracle happened. I did my first ever flat iron and Nurse Beryl was watching. I didn't get back up again but I went quite a long ways down the ice before I tipped over.

When we got home Mrs. Privett had phoned Mommy again and said Dr. Demchuk said it was touch-and-go for a while there but that Diddy is recovering well from his Hypo-thermia thanks to him having been smart enough to wrap up and climb under the straw but he had frozen his feet quite badly. Dr. Demchuk had to leave because he was needed at the hospital but he told them how to take care of Diddy and what to watch out for and he said it would be best to keep him where he is for a few days and be sure not to let him walk.

Daddy started carving the turkey and Mommy and Nurse Beryl put the mashed potatoes and gravy and stuffing and cranberry sauce and yams and jellied salad on the table and we all sat down. Mommy said "We should say grace." Nurse Beryl said "May I say it" and Mommy said "Of course" and we all bowed our heads. "Dear Lord, we thank you for sparing Diddy. We thank you for our many blessings. I thank you for Isobel, Max, Rosy and Posy who have opened their hearts and their home to me and eased my loneliness and made me laugh again. For what we are about to receive we are truly grateful. Amen."

We ate and ate and ate and when we all said we couldn't eat another mouthful Mommy lit the Christmas Pudding and spooned it nicely into the good dessert bowls but then she nearly spilled the Hard Sauce when I jumped up and yelled at Nurse Beryl "YOU

COULD GO TO FLATTE BUTTE AND SAVE DIDDY'S FEET!" "Posy!" Mommy said but I said "We could call Mr. Pankhu—" but Daddy said "ENOUGH Posy" but Nurse Beryl said "No, it makes perfect sense, it's barely out of my way and Lord knows I'm used to town-hopping" but Mommy said "The roads around Flatte Butte will be terrible from the blizzard" but Nurse Beryl said "They'll have been clearing them ever since, so if I leave at dawn I could be there by early afternoon and start Diddy's treatments right away" but Daddy said "Dr. Demchuk told them what to do for his feet" but Nurse Beryl said "But I'm a trained Physiotherapist" but Mommy said "But they're expecting you in Battleford" but Nurse Beryl said "I'll call the Queen's Court and change my dates. It's settled" and Mommy said "Beryl, you are a ministering angel."

30. Mine And Nurse Beryl's Secret

I was sitting on the bed helping Nurse Beryl pack when Mommy poked her head in and said "Mr. Pankhurst said they'll have a room ready for you and to please tell you they're all so very grateful you're coming to help" and then she went off to make Welsh cakes for Nurse Beryl to eat on the road. I was carefully folding her new green velveteen dress for her when she said "In Diddy's letter he mentioned your lucky neck crack. Did you maybe try to make him lucky by cracking his neck?" I said "I might have." She said "Think hard" and I said "Yes. One crack to the left." She said "When I was a very young nurse I left my home in Chester, Cheshire, England and trained for three full years in Manchester to get a special Degree so that I could do treatments on soldiers and other people who were in pain. Cracking someone's neck can cause serious, lasting harm if you don't know exactly what you're doing." "I'm sorry. I didn't know." "Of course you didn't and I should have told you not to try it, but back then I didn't know what a helpful little girl you are." I said "Do you think you could check and see if Diddy's head is on straight and if it's not would you crack it back to the right?" "Yes, I promise I will." "And while you're there could you make sure Eleanor Privett's is on straight too?" "Oh goodness, yes, yes of course." "And Bunny Cruickshank's and Essie Cohen's and Bucky Beddoes'?" "Tell me those names again so I don't miss anyone" and she got out her pen and a little book and I told her and then I said "I'll see if I can think of a sneaky way to get them to The Hotel so you don't have to run around town finding them." "Good idea. Anyone else?" "No just the five of them" and I handed her the perfectly folded green dress. "Like the cat?" "Pardon?" she said. "Is

142

Chester Cheshire England the same Cheshire that the Cheshire Cat is from?" and she said "Actually, yes."

I woke up with Nurse Beryl bending down kissing my forehead and then Rosy's on our mattress in the Basement. She said "Don't get up. I just didn't want to leave without saying good-bye" and she tiptoed away but we jumped up and ran up the stairs after her and put our parkas on over our evening-gown nighties and stepped our bare feet into our snow boots and walked her in the pitch dark to her car which Daddy had already brushed the snow off of and started the engine running so both her and the car would be warm. When she drove off and we came back inside Mommy said "Happy Boxing Day girls, here's breakfast" and she took the wax paper off the other half of the Welsh cakes and dumped them on the table and went back to bed and Daddy fell asleep on the chesterfield.

I asked Rosy "Would you please help me write a thank you letter now so I can mail it as soon as the Post Office opens tomorrow?" "Sure but why so fast?" "So it gets to Flatte Butte while Nurse Beryl is still there" and I ran and got our writing pad.

Monday, December 26, 1949

Dear Essie,

I'm glad you liked my Cadbury-Caramilk-barrette-noisemaker-glass-angel decoration. Thank you for the exquisite box of Black Magic Chocolates which I JUST LOVE.

I got a bride gown and a trousseau and a dresser for Pansy Daisy and a pink angora skating hat and matching scarf and an evening-gown nightie and almost all The Bobbsey Twins books and a bow and arrows and other stuff.

What did you get under the tree from Santa and your Mom and Dad and David on Hanukkah morning?

As soon as David reads you this letter you should pick up Bucky and the two of you go to The Hotel to visit poor Diddy who nearly froze to death and still has time to lose his feet. Bunny can't go with you since she's home sick as usual. My friend Nurse Beryl will be upstairs doing treatments on Diddy's feet. Be sure to say to her Hello I'm Posy's friend ESSIE COHEN and this is my friend BUCKY BEDDOES.

On top of paying for SPECIAL DELIVERY I'm putting one dollar of my Christmas money in this envelope for you and Bucky to each have pie with ice cream and a pop at The Hotel to make sure he'll go with you. You can also see Mr. Pankhurst's puppies which is another good reason for going.

Your friend Posy

P.S. Remember don't leave The Hotel until you've said hello from me to Nurse Beryl and TOLD HER YOUR NAMES.

I asked Rosy if she'd mind writing another thank you letter this one being for Bunny and she said no she didn't mind one bit.

Monday, December 26, 1949

Dear Bunny,

I'm glad you liked my Dubble-Bubble-barrette-glass-angel-pine-cone decoration. Thank you for the wonderful All Day Sucker and the yellow book mark you knitted yourself which I JUST LOVE.

I got a bride gown and a trousseau and a dresser for Pansy Daisy and a pink angora skating hat and matching scarf and an evening-gown nightie and almost all The Bobbsey Twins books and a bow and arrows and other stuff.

144

What did you get for Christmas? I mean besides Strep Throat. Ha-ha.

Your friend Posy

P.S. I'm sorry I made that joke. Strep Throat isn't funny. You should gargle with warm salt water or it could turn into Smallpox or worse.

I was going to ask Rosy to do one more letter for Eleanor but then Daddy woke up and she quick asked him to please carry her bookcase into the bedroom and away they went to decide where to put it and then down he went to bring up her box of books and I figured all she'd want to do for the rest of the day is try different books on different shelves and I was right.

But then in the afternoon the phone rang and I answered it and The Operator said "I have a Long Distance call for a Miss Paulette Kohler" and I said "I am a Miss Paulette Kohler" and the Operator said "Go ahead please" and a girl said "Hi Posy" and I said "Hi Eleanor I was going to get Rosy to help me write you a thank you letter to thank you for your thank you letter and for the ink pad with six rubber animal stamps which I JUST LOVE" and she said "You're welcome. Mr. Pankhurst says I can talk to you until Beryl comes to the phone to chat with your Mom. He said to say Hello to Posy for him so Hello" and I said "Tell him Hello Mr. Pankhurst" and she said she would and then she told me all the things she's heard that Diddy said since he came to.

"He said he didn't run away that he was just going to sneak out when everybody was asleep and go to Midnight Mass and light a candle and come straight home without anybody knowing and getting mad at him but he waited and waited at the church door for it to open but nobody came and I asked if he saw the sign on the door and he said yes but the words were too hard for him and he got so cold he went and stood inside The Holy Mary's robe but he got colder and colder and the snow started blowing right at him and he said he was sorry to do it but he put the Baby Jesus nicely on the ground and he took The Holy Mary's and Joseph's robes off them for blankets and he climbed in the manger under the straw and pulled his shiny star ornament out of his pocket and put it in his mitten and that's all he remembers." I said "Does he have Gang Green?" and Eleanor said "Not yet." And then she said "Guess what" and I said "What?" and she said "I got brand new figure skates for Christmas" and I said "HOO-HOO-HOORAY FOR YOU" and she said "And do you know what else?" and I said "What?" and she said "The puppies can wag their tails now and I think Promise knows me when I hold her. Oopsie, here comes Beryl so you better run and get your Mom, Bye."

Mommy let me put my ear on her face to listen and Nurse Beryl thanked her again for Christmas and then told her everything about Diddy that I already knew from Eleanor but she also said "Isn't it a small world, it turns out Cyril and I grew up not fifty miles from each other in England."

31. This Time It's Forever

A thick envelope came in the mail that said TO POSY KOHLER on the front and on the back I could tell it said FROM MR. CHARLIE BUCKLER & MISS PENNY PAISLEY. I ran it straight to Rosy's Study which is the corner of our bedroom where she had asked Daddy to help her set up her bookcase with its back to the rest of the room – lucky for her I painted the back of it the same nice white as the front – and far enough away from the wall to leave room for the hardly ruined antique Victorian Side Table with a drawer that locks that I accidentally knocked over playing Madam that she calls her Writing Desk and a small chair Daddy found at Sally Ann that I'm going to show her how to paint white and a picture on the wall of Jane Austen in a frame. She opened the envelope and said "There are two letters in here, one from each of them and hers is pretty long. You'd better take a seat." So I had to leave the Study and sit on the bed that now has my side shoved up smack against the other wall which means it's very hard to make the bed but Rosy said if I let her keep the extra space for her Study WITHOUT ANY ARGUMENT EVER she'll make the bed by herself every morning until the end of time. I said "Oh alright if I have to" but really I think it's a very good deal for me.

Wednesday, December 22, 1949

Dear Posy,

That was the craziest most exciting letter anybody ever sent me! It got here in 2 days thanks to you paying for Special Delivery and I told Curly the owner that his 3-piece house band would have to play a couple nights without their singer-guitar player and I borrowed his truck with chains and headed up the 91 as fast as it would crawl. I made it to Cardston in the middle of the night and waited until 5 o'clock when I figured it wasn't too early to knock on a person's door. An old lady in a housecoat answered and I said "Are you Miss Pearly Pitt?" and she said "Yes and I'm betting you're Charlie". She gave me directions to the Paisley farm and half an hour later Penny Paisley was back in my arms – only this time it's forever.

Pen and me are both working at Fort Lively Hotel for now. Curly's getting on in years so he's happy for the help and it's close enough to Cardston that Pen and her family can visit back and forth. The luckiest thing I ever did was pull up to that cook shack outside Jasper last summer.

A big THANK YOU,

Charlie

P.S. The $2 bill is for you and Rosy to get yourselves a couple of banana splits. I remember you telling me you'd live on them if your parents would let you.

I said "Do you want to go get them now?" and Rosy said "No I'm still a little sick from us finishing off the divinity fudge and besides I'm going to that party soon" and she un-folded the other letter.

Wednesday, December 22, 1949

Dear Posy,

I am sorry for not answering your nice letters. Yes my booklet arrived but I was too unhappy to get past Step 1. I wasn't even going to go to the show at the hotel you told me about but then I thought oh why not. I'm sure glad I did or I wouldn't have met Charlie who is the kindest and most wonderful man I've ever known.

Mostly I'm writing to thank you for caring so much about me that you went to all that trouble to find me. I have tears in my eyes just thinking about that.

You deserve to know the truth. When I was 17 my Dad said if a daughter of his becomes a dancer in a Chautauqua she isn't welcome in his home again. I ran off and did it anyway. Mom and my sister and brother and Great Auntie Pearl wrote me over the years but no one was allowed to even say my name at home. I was on my way back out West to ask Dad's forgiveness and I made it as far as Flatte Butte but I couldn't go on. I'd have to tell them all I lied in my letters about being a famous tap dancer and that I've mostly just been working odd jobs for 10 years. Then I thought maybe if I went to Hollywood and got discovered I could come home a big success. But after being with Charlie every day for 3 weeks I knew I had to go and tell my family how much I loved them. I got there in time to have some long talks with my Dad and we made our peace. But then I couldn't bear to leave my Mom right away or my sister and brother and the nieces and nephews I'd only just met but I knew Charlie was itching to get to Hollywood so even though it broke my heart I sent him a telegram telling him to go ahead without me.

Just so you know, I wrote your little friend Bunny Cruickshank's Mom to say I was sorry for taking off without telling her after she'd been so good to me and I put in enough money for the week's board I owed her plus $3 extra if she could find it in her heart to mail me my belongings especially my warm clothes. But I guess she's still mad at me and I don't blame her one bit.

Thank you again,

Penny Paisley

P.S. You have a free room any time your family wants to visit us here at Fort Lively Hotel and you can write me anytime and I promise I'll answer.

32. **Maybe Even Jail**

Rosy said "I suppose you'd like to write a letter about this right away?" and I said "Yes please." She unlocked the drawer of her Writing Desk and got out our writing pad and I said "I better send it SPECIAL DELIVERY" and she said "I hope you don't think you're going to pay for that out of our banana splits money" and I said "Okay I'll use some more of my Christmas dollars money."

SPECIAL DELIVERY

Tuesday, December 27, 1949

Dear Bunny, Essie, Eleanor, Darlene and David,

Well you're all in big trouble. It turns out the $10.00 in Miss Paisley's letter was $7.00 for the one week's room and board she didn't pay and the other $3.00 was for Mrs. Cruickshank to find it in her heart to mail her warm belongings to her.

Rosy says you have 4 problems: #1. If Bunny gives her Mom the money WITHOUT the letter she'll say "Where did you get that kind of money and what am I supposed to do with it?" #2. If she gives her the money WITH the smeared letter she'll say "You ruined MY letter so now I don't know what this ten dollars is for." #3. If you tell her the WHOLE TRUTH she'll say "You STOLE my letter and you STEAMED it open and RUINED it and you HID the money for WEEKS so Miss Paisley thinks I TOOK the money and I KEPT her belongings and besides she's FREEZING." And #4. If you don't give her the money OR the letter and the Post Office ever finds out YOU 5 MIGHT ALL GO TO JAIL because a person's mail is a person's mail.

Rosy says we've all made such a mess of this she's washing her hands of all of it. But here is my very good advice.

Bunny the MINUTE your Mom goes out somewhere you should phone Eleanor and then Eleanor you get all the rest of you to quick go to Bunny's house and sneak in the back door so no Boarder sees you and then Bunny you take them down to the cellar to get the big box of Miss Paisley's things and then give them 3 of the $1.00 bills you hid and then the rest of you help each other carry the box up the stairs and to the Post Office and mail it to Miss Penny Paisley, Fort Lively Hotel & Saloon, Somewhere between Coutts and Shelby, On Highway 91, MONTANA, United States of America so at least she'll be warm.

I will write you again when I think of what to do about the other $7.00 and the smeared letter.

Your friend Posy

P.S. Make Bucky go to Bunny's with you to help because he's the strongest.

I said "PHEW. That's done" and Rosy said "There sure is a lot of fibbing and sneaking happening. I bet you're going to be sorry" but still she said she'd help with another letter as long as I made it quick because her friend Betty-Lou was coming over soon so they could change into their National Dress outfits Mommy had made them and walk to their Peoples Of The World Club party together. Rosy was going as a Maori from New Zealand and Betty-Lou as Cleopatra from Egypt.

Tuesday, December 27, 1949

Dear Mr. Pankhurst,

PRIVATE & CONFIDENTIAL

I've never had this much to tell in a letter before and Rosy's going to her Peoples Of The World Club party with Betty-Lou soon so I'll just get to it.

152

1:15 pm: Thick envelope comes for me with one letter from Chuck
             The Buck, one letter from Miss Paisley and one $2.00 bill
             in it.

1:16 pm: His says he gets my crazy letter. Borrows Curly's truck
             with chains. Crawls to Cardston. At 5:00 in the morning
             Miss Pearly Pitt tells him where to go. Gets Penny Paisley
             in his arms forever on the farm. They're both working for
             Curly the old man who's tired of owning the hotel. The
             luckiest thing was the cook shack. The $2.00 is for banana
             splits.

1:20 pm: Rosy gets ready to read Miss Paisley's letter to me.

1:21 pm: Miss Paisley says sorry she was too sad to ever write me.
             Nearly didn't go to the gig. Chuck The Buck's wonderful.
             She's crying because I found her. Ran away to be a
             Chautauqua dancer but did odd jobs. On her way to say
             sorry to her Dad. Stops at Flatte Butte. Decides to be
             discovered in Hollywood. Leaves Chuck The Buck to tell
             her family she loves them. Her Dad dies. Can't leave her
             Mom. Breaks her heart and tells Chuck The Buck to go to
             Hollywood without her. And that's all she wrote. Except
             for Private & Confidential things to me only. And this
             excerpt from the P.S. (I've underlined the astonishing bit.)

1:32 pm: Rosy reads excerpt. <u>You have a free room any time</u> your
             family wants to visit us here at Fort Lively Hotel etc., etc.,
             etc.

Betty-Lou just got here.

Your friend,

Posy

P.S. Oopsie I almost forgot to ask you to thank Nigel for driving to Cardston and for buying that Obituary at the News Agent's with his own money.

Nurse Beryl phoned and Mommy let me snuggle up to listen. She said Diddy's feet were so much better they took him home to the Wolff's house early that very morning and the reason she was calling a day early to tell us Happy New Year is because Cyril invited all of Diddy's Searchers to a New Year's Eve party at The Hotel and she's staying to help with it and then driving to Battleford New Year's Day. Then she said "Are you listening in Posy?" and I said "Yes I am" and she said "Your jolly little friends Essie and Bucky came by the hotel too late today to catch Diddy but they introduced themselves to me LOUD AND CLEAR. They seem like sensible children with their HEADS ON STRAIGHT just like DIDDY'S and ELEANOR'S ARE and I said "Good. My plan worked" and Mommy said "What plan?" and Nurse Beryl quick said "So Isobel, what are you doing New Year's Eve?"

33. Should Older Patients Be Forgot

Mommy woke Marji and Rosy and me up where we were sleeping on the coats on Mr. and Mrs. Gilroy's bed and said "It's almost midnight" so we came back out to the party and Mr. Gilroy was pouring something fizzy into Daddy's glass and he opened another bottle for the other people's glasses and he gave Rosy and Marji and me some cream soda and we all watched their big clock and counted backwards "FIVE FOUR THREE TWO ONE" and we all yelled "HAPPY NEW YEAR" and we clanked each other's glasses and everybody kissed everybody else and Mrs. Gilroy and Daddy started up playing a song on her piano and his sax and all the grown-ups sang "SHOULD OLDER PATIENTS BE FORGOT AND NEVER BROUGHT TO MINE, WE'LL DRINK A CUP OF KINDNESS YET TO THE DAYS OF OLD LANG'S EYE." When they finally stopped singing Daddy held his glass up and said "HERE'S TO THE NINETEEN-FIFTIES AND A WORLD WITHOUT WAR."

After New Year's Day dinner which was a ham cooked with pineapple rings on it and all the trimmings Mommy called the Queen's Court to make sure Nurse Beryl had got to Battleford safe but the lady said "Miss McKenna called earlier to say she wasn't well and would have to postpone her arrival again" so Mommy quick called The Flatte Butte Hotel and Mr. Pankhurst told her "Beryl's feeling quite poorly. She's running a fever and has a sore throat and has gone up to lie down but I'm sure she'll call you back when she wakes up" but she didn't.

Mommy called again the next night and Mr. Pankhurst said "Poor Beryl is feeling worse than ever. And George Privett called this morning to say he and his whole family are sick in bed and then Dagmar Mosbeck the cook called in with a high fever and just now her daughter Myrtle our waitress phoned with nausea" and Mommy said "Oh dear" and he said "I'm the last one standing and now I seem to have the chills and an iffy throat so I'm not sure I won't be next—oh just a moment" and he said "YES IT'S ISOBEL CALLING FROM EDMONTON" and Nurse Beryl picked up the Guests' Telephone upstairs and said "How sweet of you to check in. What a palaver we're in here" and Mr. Pankhurst said "Thankfully the last guests checked out yesterday" and Nurse Beryl said "And you're stuck looking after your only non-paying guest" and Mr. Pankhurst said "I'm enjoying your company" and Nurse Beryl said "Cyril did you tell Isobel what Dr. Demchuk said when you called him about me?" and Mr. Pankhurst said "He said first Mr. Slager from the Post Office called with a crashing headache that won't go away and then Mrs. Cohen rang to say the whole family had lost their appetites and the next call was Albi Alvarez with swollen tonsils and within hours ALL HECK BROKE LOOSE" except Mr. Pankhurst didn't say HECK. "The Beddoes from the Funeral Home are so ill they had to cut short a Viewing and Mrs. Youngman from the General Store can't even swallow water let alone eat anything and who knows who'll be next?" Nurse Beryl said "Dr. Demchuk is ninety-nine-percent sure we all have Strep Throat" and Mr. Pankhurst said "The hospital's shipment of Penicillin was held up by the bad weather and it could be a week before it gets here" and Nurse Beryl said "So people are making do gargling with salt water and eating raw garlic and most have gone to bed with a mustard plaster" and Mr. Pankhurst said "What Dr. Demchuk finds so puzzling is that before this outbreak the only person in town with

156

Strep Throat was little Bunny Cruickshank and Nurse Beryl said "And her mother swears Bunny hasn't been near the Boarders or anyone else – or even been out of the house in days."

34. STEP 6

Lucky that Daddy had already taken the Gilroys' mattress back to them because one minute after Rosy and me got home from seeing Esther Williams in her new swimming musical Neptune's Daughter I was back in the Basement practising on my tumbling rug and just like Mommy said would happen I got right back on my Your Stairway To Stardom.

STEP 6

Get In With The People Who Know The Right People.

Here's a **startling**, little-known, **hush-hush** piece of unexpected insider information that we share with each talented Hopeful in our **Your Stairway To Stardom program**: "It's not always **WHAT** you know, it's **WHO** you know."

Of course the best way to get close to the **producers**, **directors** and **casting agents** who rule the entertainment kingdom is to move to **New York or Hollywood**.

If that's not possible, start a correspondence with someone you know who is a well-connected **'In' in the Industry** and ask them to help make things happen for you. But what if you don't know an influential 'In'? Well have we got an off-the-record, **behind-closed-doors**, eye-opening, **exclusive tip** for you! Ready? "It's not only **BIG WHEELS** who can get careers **ROLLING**."

We've known many a **Hopeful** whose show biz **Intro** was orchestrated by a bandleader, whose **Leap** to fame came via a choreographer's leg up, who became a **Household Word** thanks to a script assistant – and even a few who flashed onto the scene through blatant **Exposure** by a costume designer. We strongly recommend that you **write letters** introducing yourself to Small Wheels who might **know a Somebody** who knows a **Poobah** who could introduce you to a **Big Fish** who's close to a **TOP BANANA**. And that, my talented **Hopeful**, is how things get done in the high-flying, **winner-takes-all** World of Entertainment!

BONUS TIP: Start looking for a good agent. The best ones hobnob with all the **bigwigs** to find jobs for their clients, so they're well worth the exorbitant percentage of your earnings you pay them. And at least they can't bill you up front!

When you drop those letters of introduction in the mailbox (don't forget a headshot), you'll have **conquered Step 6** and reached the top of **YOUR STAIRWAY TO STARDOM!** All you'll have left to do is wait for your **BIG BREAK!**

The first thing I did to work on Step 6 was ask Mommy and Daddy if we could move to Hollywood. Daddy said "Not until you're older." "How old?" "At least ten." I said "That's FOUR YEARS away!" Rosy said "Three and seven-twelfths." Daddy said "You'll still have youth on your side." I said "Shirley Temple was already a STAR when she was FIVE." Mommy said "She was born down there. Her family didn't have to move." I said "It's not FAIR!" Daddy said "It costs a lot to live in Hollywood." I said "I'll sell ALL MY JEWELLERY." Mommy said "We're sorry sweetie." I said "But my CAREER!" They didn't care.

Rosy said she'd help me with the letters. I went out and bought one dozen large envelopes at The Metropolitan Store and twelve stamps to The States from The Post Office. It all came to one dollar and 30-cents which I paid for out of the two-dollars-and-eighty-five-cents I'd kept safe in my official strongbox for Other Expenses. Then Daddy drove me to Jackson's Cameras & Photography and waited in the truck while I explained to Mr. Jackson what a headshot was in case he didn't know and told him who I was sending them to. He said "Well I must say I'm wildly impressed." I showed him the picture everybody thought was my best pose and he said "The perfect choice. Wholesome, but pure Show Business." I gave him the negative and asked if one dollar and fifty-five-cents was enough to get one dozen eight-by-tens printed up and he said "Sadly no, but I can do you two if I charge half price and I'll throw in a free one for you helping me break into the tough Hollywood market." So only three altogether. I told Daddy it's too bad I wasted my resources buying so many envelopes and stamps but he said I could always get more headshots printed up once the Big Money starts rolling in and then those extra supplies will come in handy.

Rosy and me went to see the Mormon Librarian who just got back from Christmas in Cardston where her Mom said the whole town was talking about Penny Paisley being back with her family even though Percy had sadly gone to wherever people go who aren't LDS, and we asked her if she could help us find certain people's addresses and everything and she did and Rosy copied it all down in her green real leather Nogga-hide Notebook Joy gave her for Christmas.

Rosy got herself all set up at her Writing Desk with her Notebook and her new fountain pen and ink and our newest writing pad and my Your Stairway To Stardom booklet and her Dictionary from the bottom shelf of her bookcase where she'd lined up her heaviest books and I sat on the floor just outside of her Study. We worked harder on those letters than on any ones we ever wrote but it was worth it. They came out perfect.

Wednesday, January 4, 1950

Dear Mr. William Morris,

My name is Paulette De Kohler. I would like to hire you to be my Agent especially if you hobnob with bigwigs who could give me a leg into a big movie as the Girl Tumbling Star or even not the Star as long as I can be exposed for people who will make things happen to me in Hollywood.

I live in Edmonton, Alberta, Canada but don't let that worry you because so were Yvonne De Carlo, Fay Wray, Deanna Durbin and Mary Pickford all born in Canada like me. Besides I can come to Hollywood for an audition any time you think I would be perfect for a quite big part in a movie especially if it's a musical.

I am six-and-a-half years old albeit that means I will have a very long career for you to keep getting an exorbitant percentage of my earnings from – after I get paid that is.

I have already performed as the head tumbler in The Lucky Tumbling Club and I was the Conductor of the Combined Rhythm Band of Grades One and Two at the Lord Strathcona Elementary School Christmas Concert. I am also a figure skater and I can sing, dance, swim, juggle, play a musical instrument, do magic tricks and archery.

Please let me know when you would like to start.

Yours truly,

Paulette De Kohler

P.S. When you're finished looking at this headshot please mail it to Benny Goodman the bandleader. I put a nickel in the envelope so it won't cost you a thing.

Wednesday January 4, 1950

Dear Mr. Benny Goodman,

*My name is Paulette De Kohler. I am the Conductor of The Combined
Rhythm Band of the Grades One and Two musicians at Lord Strathcona
Elementary School in Edmonton, Alberta, Canada. I saw you conducting
the band and playing a clarinet in the very good Busby Berkeley movie
Hollywood Hotel starring Dick Powell and Rosemary Lane. I thought you
were just an actor pretending to be a musician and a bandleader but my
Father who plays a saxophone says that was really you playing the clarinet
and that you are also the best bandleader in the business and he should
know because he used to have his own dance band that performed almost
all over Saskatchewan.*

*I am hoping to be a Girl Tumbling Star in Hollywood musicals but I don't
mind doing something else before my Big Break. Since you and I are both
bandleaders maybe we could help each other out starting with you telling
your friend Busby Berkeley all about me.*

Yours truly,

Paulette De Kohler

*P.S. You will be getting a head shot of me pretty soon from William
Morris. After you finish looking at it would you please mail it to Busby
Berkeley so he'll know it's me when I visit him next time I'm in
Hollywood? I put a nickel in the envelope so it won't cost you a thing.*

Nurse Beryl called and I ran to listen like always. She said
"Believe it or not I'm still in Flatte Butte" and Mommy said "No!"
and Nurse Beryl said "I'm about halfway better and so is Cyril
although we're both drained of energy" and Mommy said "You

poor things" and Nurse Beryl said "We're all alone in the hotel" and Mommy said

"Dear, dear, dear" and Nurse Beryl said "We've been taking turns making tea and soup and soft-boiled eggs and the occasional custard" and Mommy said "He can make a custard?" and Nurse Beryl said "Oh yes, Cyril's surprisingly good in the kitchen. We spend most of our waking hours just cuddling puppies, sipping ginger tea and talking about growing up in England and about both of us losing our parents in the War and about him selling the family inn in Shropshire and making a fresh start in Canada and me losing my husband I barely knew and, well, about anything and everything really" and Mommy said "It's good that you have someone from back home to talk to" and Nurse Beryl said "Oh and Cyril and I showed each other the marvelously precocious and madcap letters we've each received from Posy" which made me proud and Rosy too when I ran back to her Study and told her that both Nurse Beryl and Mr. Pankhurst think we're marvelous. And then we got right back to writing the next madcap career letter.

Thursday, January 5, 1950

Dear Miss Edith Head,

My name is Paulette De Kohler. I am writing to you because I know that even a costume designer can blatantly expose a Hopeful in Hollywood.

I am working harder than anyone else in my field to be a Girl Tumbling Star in movie musicals but I don't mind starting at making costumes until I get discovered. Well not making them exactly but drawing them for somebody else to sew. I am sending you 2 pictures taken of me in my Gypsy costume that went UNDER my snowsuit so I could wear it all day at school which I won Best Girl's Costume for and then in the same

*costume OVER my snowsuit for going out Hallowe'ening at night. I am
also putting in a drawing of a costume I came up with for me to wear in a
tumbling musical. You can keep the pictures of me because my Mother has
extras but please send the drawing back since it's my only one. I put a
nickel in the envelope so it won't cost you a thing.*

*You must be very busy since you make costumes for just about every
Hollywood movie, so if you ever need a costume design done just ask and
I'll do you one up FOR FREE. Then in trades-ies maybe you could tell a
Poobah or a Big Fish or even a Top Banana all about me.*

*My Mother and I love every costume you ever made and we've seen them
all.*

Yours truly,

Paulette De Kohler

*P.S. I would have sent you an 8x10 headshot of me but I only have 2 left so
I'm saving them for a director and a producer.*

It took us most of our time for two days to write the letters and
after we put them in my big envelopes with stamps to The States
from my supplies and took them to the Post Office and mailed them
we walked straight across Whyte Avenue and paid for banana splits
with Chuck The Buck's money to celebrate me finishing all Six Easy
Steps which weren't easy at all and making it to the top of my Your
Stairway To Stardom. Rosy held up her spoon with her maraschino
cherry in it and said "Congratulations Paulette!" I'd already eaten
my maraschino cherry but I held up my empty spoon and said
"Thank you Rosalind. All I have to do now is wait."

35. **Etc., etc., etc., etc., etc.**

I got a letter from Essie that she sent December 29 but it came late because the Post Office forgot to hire extra people at Christmas saying they all went over to Bunny's right after she called to say her Mom was out doing errands and Bunny snuck them in the back door and took them down to the cellar and over to where she hid the money and gave them three dollars of it and then took them over to where the big box of Miss Paisley's belongings was and they helped each other carry the box upstairs and then all of them except Bunny took it to the Post Office but Mr. Slager sent them to Youngman's Store to get a stronger box from Mrs. Youngman and then Mr. Slager helped them pack it up and tape it and Darlene wrote on the box who it was going to and what address and then under Name Of Sender she wrote all of their names and that was that.

The next day I got a letter from Eleanor that Darlene wrote for her when they were both home sick saying that people are saying it looks like the only person who could have passed Strep Throat around to everybody was The Public Health Inspector Mr. Orson Ball who they remember having a scratchy voice when he inspected all the shops that sell food and The Hotel two days before Christmas. Eleanor said the whole town was SHOCKED and UP IN ARMS that it was The Public Health Inspector OF ALL PEOPLE but she said SHE wasn't shocked at all because she saw him herself and that's just the kind of person he is and to prove it she said when he opened the door to the little room off the kitchen and saw Maggie and Dizzy and the four puppies he yelled "WHAT ARE THESE FILTHY MUTTS DOING IN THE KITCHEN?" which she said was three big lies because they're not mutts they're German Wirehaired Pointers and they're not exactly IN the kitchen and she and Darlene keep the little room and the dogs clean as a whistle. Well she said when Orson Ball yelled, Dizzy growled at him and Orson Ball KICKED him HARD so Dizzy bit him because WHO WOULDN'T? She said then he just about closed The Hotel down but Mr. Pankhurst talked to him for a long time and then Orson Ball watched while her Dad packed the whole dog family up and put them in their car to take home to live at their house which they did for a few hours until he left town. After Dr. Demchuk figured out who gave everybody Strep Throat he told the Mayor and the Mayor called the Head of The Public Health Inspectors in Regina to complain and the Head said the Balls had gone off to spend two weeks with his sister's family in Walla Walla Washington but he said "You can rest a sure we will be talking to Mr. Ball the minute he gets back from Walla Walla and you can also rest a sure he won't be back in Flatte Butte any time soon."

The phone rang and Daddy said "Run and get that Posy, it's never for me anyway" and he was right it never ever is. But this time it was. The minute he hung up he said to Mommy "That was Gil Gilroy. He says Amer-Cana Drilling is landing so many jobs it's hard to keep a handle on day-to-day operations, and that what he needs is a central Depot where crews can pick up and drop off tools and equipment so he'll always know where everything is. Just a bare-bones building, not too big" which none of that was interesting but then he said "And he needs it yesterday." I said "Yesterday?" and Rosy said "But that's not even possible!" and Daddy said "It's just a figure of speech, he meant he needs it fast." Rosy stood up. Daddy said "No-no, sit down sweetie, not everything has to go in your notebook." She sat back down and he said to Mommy "He doesn't want to lose time putting it out to tender. He said he's talked to me enough he can tell I know my stuff and he asked would I be interested in dropping everything, rounding up a crew and starting on it right away. I told him 'You bet your boots I'd be interested' and he said 'Why don't you pop by the house and we'll talk turkey over a beer'." Rosy and me both said "Talk turkey?" but Daddy just laughed and went and got his coat.

Mommy took me shopping the reason being that school had started back up again and she told me she'd come up with a good idea. When we got to Kresge's she said "I don't suppose you know where the Jewellery counter is?" and I said "Right this way." She bought me a bracelet that had some green beads strung on elastic which was not the one I would have picked but you don't say so when it's a gift. While we were having cinnamon buns with icing at the Lunch Counter she told me her idea. She said that the bracelet is for wearing to school every day and whenever I find myself talking when I shouldn't be I'm supposed to snap the elastic to remind myself to stop.

WELL THEY GOT CAUGHT. About the smeared letter and about the ten dollars and about sneak mailing the box of warm belongings to Montana. Essie said in her letter that it was all because her and Eleanor were finally over their Strep Throat so they were in Bunny's back yard making snow angels at the same time Mrs. Cruickshank was watching out her front window for Mr. Alvarez to come for tea when the mailman put something in their mailbox and even though it's always Bunny's job to bring the mail in Mrs. Cruickshank went out herself and got it and it was a Thank You note from Miss Paisley. Well right away Mrs. Cruickshank called the girls into the house and sat them down and phoned Mrs. Privett and Mrs. Cohen and Mrs. Beddoes to send Darlene and David and Bucky right over and when they got there she read out loud Miss Paisley's note thanking her for giving the money she sent her to the kids to go and mail her box of things which Mrs. Cruickshank figured out pretty quick they must have snuck and done behind her back so she was all mad in the face and getting ready to give them BIG HECK but Mr. Alvarez had come in the door and heard everything. Essie said he snorted trying to hide a laugh but it didn't work and he said "It was BUNNY!" Snort. "BUNNY WAS TYPHOID MARY!" which didn't make any sense at all. But just like that Mrs. Cruickshank gave up being mad and Bunny quick ran and brought her the other seven dollars and the kids all said "I'm sorry I'm sorry I'm sorry" and then Mr. Alvarez sent every one of the kids off to The New Movie Of The Week for FREE and Essie said that Bunny said that when she got home from the movie her Mom was smiling and didn't say another word to her about any of it.

Daddy went out and got K.F.C. Kohler Fine Construction painted on both doors of our truck for good cheap advertising wherever he goes.

Tuesday, January 10, 1950

Dear Miss De Kohler,

Mr. Goodman is busy recording but he asked me to tell you that it's always a pleasure to hear from a child who loves music and it was a special honor to receive such kind words about his work from another bandleader. He encourages you to keep in touch because you never know when you can help each other out in the music business.

168

Good luck!

RLJ for Benny Goodman

P.S. As soon as your headshot arrives from William Morris I will forward it to Busby Berkeley. I'm sure Mr. Goodman appreciated the nickel. Every little bit helps when you make your living as a musician.

I don't know why Daddy did it because it's not like I got my Big Break from Mr. Goodman yet but he put the letter in a nice frame and hung it up on the wall.

Wednesday, January 11, 1950

Dear Paulette,

I am writing on behalf of Miss Edith Head who is busy designing the costumes for six more movies this year and getting started on thirteen for next year. She asked me to tell you that she thought your Hallowe'en idea was very clever and that your tumbling costume is delightful. We will keep you in mind if Miss Head needs help with costume ideas.

Wishing you a brilliant career in tumbling and/or costume design.

The Office of Edith Head

This time it was Mommy who put the letter in a frame and she hung it up over her sewing machine.

I still had not heard ONE word from William Morris.

I remembered to snap my Talking Bracelet for the first time when I caught myself turned around in my desk explaining to Ollie Orviss how to keep the suction cup end of your arrow up and touching your bow without it dropping down every time. But I snapped it so hard I yelled "OWWW" which I got looked at by Miss

Semonick for. Since then I've been snapping it softer. It seems to be working.

36. La Plume De Ma Sister Is Sur La Writing Desk

Didier Desjardins,
c/o Miss Helen Talbot,
Flatte Butte Elementary School,
FLATTE BUTTE, Saskatchewan,
Canada.

Lundi, January 23, 1950

Cher Didier,

Merci for your letter which you printed almost half of the words yourself in. Good for you.

Eleanor Privett says her Dad said that Dr. and Mrs. Demchuk came to La Hotel for Dinner after curling because the food and service at the Curling Rink had gone downhill and he told him your les pieds are back working tickety-boo. So YIPPEE you might get to be a world famous figure skater after all! Eleanor says she and Darlene see you standing outside the boards watching classes and then practising like crazy during Free Skates. I hope you are proud of yourself because you should be.

Your amie Paulette

P.S. Cheer up. I bet Eugene Turner had to start out with tube skates too when he was a little garcon.

P.P.S. Rosy's helping me learn to talk French from a Library book in case you and I ever see each other again.

Then I had a very good idea and Rosy agreed that it was so we went to the Library and asked the Mormon Librarian if she could help us and she said "I know exactly what you need" and she gave us the Montreal Yellow Pages opened up at Dance Studios.

Madame Delphine Desjardins,
Madame Desjardins Studio de Ballet,
26 Trevegat Street,
MONTREAL, PQ,
Canada.

Wednesday, January 25, 1950

Cher Madame Desjardins,

My name is Paulette Kohler. I am a good friend of Didier Desjardins who is your petit-fils who misses you very much because you are the only person left in the world who loves him.

I bet you are saying to yourself WHAT OH WHAT can I get Didier for his birthday that's coming up not next week and not the week after but the week after that on Valentine's Day. You might not know this but Diddy wants to be a world famous figure skater like Eugene Turner. Well that sure wasn't going to happen if he had gotten Gang Green and his feet fell off after he froze them sneaking out to Midnight Mass on Christmas Eve without Uncle Wally catching him so he could light a candle in order to be happy again but PHEW they didn't and he is back skating again.

Just so you know how bad he wants to be a famous figure skater I will tell you the secret that because the dumb Flatte Butte Rink rules won't let boys be in Figure Skating Classes Diddy stands outside the boards and watches every single Beginners and Intermediate class and then practises and practises the moves during Free Skate times even though the other kids make fun of him especially his cousins. The trouble is he only has his cousin Howie's old hockey skates and you need picks for good bunny hops

172

and stopping but Uncle Wally says he's not wasting good money on sissy
skates for a boy.

So my very good advice is that I think you should send him a pair of Boys'
Figure Skates in the mail as a Birthday present if you can afford them.

Yours truly,

Paulette Kohler

P.S. Get them for an eight-year-old even though he's only turning seven.
That way he can wear two pairs of socks now and they'll still fit with one
pair of socks next year.

Wednesday, February 1, 1950

Dear Mr. William Morris,

It's been exactly 4 weeks and I still haven't got a letter from you saying if
you are going to be my Agent or not. Remember I told you about Yvonne
De Carlo, Fay Wray, Deanna Durbin and Mary Pickford all being from
Canada like me? Well some lucky Agent must have been shocked at how
much money he made after he discovered them!

You never know if I might be your Big Break.

Yours truly,

Paulette De Kohler

P.S. Benny Goodman and Edith Head both said they are thinking about
hiring me. You can ask them.

When we showed the Mormon Librarian whose name she told us
is Miss Alma Nielsen our letter before we mailed it she said "Well
we'll just wait and see if that works. If it doesn't you can be sure

that snooty Mr. William Morris isn't the only Agent I can find in Hollywood. Not by a long shot."

I made my five best Valentines ever. The drawing and colouring and over half of the printing was all mine and then I quick mailed them to Flatte Butte early so my friends would get my Valentines before anybody else's.

TO BUNNY
    I HERD you like me.
    I like EWE too.
HAPPY VALENTINE'S DAY
From Posy

P.S. Get it? I drew 3 deer and a sheep and then we spelled HEARD wrong on purpose and a EWE is a girl sheep.

TO ESSIE
    Roses are red
    Violets are blue
    I left Flatte Butte
    You can too.
HAPPY VALENTINE'S DAY
From Posy

TO ELEANOR
    My heart BEETS for you.
HAPPY VALENTINE'S DAY
From Posy

P.S. Those are beets I drew so don't think they're radishes or you won't get the joke.

TO DIDIER

> *Bonne Anniversaire to you*
> *Bonne Anniversaire to you*
> *Bonne Anniversaire, Bonne Anniversaire*
> *AND HAPPY VALENTINE'S DAY TOO.*

From Paulette

P.S. Here are 7 Valentine cinnamon hearts to eat and 7 Birthday candles to light one at a time for 7 prayers you don't have to tell anyone about.

For Bucky's I drew a yellow and black bumble bee with a mean face.

TO BUCKY

> *If you won't BEE mine*
> *you can just BUZZ off.*

HAPPY VALENTINE'S DAY

From Posy

P.S. You never answered me once so this is almost your last chance of getting another card or letter or anything.

I got five letters in one day and they were all about the same thing only different. We opened the one from Madame Desjardins first.

Monday, February 13, 1950

Chère petite Paulette,

Thank you for your most kind letter and the very clever idea of a gift for Didier's birthday. I did not reply soon as I have been very busy since I receive it. You see I made a very fast decision to surprise Didier with giving his gift from my own hands. And so I write to you from the train with grand excitement that tomorrow I will embrace my beautiful daughter Veronique and my six precious grandchildren.

Didier is a lucky little boy to have such a good friend as you are.

With warm regards,

Delphine Desjardins

The next one was from Miss Talbot and here is the shock.

Friday, February 17, 1950

Dear Posy,

Diddy asked me to please write a letter telling you all his big news. First, you will be happy to hear that Dr. Demchuk says he is in perfect health again and that his feet will be better than ever very soon.

The other news is that Diddy came to school today with his very elegant grandma that you could sure tell used to be a ballerina in Paris! They were here to get his exercise books and artwork to show his new teacher and to say goodbye. Yes, he is leaving us. Madame Desjardins told me that she had been wrong and selfish to think Didier would be better off with his young Aunt and Uncle who have four boys and a new baby plus a business and a house to look after, while she lives alone in a large apartment. Besides she has been very lonely since the tragic loss of her dear son and daughter-in-law and she misses Didier very much. She said that her tender-hearted daughter Veronique and her generous son-in-law Wally have agreed to make the very great sacrifice of letting her take Didier back to live with her in Montreal if she promises to bring him back every summer for a visit with his loving cousins who will miss him desperately.

I have never seen Diddy so happy!

Yours truly,

Helen Talbot

P.S. He said you will be shocked to hear that he got boys' figure skates for his birthday.

The other three letters were from Bunny saying that I would never guess the news but Diddy is going to Montreal to live with his Grandma and from Eleanor saying that I would never guess the news but Diddy is going to live in Montreal with his Grandmother and from Essie saying I would never guess the news but Diddy is moving to Montreal to live over his Grand-mère's Ballet Studio and also telling me that Eleanor Privett is the TALK OF THE TOWN because her Moon Over Loon Lake solo was the best thing in the Flatte Butte Ice Carnival this year.

Mommy just said "Hmm, I wonder why there's been no word from Nurse Beryl for a while" and POOF the next day a letter came from her for Mommy and she read it to us.

Monday, February 20, 1950

Dear Isobel,

I didn't want to say anything until it was official but I can now tell you my happy news. I have accepted a full-time position with an excellent clinic in Regina.

Three weeks ago when Cyril popped up to visit me while I was working in Paradise Hill, he showed me a notice he'd clipped out of the Regina Leader-Post advertising for a qualified Physiotherapist. I called the clinic to discuss the details and then drove down to meet with them. They said they were very impressed with my Degree and my wartime experience and also with my enterprising self-employment here in Saskatchewan. It sounded promising but of course I had to wait for them to verify my qualifications and references.

I received the call this morning offering me the position and asking if I could start right away. By the time you read this I'll be on the job. I can't tell you how happy I am that my roving days are over. Cyril is going to help me find an apartment but in the meantime, bless him, he's insisting that I stay in his ever so charming hotel, Hawthorn Manor.

Say Hi to Max and the girls for me. I miss you all.

With warm regards,

Beryl

P.S. Please give Rosy and Posy the address of Hawthorn Manor in Regina and tell them I expect letters!

37. Turning Pro

The Edmonton Journal said "LOCAL CHILDREN TO SKATE WITH BARBARA ANN SCOTT" and then the man on CJCA Radio said "Some very lucky little figure skaters from city rinks will be performing with none other than Olympic Gold Medalist BARBARA ANN SCOTT when the Hollywood Ice Revue gli-i-i-des into Edmonton Gardens later this month" so I figured it had to be true but after school when I saw the sign in the skating shack it proved it. CHILDREN IN FIGURE SKATING CLASSES AGES 6 TO 12 WHO WOULD LIKE TO SIGN UP TO AUDITION FOR THE HOLLYWOOD ICE REVUE'S EDMONTON PERFORMANCE SEE JACKIE.

Mardi, Mars 7, 1950

Cher Didier,

Merci for your letter. HOO-HOO-HOORAY to vous for all the good news you told me. You are the only kid I know who has ever gone farther on le train than Winnipeg and the only person even a grown-up I ever met who lives in Montreal and who has his own bedroom and takes Figure Skating AND Ballet classes and is allowed a whole bowl of le chocolat every jour.

The big news here is that BARBARA ANN SCOTT is coming to Edmonton and I might be skating with her in the Hollywood Ice Review. Audition Day for Strathcona Figure Skaters is this Saturday. I will let you know as soon as I find out if I got picked.

Your amie Paulette

P.S. Merci for the très handsome picture of you doing your first Ballet class which I put on our dresser.

P.P.S. I'm glad 5 of your birthday candle prayers came true. I'm putting 2 more candles in this envelope so you can try again on the ones that didn't work.

P.P.P.S. Oui I do know that it is lucky to be cuddled whenever you want.

I got to the rink so early on Audition Day morning the skating shack was still locked and by the time Jackie and the lady from the Hollywood Ice Revue got there to open it I couldn't feel my feet but then Rosy showed up and took my skates off and warmed them and my feet by the oil stove so by the time it was my turn I could do everything perfect and PHEW nobody asked for a flat iron.

Wednesday, March 15, 1950

Dear Bunny, Essie and Eleanor,

Well the list got put up at the rink yesterday saying who gets to be in the Hollywood Ice Review with BARBARA ANN SCOTT and I GOT PICKED and so did my friend Marji and so did Rosy and so did her friend Joy. It was very hard not to yell and jump when I saw my name but Peggy and Becca were there and they didn't get picked probably because they're not very graceful and they can only stop by skating into the boards.

We got given a letter for our parents saying where to take us for rehearsals and what are the rules. The theme is A Visit To The Zoo. Marji and me are going to be Children Visiting the Zoo, Rosy is a Bluebird and Joy is a Penguin.

Your friend Posy

P.S. I am supposed to wear a bright coloured outfit you would play outside in on a summer day. There was a pattern in Rosy's envelope for Mommy to make her a Bluebird costume.

180

Rosy made it to the last twelve kids trying out the next day for the Lord Strathcona Elementary School Spelling Team. Only four kids get to be on the team and every other try-outer but her is in Grade Six so all through dinner and up to bed time she got Mommy and Daddy to take turns flipping open the dictionary at any page and asking her to spell a hard word on it so when I told her that I forgot to tell Diddy my big news and asked would she help me write him she said "Only if it takes one minute."

Dear Didier,

I GOT PICKED TO SKATE WITH BARBARA ANN.

Paulette

P.S. Well that's all for now.

YIPPEE! Rosy beat out eight Grade Six-ers and got on the Lord Strathcona Elementary School Spelling Team and in case she did get on it or even if she didn't Mommy had made a special dinner of Rosy's favourites to celebrate but when Daddy got home and heard Rosy's big news he said "Put it in the refrigerator for tomorrow Isobel, we're all going to the Ling Nan for Chinese food." Mommy said "Are you sure?" and Daddy said "I sure am sure."

On our way back from me helping Daddy do Stock hunting at The Sally Ann he said "I'm sorry to hear you've abandoned your tumbling career but what with the dangers of doing the splits I think you've made a wise decision." I said "Yes I didn't feel safe." And he said "Have you chosen a new career yet?" and I said "I'm thinking about switching to being a Figure Skating star" and he said "Well you're off to a good start, I mean how many young skaters have been chosen to perform with Barbara Ann Scott?" and I said

"Only two hundred-and-forty kids in all of Edmonton" and he said "Well there you go, you're already special" and then he said "Does this mean you'll have to start Your Stairway To Stardom all over again?" I said "Lucky for me Steps 2, 3, 4 and 5 are exactly the same for a Figure Skater as for a Tumbler so all I have to do over again is Step 1 and then for Step 6 just send out some new career letters as soon as Rosy and me have time after rehearsals and performing with BARBARA ANN" and he said "I see." I said "I don't know if you have to be able to get back up from a flat iron to get into The Olympics or not but if you do then I will probably just skip the National Team and turn Pro as soon as I'm done High School or even before if you let me and then it might take me a year or even a bit longer to skyrocket to international famousness but after that I will have just as good a chance of Hollywood stardom as Sonja Henie did even with all her Gold Medals" and Daddy said "Mm-hmm". "Did you know I saw three Sonja Henie movies at SONJA HENIE TUESDAY in Flatte Butte? The girls at the rink are beside themselves at the Show Stopper skating routines I make up. The good thing is that even though I haven't landed a jump turn on my feet yet and my spins aren't as fast as some people's my spirals are getting higher every week and I'm still quite young." Daddy said "Mm-hmm." When we got home I went straight downstairs to the Basement to do Step 1 over again.

"I want to be a Girl Figure Skater Pro in a big Ice Revue."

"I am going to be the Head Liner Pro like BARBARA ANN SCOTT in a big Ice Revue."

"I AM GOING TO BE THE HEAD LINER PRO IN A BIG ICE REVUE AND THEN I'M GOING TO SKYROCKET TO BEING THE MOST FAMOUS MOVIE STAR IN THE BIGGEST HOLLYWOOD FIGURE SKATING MUSICAL EVER."

38. BARBARA ANN SCOTT
Touched Me

Daddy dropped Rosy and me off at the Drop Off Door and he and Mommy went to their seats to wait. Rosy went off to get her Bluebird head to go with her Bluebird costume that Mommy made and I lined up in The Holding Area with the other Children Visiting The Zoo in the right order for our Entrance. My bright coloured outfit you would play outside in on a summer day was going to be my red-and-white striped tumbling romper but it must have shrunk in the wash because it was a little tight around the middle so Mommy quick made me a short frilly blue skirt to go with a white blouse of Rosy's and Mommy's black cummerbund pulled tight plus a blue hair ribbon and blue skate laces Mommy bought which no other girl had coloured ones.

Pretty soon the man announced loud over the P.A. that a world famous act was coming out to dazzle us which we couldn't see from The Holding Area and then another world famous act we couldn't see and then another one. Then OUT OF HER DRESSING ROOM CAME BARBARA ANN AND SHE WALKED RIGHT OVER TO US CHILDREN VISITING THE ZOO WITH HER SKATE GUARDS ON JUST TO SAY HELLO TO US which she didn't have to do so it shows what a nice person she is for a Star. I said "EXCUSE ME" and she said "Yes" and I took my Autograph Book out of the pocket Mommy had sewn on my skirt especially for holding it and my bag of lucky teeth and I asked would she sign it on the front page that I've been saving for her since I got it and she said "I'd be happy to." While she was bending over doing that I leaned in and sneak-touched her Olympic Gold Medal that was hanging down. Then

BARBARA ANN SCOTT PATTED ME RIGHT ON MY HEAD and went on to the next row of kids. I said to the lady walking behind her "If I write to BARBARA ANN would she send me an autographed picture?" and she said "Yes she would" and she gave me a card saying where to write to on it and I quick said "Would she send me two more for my friend who froze his feet and my other friend who did the Moon Over Loon Lake solo in the Flatte Butte Ice Carnival?" The lady was already three rows of Children Visiting The Zoo behind me by then but she said loud enough for me to hear "I don't know, maybe" so here's hoping.

Finally the man announced "LET'S GO TO THE ZOO" which was our Cue to file out of The Holding Area and wait quietly for our music to start up. As soon as it did two men pulled open the curtains just wide enough and out through them into the bright light went the six shortest Children Visiting The Zoo holding hands one being Marji in her red-and-white striped romper. Next was my six and behind us six more and six more and six more and six more and six more and six more and six more. As soon as all one hundred and twenty of us were out, two girls in each group of six with me being one of them made arches with our arms and the other four skated through them and then we did it again facing the other way and again facing the other way and again facing the last way and then we followed our own six's leader until we were all in a big circle around all the boards and then we skated around the rink one whole time waving our arms like we were excited which we were and then when the cymbals clanged we all stopped dead by quick turning around and going up on our picks and then we didn't move again. Out through the space between the curtains came Joy and the other Penguins and then some other animals after that but I was mostly looking for Mommy and Daddy and then came the Bluebirds with their wings held out doing circles which I watched because Rosy was one of them and they bunny hopped the whole way across the ice without one Bluebird falling and then we all bowed and everybody clapped and we all filed out and we took our skates off and put our boots on and people in red jackets took us to where our parents were sitting so we could watch the rest of the show.

Pretty soon the man said "AND NOW, THE MOMENT YOU'VE ALL BEEN WAITING FOR" and the audience already started to clap. "LADIES AND GENTLEMEN, BOYS AND GIRLS, HOLLYWOOD ICE REVUE IS PROUD TO PRESENT CANADIAN CHAMPION, NORTH AMERICAN CHAMPION, EUROPEAN CHAMPION, WORLD CHAMPION, OLYMPIC GOLD MEDALIST AND CANADA'S SWEETHEART, INTERNATIONAL SKATING STAR BARBARA ANN SCOTT." None of us in the whole audience could have guessed what would happen next. First they KILLED THE LIGHTS except for one spotlight shining on where the curtains that had been open for us kids to skate through were now closed. The music turned all quiet but scary-exciting and then *WHOOSH* through the curtains came BARBARA ANN doing a perfect spiral. She swerved to the left until she was almost at the boards and then she swerved right and kept going and going and going along the boards and swerving around every corner, always with the spotlight on her alone, all the way around the whole huge Edmonton Gardens until she got all the way back to where she started from without ever once jerking her right knee to show what kept her moving along and NEVER ONCE PUTTING HER LEFT

LEG DOWN. By then we were all standing and clapping and cheering until you couldn't hear yourself think or the music.

Saturday, March 25, 1950

Dear Miss Edith Head,

Remember I sent you that drawing I did of a red costume for when I'm in a Tumbling Musical? I didn't get it back from you so you must still have it. Well if you look at it again you will see it would be just as good for my new career as a Figure Skating Star if you pretend the bare feet have skates on them.

I'm putting a new picture of me in this envelope dressed as a Child Visiting The Zoo for my performance in The Hollywood Ice Revue where I skated with BARBARA ANN SCOTT. I'm not a tattle-tale but one of the other Children Visiting The Zoo did not even come close to obeying the costume rules. She showed up wearing a pink satin and net skating dress with a tiara. I have been to The Calgary Zoo and I don't have to tell a famous costume designer like you that nobody was wearing a tiara there.

Yours truly,

Paulette De Kohler

P.S. Or I bet not at any other Zoo in The World either.

Saturday, March 25, 1950

Dear Mr. Busby Berkeley,

My name is Paulette De Kohler. I have just performed in the Hollywood Ice Revue with BARBARA ANN SCOTT and I was wondering if you are going to be doing any musicals that need a Girl Figure Skating Star or I don't even have to be the star if you think I'm too young which is 7 in July.

You probably already got my 8x10 headshot in the mail from Benny Goodman who was in your very good movie Hollywood Hotel starring Dick Powell and Rosemary Lane.

I drew and coloured a perfect costume that I could wear in a Figure Skating Musical so you won't even have to pay a costume designer. It's at Edith Head's. Phone her and tell her I said it's okay to send it to you.

Yours truly,

Paulette De Kohler

P.S. Just pretend the bare feet have skates on them.

39. We're Out Of The Woods

I could tell that richness was starting up for our family when I was sitting on the floor changing Pansy Daisy into her nurse's uniform Nurse Beryl sent me because she said she couldn't resist buying it when she saw it in a shop near Hawthorn Manor and I heard Mommy say on the phone to Auntie Fern "I just had to share our good news with you. You know the Depot Max just finished building for that drilling company I told you about? Well the owner of the company is up here from Dallas Texas and he's so pleased with Max's work that he wants him to build their new three-story office building on Calgary Trail... Uh-huh, a SIZEABLE contract... thank you Fern, I'll pass that along to him. Well the owner, Beau Hughes... yes B.E.A.U. It must be short for Beauregard ... I know! It's right out of a southern novel. Anyway he's invited Max and me to join Jeannie and Gil Gilroy and him for dinner Tuesday night at – are you ready – Hotel Macdonald... I KNOW. Now here's the other reason I called. I have nothing to wear. Well nothing special enough and I was wondering if you'd come dress shopping with me" which I never heard Mommy say before because she always makes everything herself.

Then when Daddy got home and I said "HOO-HOO-HOORAY FOR YOUR NEW BUILDING" and he said "Thank you Posy", from behind his back he brought out a TWO POUND BOX of Black Magic Chocolates which I didn't even know they made them that big! During dinner which was meatloaf and mashed potatoes with gravy and then raisin bread pudding for dessert because Mommy didn't know chocolates were coming Daddy said to her "This is way beyond anything I've done before. I'm going to need professional advice on building an elevator shaft and installing all that over-size glass. And you don't use run-of-the-mill blueprints on a job like this. I'll have to somehow get really good architectural drawings done up" and I said "You mean like Mr. Cohen probably does up?" and Daddy said "Um, yes exactly like Mr. Cohen probably does up as a matter of fact."

And then although IT WASN'T EVEN OUR MOVIE SATURDAY Mommy gave Rosy and me each fifty-cents to go see Easter Parade starring Judy Garland and Fred Astaire who I've seen both of them hundreds of times and he danced as perfect as he always does and she danced almost as good as Ann Miller even though in the movie they pretend Hannah Brown who was Judy can dance better than Nadine Hale who was Ann but WHO COULD? We stayed and watched it two times through and when we got home we told Mommy how perfect Judy and Ann's costumes were and we told Daddy that his favourite Irving Berlin wrote all the songs so now all four of us are going right after dinner to see it again and Daddy says we can have Cracker Jacks AND Twizzlers during it and he's buying.

My empty Easter basket was sitting on top of our dresser when I woke up. I searched all over the house in the dark with no luck finding a single Easter egg which I'm usually very good at. When Rosy woke up after I accidentally bumped the bed a few times she said "I looked out the window late last night and I think I might have seen something with big ears and a flashlight going into our playhouse." We quick put our boots and housecoats on and boy-oh-boy was she ever right. Behind just about everything out there we found two big hollow chocolate bunnies, four filled eggs, eight small solid ones, ten little coloured ones and six dyed hard boiled eggs for Mommy to devil which was our most stuff ever. Then after Hot Cross Buns for breakfast I put on my brand new blue-and-white striped dress under Rosy's blue spring coat she'd grown out of and my good hat with new daisies on it and my white gloves and last of all my NEW RED LEATHER SHOES WITH TEENY HOLES IN THE SHAPE OF A HEART ON THE TOES AND BLACK PATENT BOWS AT THE BACK because Jesus finally answered my prayers. Then off we went to Sunday School with Rosy wearing everything new too only in green her new favourite colour.

40. Chassé, Pivot, Shimmy-Shimmy

Easter Sunday night Mr. Cohen phoned to talk some more about the building and Daddy said "You know what Nate, this would be so much easier if we could spread the plans out and work through all the details in person. Tomorrow's a holiday, how about you take Tuesday and Wednesday off as well, I'll book a couple of hotel rooms in, say, Lloydminster and we can meet there tomorrow morning?" Mr. Cohen must have said yes because Daddy said "What do you say we bring Isobel and Sara along? They can see the sights, shop, get to know each other better?" One second after he hung up Mommy was off next door to talk to the Beagles. When she got back she said "It's all settled. Bonnie will look after you girls and sleep over here the two nights we're gone. Mrs. Beagle will have you over for your dinners and you girls and Bonnie can rustle up breakfasts and lunches and keep each other amused until we get home Wednesday night." Then she started pulling clothes out of her closet all excited about going on a holiday.

Bonnie Beagle is in Grade Eleven and she turns seventeen on Ginger Rogers' birthday July 16. She is very pretty and wears Saddle Oxfords and bobby socks and she's held hands and skated with two different boys at the rink that we've seen but there might have been more. She always says Hi nicely to us even if she's with her High School friends. We love her.

The first morning after the three of us finished eating all of the snacks Mommy had left for us Bonnie said "Is there some place here where I can practise my jazz dancing? All our classes and rehearsals got cancelled over Easter holidays and I want to work on my routines for the big Recital especially since I'm the Dance Captain now." I said "Follow me" and I took her lickety-split down to my tumbling rug and said "Right here." She said "Gee that's nice of you Posy but I can't dance on a rug" and I said "Um, well, okay then I can put it away" and she said "Thanks that'd be peachy keen." While she ran next door to get her records Rosy carried the record player carefully down the stairs and I rolled up my tumbling rug and dragged it over to where Daddy keeps his Stock.

Bonnie brought three records she dances to which Daddy has all three of the exact same ones. She said she likes the Benny Goodman one best and I told her that he and me write to each other which she didn't believe until I quick took her upstairs and showed her the letter in the frame. We asked if we could watch her dance and she said yes that it would be good to rehearse in front of an audience. Well she put on Sing-Sing-Sing and started to jazz dance and WE COULDN'T BELIEVE IT. She could be on Broadway or in Hollywood or anywhere. Then she danced to It Don't Mean A Thing If It Ain't Got That Swing and WE COULDN'T BELIEVE IT EVEN MORE. I asked does she have a stage name yet and she said she's thinking about maybe Bonbon Beagelle. And when we asked would she show us how to jazz dance she said she would.

She put on Alice Faye singing Everybody Step which I know all the words to from Daddy's record and she taught us Chassé-ing and how to wiggle a Jazz Walk and then she got us doing Pivot-Turns that are quite a bit harder. In the afternoon she said we were ready for some trickier moves and she put on her Duke Ellington record. For the Lindy Hop you have to do Gallop step to the left, right foot behind, step on your left foot and then quick do Gallop step to the right, put your left foot behind, step on your right one and then do it all over again and again except faster and faster. Rosy got it right after three tries. I was just about ready to give up jazz dancing for good but then she showed us the Shimmy-Shimmy and from then on all we did for the whole three days was practise, practise, practise, practise and practise.

On Wednesday Mrs. Beagle had us over for dinner for the last time which was something new called Tuna Casserole and then she gave us a package of chocolate covered marshmallow cookies and we took them out to our playhouse and played Fish and ate them until it got too dark to see the cards so Bonnie started telling ghost stories that were so scary Rosy and me held onto each other and Wiggy for dear life. All of a SUDDEN there was a LOUD KNOCK on the playhouse door. All three of us SCREEEEEEEEEEEEEEAMED. The door opened...

And PHEW it was just Mommy and Daddy home from Lloydminster. The first thing they did after hugging us was thank Bonnie for looking after us and give her a twenty-dollar bill which I knew was five dollars too much because I'd heard Mommy say let's give her a whole five dollars a day for the three days even though she's only sleeping over two nights. Bonnie said "Are you SURE?" and Daddy said "Absolutely" and Mommy said "We really appreciate you doing this for us on your Easter holiday" and only I knew Bonnie got exactly how much she needed to buy a skimpy shimmy-shimmy costume with fringes on it that her parents would NOT approve of at Malabar's Costumes & Dance Wear and one penny back. They brought Rosy a desk set for her Writing Desk and I got a pair of sunglasses. My first. They have Plastic frames which is so modern the lady who owned the store said she had to order them from The States. They're red.

Then they told us the biggest news we couldn't believe. MR. AND MRS. COHEN ARE MOVING TO EDMONTON AND ESSIE AND DAVID ARE COMING WITH THEM. They said as soon as school got out in June the Cohens would pack up everything they own which isn't much because of only living in two rooms above Mr. Cohen's cousin's family and move into a house Mommy and Daddy would find for them to rent in Edmonton.

I got a postcard from Bunny that she mailed from Saskatoon where I didn't even know she was going with a picture of a Saskatchewan castle on it called The Bessborough Hotel which she said is haunted by ghosts and they put a bowl of free chocolate Easter eggs on the Lobby Desk for Children Of Guests Only which meant her. She said Mr. Alvarez took her and her Mom there for Easter Sunday and Easter Monday to see the sights. Mommy said "Well, well, well, well, well" and I said "I KNOW! Lucky Bunny eh?"

I only take my sunglasses off late at night when I can't see out of them anymore.

41. Tricky Moves

Mommy took Rosy and me to Bonnie Beagle's big Recital where she was in three numbers being a Tap Extravaganza and two Jazz Dance routines which one of them was the Sing-Sing-Sing solo wearing her skimpy shimmy-shimmy costume and everybody stood up and clapped for her which her Mom told us is called a Standing Ovation and I heard three people say "She's going to go far." But next morning she was right back in our Basement teaching us more moves. That proved how nice she is to everyone which I told her is good because she'll meet the same people on the way down.

Lundi, Avril 17, 1950

Didier Desjardins,
Madame Desjardins Studio de Ballet,
26 Trevegat Street,
MONTREAL, Quebec,
Canada.

Cher Didier,

Here is a big surprise for you. I wrote BARBARA ANN SCOTT and asked her for an autographed picture of herself saying For Didier on it and at last she sent it. So here it is in one of my big envelopes that I invested in for my career.

Your amie Paulette

P.S. Rosy and me have a Studio de Jazz Dance in the Basement where we practise Pivot Turns and the Shimmy-Shimmy and other tricky moves.

Monday, April 17, 1950

Dear Eleanor,

Here is a big surprise for you. I wrote BARBARA ANN SCOTT and asked her for an autographed picture of herself saying For Eleanor on it and at last she sent it. So here it is in one of my big envelopes that I invested in for my career.

Your friend Posy

P.S. Our almost 17-years-old good friend Bonnie Beagle taught Rosy and me how to Jazz Dance and we're going to give free classes to Peggy, Becca, Marji and Joy.

P.P.S. Thanks for the picture of Promise eating your chesterfield. Ha-ha.

Mommy got phoned all excited by Grandma who said they are putting the farm up and if it sells, THEY ARE MAKING THE MOVE TO EDMONTON maybe even this summer which would make my life perfect forever. She said tell Posy I promise we'll make sure Wee Teats and Strutter go to good homes before we leave.

Eleanor wrote me back to thank me for the autographed picture of BARBARA ANN SCOTT and she told me the BIG SECRET that Darlene and her were sitting on the floor behind the counter re-stocking cigarettes when Mrs. Cruickshank and Mrs. Beddoes came in The Hotel for coffee and pie and they heard Mrs. Beddoes say "Now Connie Cruickshank you sly suzy I've been waiting for you to tell me yourself but you haven't said a word so I'm just going to come right out with it and say that a little birdie told me – although I'll admit I was starting to wonder myself about how often I've seen you two out and about together – that you and Albi Alvarez are getting MARRIED!" Eleanor said she snuck a look through the glass counter and Mrs. Cruickshank was blushing AT HER AGE and that she said "I guess the secret had to come out sooner or later. Yes Loretta you heard right" and Mrs. Beddoes said "Congratulations! So how did it all start?" and Mrs. Cruickshank said "Well of course I've seen Albi going in and out of his Photography Shop for years and even said hello on occasion but who'd have dreamt when he knocked on my door that day right after Miss Paisley disappeared to show me a letter from of all people little Posy Kohler in Edmonton that we'd get to talking and talking and having tea together and that he and I would end up falling hook-line-and-sinker for each other?" and Mrs. Beddoes said "You just never know when it's going to happen do you? Geoff and I never even looked at each other all through High School and then seven years later wouldn't you know it we bumped into each other at of all places Whoop-Up Days in Lethbridge and he'd just got his Embalming Diploma and I'd just qualified as a Makeup Artist so of course it was a perfect fit."

I said to Mommy that I better quick write and tell Bunny the news but she said "NO-NO-NO dear, let her Mommy tell her."

42. Under The Knife

Monday, May 15, 1950

Dear Nurse Beryl,

This is the worst thing I have ever had to tell anybody and the reason I am writing to you instead of somebody else is because you are a Physiotherapist so you will understand what I am going through but it will still come as a shock to you.

I AM IN THE EDMONTON GENERAL HOSPITAL AND THEY'RE GOING TO TAKE MY TONSILS OUT TOMORROW MORNING.

Nobody tells you anything around here but this is not the first time I've been in a hospital because you remember about my 7 teeth getting pulled on my birthday. I am pretty sure there will be needles and chloroform and blood and there could be even worse things. Maybe even the WORST thing. Mommy says I'll just go to sleep and when I wake up she'll be here with ice cream and the operation will be all over and it'll be like nothing happened. But I have known 2 people who went under the knife in the hospital and never came out again being Auntie Clara and Mrs. Moody.

Pray for me.

Your friend Posy

P.S. I didn't bring my bag of lucky teeth in case somebody steals them or throws them out by mistake so now anything could happen.

Wednesday, May 17, 1950

Dear Bunny,

I am writing to you because nobody else will understand what I am going through like you will. It is now the next afternoon after having my tonsils taken out. I can barely talk enough to tell Rosy what to put in this letter but I will try.

I didn't know where I was when I woke up and I felt dizzy and sick and my throat hurt and then I remembered the awful things they did to me before they put me to sleep and boy-oh-boy I got really mad because Mommy lied to me about everything. Rosy didn't want to write that but I made her because it's true and it's my letter. I can't swallow what the nurse brings me. I can't even look at ice cream without almost throwing up in the bed. It's like I have steel wool in my throat even if all I'm sucking is ice.

You have never known such pain and I hope you never do.

Your friend Posy

P.S. I just this minute got given your letter saying you have Scarlet Fever. Mommy was wrong. Gargling with salt water didn't save either one of us.

P.P.S Whatever you do don't let them take you to the hospital.

Mercredi, Mai 17, 1950

Cher Didier,

Here is the shock. I could have died having my tonsils out yesterday. It was touch-and-go for a while there but I pulled through. The reason I am telling you instead of somebody else is because you are the only person who has been through anything almost as bad when you nearly died and froze your les pieds. I have been in Le Hospital for trois days and it's not over yet but if she's not lying again Mommy says I will be home with my famille by Vendredi afternoon.

The nurse just got here with my dinner on a tray so we'll see what happens with that.

Your amie Paulette

P.S. I was able to eat 3 bowls of jello and an orange popsicle that Daddy just brought me and I haven't thrown up yet but that could all change in a minute.

Well they finally let me out of the hospital and I got carefully brought home and put on the chesterfield under the Aff-gan with two pillows and a bowl of Neapolitan ice cream. I got sent three bouquets of flowers being one that Grandma and Grandpa sent somehow from their farm outside St. Hildegard and one from Nurse Beryl and Mr. Pankhurst from Regina and the other one from Auntie Fern and Uncle Otto plus nine Get Well cards being six from Flatte Butte and three of them had dollars in them. Peggy and Becca and Marji came after school and brought me a grape popsicle and said they'd bring me a different flavour every day until I'm better which looked like it could be a long time. Mommy was very nice to me and she apologized for lying which she said she didn't know she was doing and I believe her.

43. On The Mend

Nurse Beryl called Long Distance from Regina and said she was glad that my surgery was a success and the agony was over and that I was at home and thankfully on the mend. I told her that I was able to eat pudding and ice cream and popsicles if I was careful swallowing and she said that was a big relief for her. I remembered to say thank you to her and Mr. Pankhurst for the nice flowers and she said "You're welcome poppet" and then Mommy started telling her about Daddy's building he's building and I thought all the interesting talk was done so I went back to the chesterfield to read my Get Well book from the Beagles about unusual dogs. But when Rosy got back from seeing The Red Shoes for the fourth time with her friends Jocelyn and Shirley and Daddy got home from a Banker meeting on The North Side Mommy got everyone to come into the living room and she told us the big news.

She said Nurse Beryl said "You'll probably think we're moving too fast but Cyril and I know without a shadow of a doubt that we're doing the right thing. So, we're getting married on the first of July." I said "NURSE BERYL AND MR. PANKHURST ARE MARRYING EACH OTHER?" and Rosy said "Didn't you guess that?" and Daddy said "That's great news" and Mommy said "I knew she was falling in love before she knew it herself, just listening to her voice that first time she called from Flatte Butte Hotel." I said "NURSE BERYL AND MR. PANKHURST ARE MARRYING EACH OTHER?" Mommy said "They're going to have a small but lovely wedding in the ballroom of Cyril's ever so charming Hawthorn Manor and they've invited us all to come and to stay there as their guests" and I said "IN THE BALLROOM?"

and Mommy said "She's asked me to be her Matron of Honour and she would like Rosy to be her Junior Bridesmaid" and Rosy said "HER JUNIOR BRIDESMAID?" "And she'd like Posy to be her Flower Girl" and I said "HER FLOWER GIRL?" and Mommy said "Because it's her second wedding she's just going to wear a simple – but knowing her it will be elegant – cream coloured, ankle-length dress with a fingertip veil and she said I could wear a summer evening suit or dress in a pastel colour of my choosing and Rosy can wear a ballerina-length dress in a complimentary shade" and Rosy said "A BALLERINA-LENGTH DRESS?" and I said "What about me?" and Mommy said "I've saved the best for last. Beryl said 'If you wouldn't mind making it Isobel, I see Posy in A CLOUD OF PINK TULLE'."

After dinner Daddy said "With Posy deep in the throes of convalescence, did anyone think to bring the Saturday mail in?" and Rosy said "Sorry-sorry I forgot" and she was off out the door and back in with an envelope for The Kohler Family from Mr. Charlie Buckler and Miss Penny Paisley and Daddy said Rosy could read it to us and she did.

Monday, May 15, 1950

Dear Isobel, Max, Rosy and Posy,

I wouldn't have believed it if you'd told me a year ago but the beautiful Miss Penny Paisley is going to make an honest man out of me. Yep we're getting married! It'll be a real small wedding Saturday, July 1ˢᵗ in Cardston, just her family and a couple of old friends and then we'll hop on Trusty Rusty and zoom up to Flin Flon for our honeymoon so Pen can meet my folks.

We asked Curly if after we get back could we have a party at Fort Lively for the handful of terrific people who helped get us together and he said you betcha. Of course we said to each other that the Kohlers have to be first on the list. Since we don't know the names of the other folks and kids who helped, we'll leave it to Posy to get the word out as only she can.

We're shooting for Saturday, July 8th. We'll have a free room for the four of you. The other rooms will be first come first serve. We'll look after all the food and drinks. Just bring yourselves and get ready for a good time with lots of music and dancing. Max be sure to bring your sax. And tell anyone who wants to be part of the entertainment they're more than welcome.

The not so good news is that old Curly's thinking of selling the hotel and moving in with his daughter's family in Billings which could put us out of work but we'll worry about that if and when the time comes.

Looking forward to hearing back from you,

Charlie & Penny

I missed school and playing kick-the-can with my friends and teaching jazz dancing and climbing trees and dogs and all the things other children were doing outside my window and I'll always have to remember the surgery and the agony but I tried not to complain. Whenever I felt up to it I'd get up off the chesterfield and go to Rosy's Study where she left out our writing pad and the letter she printed nicely so I could make copies of it for people when she was at school.

THE DATE GOES HERE

Dear PUT THEIR NAME HERE

You are invited to a party Charlie "Chuck The Buck" Buckler and Miss Penny Paisley are having on Saturday, July 8 at Fort Lively Hotel somewhere between Coutts and Shelby on Highway 91 in Montana to thank the people and kids for finding them and helping them get together.

They are looking after all the food and drinks so just bring yourselves and your musical instruments if you have one and get ready for a good time with lots of music and dancing and you can do entertainment if you want to and then spend the night there for free.

Yours truly,

POSY SIGN YOUR NAME HERE

for Mr. Charlie Buckler and Miss Penny Paisley

I thought on my first day back at school everybody would be a bit more excited to see that I was still alive but I guess they already heard the good news from my best friends.

Lucky for me Mr. Gilliland was on playground duty for afternoon recess because all of a sudden seeing him there made me think of something from a long time ago and I went up to him and said "Mr. Gilliland are you Charlie Buckler's whose stage name is Chuck The Buck's buddy named Gilliland who writes songs?"

A horrible thing just about happened. Rosy was turning TEN in the morning and I didn't have a Birthday present for her because of my surgery and the agony. And then POOF I remembered and I ran to my bottom drawer where I keep my supplies and at the back under my extra pine cones and wrapped in a hanky was the heart-shape locket I got at The Sally Ann for Rosy's Christmas present before I thought up the bookcase idea. I showed it to Mommy and she said "That's very nice dear" but when she turned it over she laughed and laughed and said "What did you pay for this?" I said "Well it would have been ten-cents but because of the HALF PRICE

FOR ONE DAY ONLY miracle I only paid five-cents" and she said "You really are the luckiest little duck. The hallmark says it's fourteen-karat gold." I said "Does that mean it's a peachy-keen present?" and Mommy said "Super-duper peachy-keen." I said "What do I tell Rosy if she asks how much it cost?" and Mommy said "I taught you girls better than to ask the price of a gift so I'd say you're off the hook."

I almost told her in the morning when she screamed from loving it so much. But I didn't.

44. Shock After Shock

This just came in the mail to Mr. and Mrs. M. Kohler and Family.

MARRIAGE ANNOUNCEMENT

Constance Mary Cruickshank (née Farris) and Alberto Tahoma Alvarez
announce the happy occasion of their marriage.
Ceremony took place Friday, the 2nd day of June, 1950
at
Oddfellows Hall, Flatte Butte, Saskatchewan,
Justice of the Peace Geoffrey T. Beddoes officiating.
Flower Girl: Bernice Cruickshank. Ring Bearer: Wilbur Beddoes
Witnesses: Dorothy Ann Farris and Ian Rolheiser
A small reception followed catered by the Rebekahs.

Thursday, June 8, 1950

Dear Bunny ALVAREZ,

HOO-HOO-HOORAY FOR YOU. Mr. Alvarez is one of the nicest men I have ever known. He will be a very good Daddy for you and teach you many magic tricks and now that your Mom doesn't have to have Boarders anymore you and her can go to movies together for free anytime you want.

The Wedding Reception in the Oddfellows Hall sounded like a lot of fun with people bringing their favourite record and making up a funny dance to it and Mr. Alvarez lassoo-ing your Mom from across the room and Liddy Frisch printing a pretend newspaper saying LAST BACHELOR IN FLATTE BUTTE BITES THE DUST. But best of all is the news that Mr. Alvarez is hiring Wilma Lutz who can't teach Figure Skating in the summer to run his Photography Shop and the Movie Hall for 5 weeks so your Mom and you and him can go on your honeymoon to New Mexico to meet your new Abuela and Abuelo and your Tias and Tios and I bet eat Tamales which you will JUST LOVE. And before that YIPPEE you're coming to Chuck The Buck and Miss Paisley's party on the second day of your honeymoon.

Your friend Posy

P.S. The Announcement was the first I ever heard that Bucky's real name is Wilbur.

P.P.S. Rosy and I just found out this minute that New Mexico isn't in Mexico but it's still pretty good news anyway.

Mr. Cohen took the train and was sleeping on our chesterfield for three nights so him and Daddy could have a big meeting with Mr. Hughes who FLEW HERE from Dallas Texas to see their Architectural Drawings and talk turkey about the new Amer-Cana Office Building. Daddy phoned Mommy and said things were turning out even better than they hoped and that they were going out for drinks and dinner with Beau and not to expect them home until late.

Mommy made us whisper and tiptoe in the morning because Daddy wasn't up yet and Mr. Cohen was still asleep on the chesterfield but they must have perked right up because while we were at school Daddy went out and bought a brand new only two-years-old car that's a Buick Super in Honolulu Blue Metallic and Mr. Cohen bought half of our truck for their family to use but the other half will still be the business truck and they got both the doors painted over again with a big K.C.F.C. Kohler & Cohen Fine Construction. Then they took all of Rosy's and my stuff out of the playhouse and put it in the basement and put the playhouse back on the truck for the Cohens to move to Edmonton in like we did

208

only instead of seeing The World on the way they're going to go to the party at Fort Lively because of Essie and David wanting to go so bad and thank goodness Daddy said as soon as they get to Edmonton and unload it we can have our playhouse back.

Mommy and Daddy got a letter from Chuck The Buck which they sat me down and read to me.

Wednesday, June 7, 1950

Dear Max and Isobel,

Don't get me wrong, I'm not complaining or anything but we've already had letters come from a Mr. and Mrs. A. Alvarez & Daughter and a George and Dottie Privett & Girls and a Mr. and Mrs. Geoffrey Beddoes & Son accepting the invitation to attend our party including a free room for the night – which was a misunderstanding but good old Curly said what the heck it's only one night. So anyway I'm just wondering if you could maybe ask Posy how many other people she's invited because we're running out of rooms and are worried we might have to send guests to the campground nearby or maybe see if some neighbors could put them up. And then of course there's the food and drinks.

Like I said, it's not a problem. Just that we'd kind of like to get a handle on how many people to expect. Thanks.

Charlie

Daddy said "Hmm, that's fourteen counting us." Mommy said "Jeannie Gilroy mentioned today they're driving to Great Falls anyway to drop Marji off for a month with her Grandma so she just sent a note accepting the invitation." Daddy said "So then seventeen all together. It may be more than the handful they expected but it could have been worse" and Mommy said "Didn't you say the

Cohens are driving down?" and Daddy said "Right. Twenty-one. Anyone else Posy?"

Wednesday, June 14, 1950

Dear Mr. Pankhurst,

I am writing to tell you that a letter came from Chuck The Buck today saying they're running out of rooms and maybe food and drinks at Fort Lively Hotel & Saloon because of all the people I invited to the party. So you better hurry up and get ahold of Chuck The Buck to say you're coming since nobody deserves to be there more than you do because of your good clues or else you and Nurse Beryl will have to sleep in the campground nearby or be put up by neighbours. Besides Old Curly is thinking about selling the hotel so this might be your last chance ever to sleep in a Ghost Town.

Your friend Posy

P.S. YIPPEE only 15 more days and we'll be sleeping in your Ballroom.

P.P.S. Mommy says she bought Silk-O-Lina right out of pink tulle but I won't tell you one more thing about my dress so I don't spoil your surprise.

P.P.P.S. Tell Nigel too or he won't have a room either.

Mercredi, Juin 14, 1950

Chère Madame Desjardins,

I am writing to tell you that they're running out of rooms and maybe food and drinks at Fort Lively Hotel & Saloon because of all the people I invited to the party. So you better hurry up and tell them you and Didier are

210

coming or else you will have to sleep in the campground nearby or be put up by neighbours.

Very sincerely,

Paulette

P.S. Diddy's letter said you and him are going to Flatte Butte to see his cousins before the party. WELL SO AM I GOING TO BE THERE THEN.

Becca came to our house just before we started eating dinner and she was puffing from running fast all the way to tell us the best news of her whole life being that her Mom whose name I know is Carlotta is ALL BETTER FROM T.B. AND IS LEAVING THE SAN IN P.A. FOR GOOD. She said her Dad was on the phone right that minute making the plans. Mommy said "Have you eaten dear?" and Becca said "No" so Mommy boxed up our pot roast dinner for the Cappellettos and Daddy drove Becca home with it and by the time he got back Mommy had made bacon and tomato sandwiches for us. While we were eating them with ketchup Becca phoned to tell us her Auntie Adrianna and Uncle Mike had just invited them all to their cottage on Sylvan Lake until the middle of August except her Dad has to drive up to Edmonton to work but he'll be back every weekend for fun. And he said because Becca's been such a good girl helping with Nico and Nina and the housework all year without ever complaining and since she wants to go so bad they're going to drive all the way from Sylvan Lake to Montana and back for Chuck The Buck and Miss Paisley's party even Nonna and the little ones.

45. Ready... Set...

I asked Mommy if she remembered exactly what the bright red costume I designed looked like before I never got my drawing back from The Office Of Edith Head and she said yes she did so I told her what I needed it for and she said "It doesn't give me much time" but she said she'd do it. Later when I told her that I forgot to say I needed six of them she said "You're kidding me right?" but after I begged she finally said "Okay but you do understand I can't start them until I'm finished our three outfits for Beryl's wedding. Then I'll do as many as I can manage." I said "BUT—" and she said "And I know you have your heart set on all those beads and feathers but sewing individual beads on takes a lot of time" and I said "I don't mind if you just buy yards and yards of fringe and sew that on instead" and she said "Oh well then, that'll make ALL the difference in the world."

Chuck The Buck called Daddy Long Distance and said he thought he better pump up the size of the band and add some numbers that aren't Western Music considering who all was coming and maybe bring in a Ringer on drums from Missoula named Sticks Kirkpatrick that everybody says is Hot Stuff and would Daddy mind being the bandleader as well as the sax player and could he maybe bring some sheet music and does he know of anyone else coming to the party who can play an instrument and Daddy said "Jeannie Gilroy can play any kind of music by ear if you have a piano at the Saloon" and Chuck The Buck said yes they do and Daddy said "And I hear George Privett's one heckuva trombone player, in fact they say when he worked at the Curling Club the touring bands playing for bonspiel parties always asked him to sit in. Oh, and add six Cappellettos to the list, three adults and three children." So that all got settled.

Just before I left for school I said to Mommy "It turns out I need four more costumes so ten all together" and she said "WHAT?" and I said "Oopsie there's Marji I'd better run" and I yelled "WAIT UP!"

When Rosy went to the Library to drop off her week's books before we left town Miss Alma Nielsen told her she was going to trade shifts with the other Librarian and drive to Cardston Friday morning the seventh of July and stay the night at her Mom's so she and Pearly Pitt could take one car and get an early start for Montana on the Saturday morning.

When Becca's Dad came to take her out of school a week early Miss Semonick gave Becca her Grade 1 final report card and said out loud "I've got good news for you Rebecca, you have passed into Grade Two" and I started everyone up yelling "HOO-HOO-HOORAY" for her and she said thank you to Miss Semonick and goodbye to the class and gave a special smile to Peggy and Marji and me and then the recess bell went and we all went outside and us three ran over to the fence and waved goodbye to Becca and Mr. Cappelletto and Nonna and Nico and Nina when they drove by in their green station wagon to go get her Mom out of the San in P.A. for good.

Mommy said "I ran into Faith Upright on Whyte Avenue today and she said that she and Ernest felt called to take the girls to a Family Bible Camp outside of Foremost Alberta for three weeks so I'm afraid you won't be seeing Peggy and Joy for a while after this Friday" but Rosy said "We might be because Joy and I just figured out it's only a one-hour-and-thirty-minutes drive from Foremost to Fort Lively so she and Peggy are going to try and talk her parents into going there for the party." Mommy said "In a SALOON?" and Rosy said "I think they're going to leave that part out when they ask them."

Chuck The Buck called Daddy again and said "So who's this Cyril Pankhurst guy?" and Daddy asked him why he was asking and he said "Because he just called Curly and they had a long talk and then Curly told me the guy's bringing a case of rye, a case of rum and a case of wine from his bar stock in Regina – can you believe it?" When I asked Daddy if he remembered to tell him about Miss Nielsen and Miss Pitt and the four Uprights maybe coming he said "You know I just clean forgot."

All day on the last day of school before summer holidays us kids said "Oh I hope I pass" and "Gee what if I don't pass" and "I just know I failed" and then we got given our Report Cards and snuck them open and PHEW we all passed. I got two H's, two A-Pluses, an A, a B-Plus and I was up to a B-Minus in Arithmetic because I had worked hard with Mommy on it. Miss Semonick's Teacher's Comment said "Paulette is an interesting child" instead of "Paulette talks entirely too much" which shows that the Talking Bracelet worked.

The MINUTE we got home Mommy had everything packed and ready to go and we got into our Honolulu Blue Metallic Buick Super and headed straight for Flatte Butte for the night because we were leaving too late to make it all the way to Regina in one go.

A Buick Super is very different than sitting four people in a truck cab. Rosy and me had the whole back seat all to ourselves with so much room we could have put four more kids in there easy. We each had our own window but we mostly just played Hangman and ate Welsh cakes since we couldn't see much outside with Mommy's lavender silk evening suit hanging from the hook on my side and Rosy's ballerina-length lilac dress hanging on her side. My Cloud Of Pink Tulle was wrapped in a white sheet and sitting on Mommy's lap the whole way so it wouldn't get squashed by suitcases in the trunk.

We got to Flatte Butte too late to go visiting anyone but the Privetts came to The Hotel and I got to see Eleanor for the first time since last summer and she brought Promise to meet me who I JUST LOVE. Mrs. Mosbeck the cook stayed and made us dinner which was roast beef and something else but I was almost asleep so I don't know what. Rosy and I got given our own room and we said goodbye to Eleanor and Darlene and told them we'd see them again Sunday afternoon.

46. Happily Ever After

Hawthorn Manor is not big enough to be a Saskatchewan castle but it's so fancy Rosy said it could be a large Duke or Knight's mansion easy. The man standing behind the Front Desk said "You must be the Kohlers" and he knocked on the door behind him and said "Your friends have arrived" and out came a handsome man with a very nice smile and I must have never looked at him in Flatte Butte because I felt all shy since I wouldn't have even known who he was if he didn't say "Hello my friends. Welcome, I'm Cyril. What a happy day this is!" and he shook Mommy and Daddy's hands and patted Rosy's shoulder and then he pinched both of my cheeks and laughed for no reason. He said to us "Beryl just called to say she's finished her last patient and will be here in two minutes" and then the man at the Front Desk said "Mr. Pankhurst I have that collect call you're expecting" and Mr. Pankhurst said to us "That'll be Nigel my Best Man. I asked him to call from a phone booth along the way to confirm he'll be here in time for the rehearsal. Excuse me for a moment."

Rosy and I said "Rehearsal?" and Mommy said "They have to make sure we know where to walk and what to do" and we said "In the Ballroom?" and she said "I'm sure it would have to be" and then I said "Rosy we get to meet Nigel" and Daddy said "Who?" and Rosy said "Nigel Oswald from Oswestry, Shropshire, England" and I said "He's Mr. Pankhurst's best mate" and Mommy said "How do you know all that?" but just then the front door opened and Nurse Beryl came in looking so beautiful with her new hair and her new makeup and her best smile ever and she said "What a happy day this is!" which is exactly what Mr. Pankhurst said and they were both right.

When Mr. Pankhurst came back he said to Nurse Beryl "Nigel's just two hours away" and to us he said "Have you eaten?" and Mommy said "Yes thank you" but I said "Just breakfast and then Welsh cakes in the car" and Mommy said "Posy!" and Nurse Beryl laughed and Mr. Pankhurst said "Why don't we let you settle in and in fifteen minutes we'll meet over there in the Chelsea Room for lunch" and then he nodded to a Bell Hop wearing a pill box who picked up our suitcases and said "Right this way please" and took us up an elevator made of shiny wood and mirrors to the top floor being Floor Number Three and the little brass sign on the door he opened said Premier's Suite.

After having lunch in the Chelsea Room and going to Mr. Pankhurst's house down the street to play with Maggie and Dizzy and then meeting Nigel and doing the Rehearsal in the Ballroom that still had dust covers on the chairs and learning what The Flower Girl had to do and then wearing my pink Dotted Swiss party dress to the Rehearsal Dinner where Nurse Beryl and Mr. Pankhurst said that since we're like their family in Canada would Rosy and me like to call them Auntie and Uncle from now on which we said yes we would and Nigel making me laugh so hard I nearly spit out my Krem Broolay and then Rosy and me sleeping in a Four Poster Bed in our own room in the Premier's Suite and then having breakfast in the Devonshire Room and going to Nurse Beryl's hairdresser to get my hair done up in curls on top of my head with bobby pins and hairspray and having a Light Lunch and Petty Forzes brought to the table in the Premier's Suite and getting into my new underwear and my new white socks with lace trim and my new black patent Mary Jane shoes and having white real carnations bobby-pinned inside my curls and then putting on my Cloud Of Pink Tulle and then the SECOND I heard the String Quartet playing the first note of our Walking Song being the first Bridal Party person to step into the Ballroom that was fixed up like a King and Queen lived there and then walking and smiling slowly down the Aisle between the cream coloured chairs with cream satin bows tied on them and sprinkling pink rose petals on the long blue rug out of my pretty white basket with carnations stuck on it and then stopping and turning around and watching Rosy walk down the Aisle in her lilac Ballerina-length dress carrying a little bouquet of white roses and baby's breath and then watching Mommy walk down the Aisle in her lavender silk Evening Suit with a bigger bouquet of white roses and baby's breath and then listening to the music change to Here Comes The Bride and seeing all the thirty people stand up and then watching Nurse Beryl walk down the Aisle in her elegant cream coloured ankle-length silk dress and fingertip veil carrying a Cascade Bouquet of pink roses, white gardenias, cream coloured lilies and white steffa-notice and then watching her and Mr. Pankhurst get married and put rings on each other's fingers and kiss on the lips and then us all going back down the Aisle with Rosy and me last and then having pictures taken of just Rosy and me and then me alone and then both of us with Mommy and both of us with Nurse Beryl and both of us with Nurse Beryl and Mr. Pankhurst and then all of us including Nigel and then once with Mommy and Daddy and Rosy and me and then going outside and doing all of the exact same pictures all over again and then coming back into the Ballroom for a fancy dinner and speeches and dancing with every single person at the wedding and helping serve little pieces of Wedding Cake to everybody and then going upstairs and getting out of my Cloud Of Pink Tulle that had quite a bit of white icing on it and getting into my Christmas evening-gown nightie, I said "Mommy I've decided that when I grow up I'm going to marry a handsome man who owns a Mansion hotel and I'm never going to leave it happily ever after."

47. Good Old Flatte Butte

Except for Nigel who had to quick hurry back to The Prince of Wales Hotel because of it being High Season and because he was taking off the next weekend too we were the only people in the Devonshire Room for that early of a breakfast which mine was pancakes with strawberries and whipped cream. Daddy told Nigel "It's going to take us five hours just to get to Flatte Butte and drop the girls off and then another four to Edmonton" and Nigel said "Ooh, that's a long day. Well drive carefully. Very nice to meet you. I'll see you at Fort Lively. Toodle-oo." After he left Daddy said "He seems like a nice enough fellow but remind me why you invited him to the party?" I said "Because he drove all the way to Cardston to find Miss Pearly Pitt" and Rosy said "And he bought Percy Paisley's Obituary from the News Agent with his own money" and Daddy said "Oh well then, it makes perfect sense" and Mommy laughed for some reason and then we took off.

Eleanor and Darlene and Promise were waiting for us in their front yard and I jumped out of the car and hugged Promise before I even remembered to go back and get my Cloud Of Pink Tulle that Mommy had rinsed the icing off of and wrapped in the sheet and said I could keep it with me to show my friends. Mommy got her tape measure out and measured Eleanor and Darlene and wrote it all down and then we heard "POSY!" and it was ESSIE and she and me held both hands and jumped up and down and then POOF it was BUNNY running up and hugging me. Mommy quick measured them both and then she and Daddy thanked Mr. and Mrs. Privett again for inviting Rosy and me to stay with them to have fun with our Flatte Butte friends and to take us with them to Montana and they told us to be good girls for Mrs. Privett and kissed us and left and we won't see them again until they drive down from Edmonton to meet us at the party on Saturday. Then Mrs. Privett took all us girls around to the back yard for a surprise.

She had a very exciting table set for us with grown-up ladies' party sandwiches and six little butterscotch puddings and bread-and-butter-pickles and raisin tarts and wiener pieces on toothpicks and marshmallow-men and radish roses to eat all in whatever order we wanted with lemonade. We already knew all of each other's news from our letters but we told it all over again anyway and then Bunny showed us her envelope of pictures of her Mom and Mr. Alvarez getting married and I asked her how come they got to use the Oddfellows Hall and she said "Because Mr. Alvarez's – I mean my Daddy's best friend Ian Rolheiser is the Past Noble Grand" and then she held up another picture and said "And this is me in my Flower Girl outfit" which was a nice blue dress with puffed sleeves and an embroidered collar and I pushed my chair back and stood up and said "I brought my—" Rosy's hand reached up behind me and pulled me back down by my blouse and she said "What a beautiful dress Bunny for your best day ever" and then she quick handed me another raisin tart and said "Posy brought—her appetite."

Next morning I pulled open the door to The Bakery and yelled "SURPRISE! LOOK WHO'S HERE" and Mr. Rolheiser said "Yes hi there Posy, Albi told me you were back in town and Dottie Privett just phoned to say you were on your way here so I put aside some chocolate chip cookies, your favourite" and he gave Eleanor and me each two free ones. After I told him all about Edmonton Alberta I explained why we needed the Oddfellows Hall during the day all week and I asked him if he would be allowed to let us use it and he said "Allowed? I am the Past Noble Grand. I would think that if I say you can use it then that's the final word, wouldn't you say?" and I said I would. He said "I've got some orders to get out but if you're out front of the Hall at one o'clock sharp I'll let you in." We were almost out the door when he said "Oh I almost forgot, Loretta Beddoes was in earlier and she saw Wally Wolff at the filling station and he said his Mother-In-Law and Diddy are in town and if I see either of the Kohler girls tell them to call the house."

At our surprise party we had all promised to meet next day in the back yard of The Hotel at exactly Noon so we would all know where we all were and what to do next and also because Mr. Privett said he'd send Myrtle out with sandwiches so everybody showed up plus David Cohen. Rosy said she was embarrassed to call the Wolff house and speak to Madame Desjardins or Diddy because of not having had time to practise her French but I said I would because I can speak twenty-three French words fluent. I went inside and asked Mr. Privett to please dial the Wolffs' number for me. When Howie answered I said "Bon-joor 'Owie. May I speak to Didier si-voo-play" and he said "IT'S FOR YOU DIDDY" and one second later my cher ami said "Hello" and I said "DIDDY IT'S YOU" and he said "YIPPEE YOU CALLED" and I said "You have to be at the Oddfellows Hall on Main Street at one o'clock sharp and it's already quarter after twelve so you better start getting ready" and he said "Should I bring the flat hat and everything?" and I said "Oui" and I hung up and asked Mr. Privett if he would please dial the Beddoes' number not the Funeral Home but where they live upstairs and Bucky answered and I said "BUCKY IT'S YOU!" and he said "Yep" and I said "You have to be at the Oddfellows Hall at one o'clock sharp and it's already quarter after twelve so you better start getting ready."

Diddy and Bucky were standing out front of the Oddfellows Hall when we got there and just like that the six of us Thick Thieves without even saying anything quick grabbled ahold of each other's hands in a circle around Rosy and did our big loud "RING-AROUND-THE-ROSY, SISTER-OF-THE-POSY" like we always used to and we ended up lying on the sidewalk laughing like crazy at "WE-ALL-FALL-DOWN." Rosy and Darlene and David told us to get up right this minute and behave ourselves or Mr. Rolheiser would see us so we got up and everybody waited nice and polite after that.

David asked Bunny where she's going to in New Mexico and she said "To my Daddy's parents' house near Alamogordo where my Daddy used to live when my Daddy was a boy." Darlene asked Essie "Will you miss Flatte Butte when you move to Edmonton" and Essie said "No." Eleanor asked Diddy how he's getting to the big party and he said "Mrs. Beddoes told my Tante Veronique to tell us that Grand-mère would be very welcome to ride in their car and that I'd be good company for Bucky" and then Diddy said to Rosy "I love your shoes!" and she said "They're Saddle Oxfords. I got them for my Birthday" and I said "All the big kids in Edmonton are wearing them but I bet hers were the only ones in an elementary school." And then Mr. Rolheiser showed up.

He unlocked the door and took us into the big main room with stairs and a balcony he said they use for parties and concerts and important Regional Meetings and told us to STAY there and not go wandering around anywhere else in the building or touch

ANYTHING. And then he left. Right away the kids started wandering around the building touching everything and when I told them to stay put in the big room and Rosy and me got things started up everybody was hardly even listening to us. Bunny wouldn't STOP getting the giggles and Essie said "I don't think we should be DOING these kinds of things" and it was plain that Darlene doesn't like taking orders from ANYONE and Eleanor thinks she's the ONLY one who's any good because of people saying her Moon Over Loon Lake solo was so perfect and David who was plugging and unplugging lights said "Am I the only one who's ACTUALLY doing anything here?" and Bucky said "I'M LEAVING" and he did.

I could tell that Rosy was getting pretty close to washing her hands of all of us again and then David who was trying out some switches accidentally turned all the lights off and we couldn't see anything and then WHOOSH the front door opened and a lady I didn't know was standing there in the sun and she said "Oh my goodness, I heard you were all here but I can't believe my eyes" and every kid but me said "GOOD AFTERNOON MISS TALBOT."

After we told Miss Talbot what we were doing she took over running things and it all went tickety-boo after that but later on she said it was looking like she'd better come back Tuesday and Wednesday to help us and maybe even Thursday but that on Friday morning she was leaving to drive to her family's big cabin on Elkwater Lake in The Cypress Hills for the whole summer.

On Tuesday morning early I took Rosy to The Flatte Butte Beat newspaper office and when we walked in the door Liddy Frisch said "Tell me I haven't lost my mind. Could this tall stranger be

NOSY POSY, THE GIRL TUESDAY? and I said "YES SHE COULD" and she said "How's life in the big city?" and I started to tell her all about Edmonton Alberta but she quick said "And you must be Rosy" and Rosy said "How do you do" and Liddy Frisch said "I don't mind saying it Posy, it's been tough keeping The Beat going without you bringing me news from the street every week. What interesting story do you have for me today?" so I told her about finding Miss Paisley and Chuck The Buck and how they're getting married now and having a party for us and she said "I'm guessing you need something from me" and we told her what and she said "How many?" and Rosy told her "Forty-five to be on the safe side" and she said "Well I'll be pretty busy getting the bi-weekly Beat out but if I can get Connie Cruicksh—I mean Alvarez to help me I might be able to squeeze it in." I opened my Pink Puppy Purse and said "I can pay" and she said "I'm afraid your money isn't good around here. I'm going to have to do it for free." Rosy said "Thank you very much" and Liddy Frisch said "Aha, here comes the Boy Tuesday" and I said "HI BUCKY!" and he said "I'm here to get the Movie Flyers." I told him I would walk up and down Main Street with him so that any business folk who haven't had a chance to see me yet could. Rosy got her Notebook out and when Bucky and I left she was showing Liddy Frisch all the names and stuff for the thing we needed her to do.

Madame Desjardins who is the most beautiful Grandma I ever saw came with Diddy to the Oddfellows Hall in the afternoon and she said "Ah sweet Paulette and clever Rosalind, I am so very happy to meet at last the little girls who have given me much happiness" and we said "Bon-joor Madame" and she said "I am here to watch the grand spectacle that Didier tells me is better than anything I have ever seen" and it was lucky for us she did come because she made some very good suggestions which Miss Talbot said she never could have thought of anything that creative herself.

Later when Mr. Rolheiser came back and locked us out onto the sidewalk Madame Desjardins said "Miss Talbot has kindly offered to introduce me to Mr. Beddoes at the chapelle funéraire so that I may speak with him about a matter" and she gave Diddy a dollar to take us kids to Youngman's Store and buy us all pops.

When we finished our pops and the other kids went home Rosy and me walked Diddy to Beddoes Funeral Home where his Grand-mère was standing outside with Miss Talbot talking to Mr. Beddoes beside his long black shiny car and we heard Madame Desjardins say "Monsieur Beddoes, I am wondering if there could be room in this magnificent automobile for a Hip of Beef?" and Mr. Beddoes said "Could there be ROOM? In a 1949 nine-passenger Cadillac Model Seven-Five-Three-Three-X Business Sedan better known as a Limousine? Oh yes Madame Desjardins, there will be room enough to spare" and she said "You are too generous Monsieur" and he said "It will be well wrapped won't it?" and she said "Certainement Monsieur. No blood will escape." Then Mrs. Beddoes came outside and said "Geoff did you remember to tell her they have to be ready to go at six o'clock Saturday morning?" and Mr. Beddoes said "It's a ten-hour drive, eleven if we stop twice to eat." Madame Desjardins said "There is one small problem with this arrangement. My son-in-law Wally Wolff informs me that a large Hip must be put on the spit not later than ten o'clock in the morning if we are to dine at six. Could we perhaps travel the day before?" Mr. Beddoes said "Impossible Madame, I have a funeral booked for Friday afternoon" and Madame Desjardins said "Mon Dieu! One week ago I telephoned from Montreal to Monsieur Chuckdabuck to say I will contribute a large Hip to the party that is making my grandson so happy. C'est une catastrophe!" and Mr. Beddoes said "One moment please Madame" and he went inside to his office and talked on the phone for a very long time and when he came back he said "The family of the deceased has graciously consented to a Friday morning service. We will pick you up at one o'clock Friday afternoon." Madame Desjardins said "You are too kind Monsieur" but Mrs. Beddoes said "So we arrive in Fort Lively at midnight with two cranky kids in the car? Is that what you're saying Geoffrey?" which is when Miss Talbot up and said "You're welcome to all spend the night in my family's big cabin on Elkwater Lake in the Cypress Hills and drive the last three hours early next morning."

48. The Big Blow

We played I Spy all the way to Biggar where we had chicken sandwiches and oranges out on a blanket and Mrs. Privett took a picture of us kids standing beside a sign where to be funny somebody painted "New York Is Big But This Is Biggar" which I got the joke because Biggar is Bigger spelled wrong. Then Mr. Privett said we better get going if we don't want to show up late and spoil the big dinner he knew his Mom would be making in Medicine Hat where we were spending the night to break the drive to The States up.

You could tell that Grandma and Grandpa Privett loved Eleanor and Darlene from how they pulled them right out of the car and kissed them and so did Morty their nice old dog and then the Grandma took us kids straight inside to the table and gave us little buttered buns to eat right away so our mouths wouldn't be empty while she and the young Mrs. Privett carried the turkey and ham and roast beef and trimmings in. The grown-ups had just sat down when Grandpa Privett said "I hate to burst everybody's bubble but I'm afraid there might be a problem with your plans. What's happening is – but here I'll let you listen for yourselves" and he stood back up and walked over to the sideboard and turned the radio on. "It's all they've been talking about today."

Right away a lady sang *"Stay tooooned for Nooooze at Six"* and a man said "Brought to you by Plundered Hills Sod Farm. NOW, our top story" and a sound went *"Bing-Bong"* and a man said "A freak weather phenomenon has been causing HAVOC today for our neighbour to the south. The trouble began overnight when an UNFORESEEN windstorm formed high over northern Wyoming and swept down without warning into an UNSUSPECTING Montana during the early hours of this morning. Gusts up to ONE-HUNDRED-AND-TEN-MILES-PER-HOUR pummeled crops south of Billings and BARRELED on to rip the roof off a barn in the state's WIND-PLAGUED Livingston area, before veering west, picking up speed, and RAGING through Butte, uprooting trees, overturning a vehicle and knocking out power to a dozen homes. When the MONSTER gale suddenly turned NORTH and gusts were clocked at ONE-HUNDRED-AND-FIFTEEN-MILES-PER-HOUR, Canadian weather authorities went on high alert, issuing the warning 'WHO CAN SAY?' In our Four O'clock Newscast brought to you by Whoop-Up Trail Deadstock Removal we reported that the FURIOUS wind had left a swath of damage on its RELENTLESS push up to Helena. *"Bing-Bong"* "THIS JUST IN. Our sources tell us THE BIG BLOW is hurtling toward Great Falls with no signs of slowing. *"Bing-Bong"* "We interrupt this Update with an UPDATE. Canadian weather authorities have this moment Updated their warning to 'YOU JUST NEVER KNOW'."

I didn't like the way Mr. Privett said "I don't like the sound of that" but Grandma Privett said "I've made lemon meringue pie and chocolate-and-vanilla checkerboard cake with double icing so I say we just tuck into that and take it for granted the weatherman got it wrong as usual" which was a big relief for me. When we finished eating as much as we could we went outside and took turns doing Fetch with Morty but the second I heard *"Stay tooooned for Nooooze at Eight"* I ran back inside.

I made it to the kitchen for "Brought to you by Ed's Stockyards And Auction, It Smells Like Profit" and got to where the grown-ups were standing by the radio on the sideboard for "NOW, more on

THE BIG BLOW." *"Bing-Bong"* "Great Falls Montana is picking up the pieces after today's freak wind blew through town shattering windows, sending shingles flying, and causing a two-car pileup on Highway 91 before it ZIG-ZAGGED over to Fairfield and – still on a RAMPAGE – charged straight up to Dutton. It now looks like this UNSTOPPABLE storm has its EYE trained on Shelby."

When Mrs. Privett said "It's way past your bedtimes girls" Darlene said "But Mom, you HAVE to let us stay up and listen to the next news" but her Dad said "That's not until ten o'clock" but Grandpa Privett said "I figure they're so worried about all this that none of them's going to sleep anyways so how about we all play Chinese Checkers until the ten o'clock news" and Grandma Privett brought the cake out again and we tried to have a good time.

"Stay tooooned for Nooooze at Ten" "Brought to you by Don's Lumber, Selling Alberta One Tree at a Time. NOW, BREAKING NEWS." *"Bing-Bong"* "Montana State Troopers have BLOCKED OFF Highway 91 to all traffic for the foreseeable future. Closer to home, Provincial authorities have just announced the CLOSURE of the Border Crossing at Coutts until further notice."

Mr. Privett said "I'm sorry kids. I know how much you were looking forward to the big party, but I'm afraid it's not going to happen." Mrs. Privett said "It's very late and we've all had an awfully long day so how about we all scoot off to bed – UH-UH-UH, no tears!" and she told Rosy and me "In the morning we'll sort out how to find your parents and get you heading home."

Nobody in the house was still up. I was lying in the middle between Rosy and Eleanor with Darlene crosswise at the foot of the bed who were all asleep except me. I crawled over top of Eleanor because nothing wakes her up and found my sundress on the floor in the dark and unbuttoned the pocket and took out my bag of lucky teeth and tiptoed down the stairs and through the kitchen and snuck out the back door and told Morty "Shhh it's just me" and I walked out into the yard and stood there for a minute with my evening-gown nightie blowing around and around my legs and then I looked up at the sky that was full of a million stars and I said "You're the only one who can fix this."

49. The United States Of America

I woke up because Mr. Privett was yelling "RISE AND SHINE EVERYBODY. NO TIME TO WASTE. WE'VE GOT A PARTY TO GO TO" and we all went running down to the kitchen and Mrs. Privett said "It's true. We just heard the six o'clock news and they said that right about midnight the wind died down as fast as it had come up and the authorities just opened the Border Crossing and the State Troopers opened Highway 91 and—" and Mr. Privett said "And if you kids can eat breakfast, get dressed, get your stuff together and be in the car before I count to a hundred we can be in The States by ten o'clock. ONE... TWO..."

We made it to Coutts fifteen minutes earlier than he said and we stopped at the Border Crossing and Mr. Privett rolled down his window and talked to the man and showed him his wallet and lickety-split we were in THE UNITED STATES OF AMERICA which looked a lot more like Canada than I thought it would. We were in The States for at least ten whole minutes before Rosy yelled "THERE IT IS" and we saw the big sign up ahead saying FORT LIVELY HOTEL & SALOON with the even bigger words ROOMS EATS DRINKS LIVE MUSIC DANCING painted above it so you could read it going either way on The 91. Sticking out of the ground when we turned in was another sign saying HOTEL WITH SALOON FOR SALE. The first thing we saw in the parking lot was a Honolulu Blue Metallic Buick Super and Rosy and me barely waited for the car to stop before we were out of it and through the door under the word SALOON.

Mommy and Daddy were sitting at a table with Miss Paisley and Chuck The Buck and an old man and we ran and kissed Mommy and Daddy and hugged Miss Paisley and said Hi to Chuck The Buck and met Mr. Old Curly Watling and in case they hadn't heard we told them all about THE BIG BLOW and about crops shattering and shingles being uprooted and then we told them about every single person and thing we saw and did and ate in Flatte Butte, Biggar and Medicine Hat.

Then we saw through the window the Beddoes' long black Cadillac drive up and park right in front of the SALOON and we all quick hurried outside. Bucky was first out and then Diddy and then his Grand-mère and then Mr. and Mrs. Beddoes and then I was shocked to see Miss Talbot get out because she wasn't even invited since she didn't help find Miss Paisley or anything but she told Rosy and me "I was worried you might have problems explaining all the changes to the Edmonton girls" which we hadn't even thought about so PHEW for that. Then Mr. Beddoes opened the trunk and Chuck The Buck helped him carry the Hip without getting too much blood on themselves over to the barbecue pit that was already hot and ready and Daddy who used to be a veterinarian on-the-side and knows a lot about animals stuck the spit through the right place in the Hip.

Just then a horn honked out on The 91 and we saw the red K.C.F.C Kohler & Cohen Fine Construction truck with our shiny silver playhouse on the back turn off and pull into the parking lot. There was barely time for Mommy and Daddy to introduce Nate and Sara and Essie and David Cohen to everybody when the Cappellettos' green station wagon full of Manny, Carlotta, Becca, Nico, Nina and Nonna drove in from Sylvan Lake.

Next came the Alvarez family on the second day of their camping honeymoon to New Mexico and Old Curly pointed to where the campground was nearby and Mr. Alvarez left his wife Connie and his daughter Bunny with us and went off to set up their tent right away in order to make sure they got the best campsite.

We heard "YOO-HOO" and in came the Gilroys who had spent the night in Great Falls with Marji's Grandma who they said was alive with no windows broke and all her shingles still on.

And then the Mormon Librarian Miss Alma Nielsen drove in and Rosy and I introduced her to everybody and she introduced all of us to Miss Pearly Pitt.

Pretty close behind them was a blue car that I knew was the Uprights getting here from the Bible Camp outside of Foremost but it stopped before it got all the way in as if maybe they didn't know if they were at the right place or not so Rosy and I ran over and waved at Peggy and Joy through the back window and yelled "YIPPEE YOU'RE HERE!"

Last of all was two very nice cars that drove in together that turned out to be Uncle Cyril and Auntie Nurse Beryl who left their Honeymoon Suite in the Palliser Hotel in Calgary that morning and stopped at The Prince of Wales Hotel in Waterton for a nice lunch with Nigel Oswald who has his own car so they drove down at the same time.

Pretty soon the grown-ups were all sitting in groups in the shade telling each other over and over again exactly where they were and what they were doing and what they were eating when they first heard about THE BIG BLOW and where they were and what they were doing and what they were eating when they heard it was all over – except for Mr. Pankhurst, Nigel Oswald and Old Curly who were walking around inside the Hotel opening and closing doors and I think talking turkey about something. Miss Talbot said it was the perfect time for her and us kids to sneak into the empty Saloon and check out the place and figure out where everything should happen and show all the changes to the Edmonton girls.

We'd been in the Saloon for quite a long time when we heard a big racket out front so we ran outside to see what was going on and Old Curly was ringing a cowbell and yelling "GRUB'S READY. COME AND GET IT" and everybody in the whole place lined up to fill their plates with barbecued Hip and baked potatoes and baked beans and corn-on-the-cob in melted butter and dill pickles and hot buns and carry them to tables inside the Saloon. When everybody was sitting down Chuck The Buck said into the microphone "RAISE YOUR GLASS TO CYRIL PANKHURST FOR THE FREE BOOZE" and we all stood up and I held my orange pop up for Mr. Pankhurst at the next table to see. "AND NOW RAISE YOUR KNIFE TO MADAM DAY-JARDANS FROM MONTREAL FOR THE BEEF" and she pretended to be scared of all the knives pointed at her and everybody laughed. Then Mr. Pankhurst walked to the microphone with his glass held up and said "HERE'S TO THE HAPPY COUPLE, PENNY AND CHARLIE BUCKLER" and I put my knife down and picked my glass up again and HOO-HOO-HOORAYED them and then Chuck The Buck went back up with his glass and said "THANKS FOR COMING EVERYONE AND HERE'S TO OUR GENEROUS HOST CURLY WATLING" and Old Curly got up and said "OH FOR CRYIN' OUT LOUD THE FOOD'S GETTIN' COLD" and everybody dug in.

When I was waiting at the Bar to get another Orange-Pop-Over-Ice I was next in line behind Peggy's Dad Mr. Upright and I heard him say "Is there a bottle of something we could have without alcohol in it?" and Chuck The Buck said "Gosh I'm afraid not. But I do keep a stock of Communion Wine here for when Pastor Tipler runs out" and Mr. Upright said "Well I guess we'll have to make do with that then. Do you have any very small glasses?" and Chuck The Buck said "As a matter of fact I do."

And then you could help yourself at a long table full of nothing but desserts that Old Curly's cook made and that Mrs. Privett and Mrs. Cohen and Mrs. Gilroy and Mommy brought with them and then the table with the Gilroys and the Privetts at it who were getting along like a house on fire started up with "WE ARE TABLE NUMBER ONE, NUMBER ONE, NUMBER ONE. WE ARE TABLE NUMBER ONE, WHERE THE HECK IS TWO" and then every single other table played along. Us thirteen kids were TABLE NUMBER FOUR which was really two tables pushed together. Then Miss Paisley went up and said into the microphone "I didn't throw my bouquet in Cardston last Saturday because the women at the wedding were either too old or already married but even though the flowers are a little worse for wear I'm going to throw it here. So you single ladies come and stand in a bunch on the dance floor" and Miss Alma Nielsen and Miss Helen Talbot ran and did that, and she threw it. They both made a good grab for it but even though Miss Nielsen was the one who already had a fiancé, Miss Talbot was quicker.

After that everybody went outside to walk off their big meal or sit on the grass for a while but pretty soon the Fort Lively House Band and the Guest Musicians went back inside and Daddy the

Guest Conductor started them up playing When It's Swingtime In The Rockies so everybody moved back into the Saloon. That's when Mommy and Miss Pitt and Mrs. Beddoes came and whispered to us kids to sneak upstairs with them.

Miss Pearly Pitt had packed her combs and curlers and hot irons and clips and elastics and barrettes and bobby-pins and hairspray and Mrs. Loretta Beddoes had brought her big Make-up Kit from the Funeral Home and they'd put a sign on the Beddoes' guestroom door saying HAIR AND MAKE-UP. Mommy and Daddy's door said WARDROBE and she had the ten costumes she'd made and Diddy's that his Grand-mère had brought all laid out plus her sewing kit and safety pins just in case. And then the three of them made it all even more grown-up and exciting by saying that us performers COULD CALL THEM BY THEIR FIRST NAMES FOR TONIGHT ONLY.

The third time Miss Talbot came upstairs to see if we were ready yet Loretta said "Only one eyebrow to go" and Isobel said "Everyone's in costume" and Pearly said "I'm just gonna spray 'em all one more time so those curls aren't goin' anywhere". Miss Talbot said "Okay then I'll go tell Chuck The Buck FIVE MINUTES and I'll send Curly up with his Master Key. Remember as soon as he switches off the upstairs lights you all run quiet-as-mice to your proper rooms and shut the door behind you and then listen hard for your Cue." David who was wearing his Stage Hand's costume of black pants and a black shirt went downstairs with her. His first job was supposed to be handing out one Program to every person in the Saloon but when Mrs. Connie Alvarez brought them with her, she told us that Liddy Frisch had got her to run off two hundred just to be on the REALLY safe side. So now David was giving everybody extra ones to take home for themselves and for their friends and neighbours as keepsakes forever.

On her way out the door Isobel kissed me and whispered "Give 'em all you got!" and I peeked out and watched her and Loretta and Pearly walk along the fancy long balcony that you can look down into the Saloon from and then turn and walk nicely side-by-side down the big wide wood stairs in their summer dresses and high heels like they'd been up to nothing at all upstairs. A minute later I saw Old Curly come up the stairs and walk along the balcony unlocking all the guestroom doors. Then he headed back downstairs and when he got to the bottom he reached over and switched off the balcony lights. I whispered "PLACES EVERYONE" and we all quick tiptoed out and each of us girls ran to the room Miss Talbot had told us was ours and shut the door behind us and Diddy snuck down the back stairs.

50. My Stairway To Stardom

I opened my door just a bit so I could see what was happening below. Miss Talbot was standing beside the stairs looking nervous, David was almost done handing out the Programs and since I've been singing Tangerine my whole life I could tell that the band was almost to the end of it. One second later Daddy whipped his hand to the side and they all stopped exactly at the same time. Then Chuck The Buck said into the microphone "I'm going to ask you people on the dance floor to please go back to your tables now because we've got such a big surprise for you that you're gonna want to be sitting down for it." As soon as everybody was sitting he said "Some very special friends of Penny's and mine have put together a big spectacular production number to help us celebrate tonight and I'm proud as punch to introduce them to you."

Sticks the Ringer from Missoula started up a perfect drum roll, David switched on the balcony lights and Chuck The Buck said "Ladies and Gentlemen, LOOK UP." Everybody did. And he said "I give you... THE CHILDREN OF THE CHORUS!

"FROM FLATTE BUTTE, SASKATCHEWAN... BUNNY ALVAREZ." Bunny quick POPPED out of Door #1 at the end of the balcony, ran to the stairs, went down four steps and over a bit to the Left and stood with her hands on her hips and her bright red lipstick lips puckered up as if she was saying 'OOH!' "ESSIE COHEN" and Essie POPPED out of Door #10 at the other end of the balcony, ran down one step below Bunny except over to the Right in the exact same pose. "ELEANOR PRIVETT", POP out of Door #2 and down one more step on the Left. "DARLENE PRIVETT", POP out of #9 down one more on the Right. "FROM EDMONTON,

ALBERTA... PEGGY UPRIGHT", POP out of #3 one down on the Left. "BECCA CAPPELLETTO", out of #8 and one down on the Right. Sticks never stopped his drum roll for one second. "MARJI GILROY", out of #4, down Left. "JOY UPRIGHT", out of #7 down Right. "AND DANCE CAPTAIN ROSY KOHLER!" Rosy stepped nicely out of Door #5, did a perfect Jazz Pirouette, swung her Right leg over the Left banister, *WHOOSH,* slid all the way to the bottom, threw her Left leg back over the post, did a DOUBLE Pirouette – which got a big cheer from the audience – and Jazz-Strutted up three steps over on the Left. "FROM MONTREAL, QUEBEC... DIDDY DESJARDINS!" Stage Hand David walked over to the door that goes into the Hotel Lobby and swung it wide open. Diddy stepped into the Saloon wearing black tights, black dance boots, a snow white leotard and a gold lamé jacket with black satin lapels and did six Grand Jetés with just one wobble nobody would notice across the Saloon to the bottom of the stairs and took one step up and stood over on the Right.

Sticks did a big Da-Da, Da-Da, Da-Da-DUM on his drums and the audience started up whistling and clapping and cheering while Diddy posed like Fred Astaire and all nine girls stood there for a long minute looking so beautiful in their skimpy snug shiny-gold satin rompers with no sleeves and one row of red fringe around their hips and one row of red fringe around their scoop necks plus bare legs and black party shoes and their hair done up in curls with shiny-gold ribbons and their make-up on good and thick with lots of rouge and turquoise eye shadow and dark eyebrows with their hands on their hips and all of their bright red lipstick lips saying 'OOH!'

Chuck The Buck said "AND NOW!" Drum roll. "THE HEADLINER OF TONIGHT'S SHOW!" Cymbals. "POSY KOHLER!" I stepped out of Door #6 right at the top of the stairs and posed for one second. Or maybe two. Then down the stairs I went, nice and slow, one step at a time, with the drum roll going and going, wearing the same costume and hair and make-up as the other girls except my skimpy snug satin romper was bright red and my fringes were shiny gold and instead of ribbons in my hair I had red feathers and I was the only one who asked Loretta for a beauty mark on my one cheek. When I got to my step being two up from the bottom I posed with both my arms straight up in the air and the audience cheered and clapped even longer than I'd figured they would.

Chuck The Buck waited for the audience to settle down and said in an important voice "Fort Lively Hotel and Saloon is proud to present The INTERNATIONAL Lucky Jazz Dance Club performing the World Premiere of MY STAIRWAY TO STARDOM."

Daddy said "A-one, a-two", Sticks started brushing a drum, the Dance Captain said "AND" and us eleven dancers did Jazz-walk, Jazz-walk, Jazz-walk, back-and-forth, back-and-forth each on our own step in time with Sticks' brushes while we all said together, not too loud:

"Practise... practise... practise... practise... practise... practise... practise... practise... practise... practise... practise... practise."

Bonnie Beagle made up the routine for us but Madame Desjardins, Miss Talbot, Rosy and me changed quite a bit of it to be on the stairs and balcony back in Oddfellows Hall as soon as we heard Fort Lively Saloon had a big Busby Berkeley Staircase.

241

Sticks quick stopped brushing, The Dance Captain whispered "WAIT FOR THE DOWNBEAT", Daddy said "Hit it" and the whole band started playing Mr. Gilliland's jazz music which was as good as if Duke Ellington or somebody wrote it or maybe even better. We sang Verse #1 while we did grapevine-grapevine-grapevine over and over along our own step. The words were mostly by Rosy and me.

"I'm on Tour, look at me, it's Opening Day,
I'm not sure, but fingers crossed, I'm on my way.
Maybe today, people will say, you'll go far,
They might even say, HEYYYY, you're gonna be a STAR."

Then Daddy quick stopped the music like we planned. Miss Talbot had to Cue two of the Flatte Butte girls – I won't say which ones – because as usual they weren't ready but as soon as we all got into our Pin-Up-Girl show-off poses we yelled:

"LOOK AT THIS MAKE-UP, LOOK AT THIS POSE, LOOK AT THIS HAIR-DO, LOOK AT THESE CLOTHES."

Then we sang Verse #2 while we did chassé-chassé-chassé-touch, chassé-chassé-cut from one end of our step to the other and back, twice.

"I can fence, I can tumble, sing and dance,
I can act, I can juggle, gimme a chance.
I can swim, I parlez French, I stand on my head,
I even do archer-REEE, to help me get ahead."

Then Darlene and Joy put their hands on their hips and yelled all bossy-like:

"YOU THINK YOU'RE SO GOOD. WHAT IF SOMEBODY'S BETTER? AND NOTHING IS FOR FREE!"

And the rest of us yelled back just as bossy:

"HOLD YOUR HORSES, WE'VE GOT RESOURCES, JUST YOU WAIT AND SEE!"

Next came the CHORUS which we sang doing Hip-walk, Hip-walk, Hip-walk along our step that's almost a Jazz-walk only you wiggle your hips a lot more. Madame Desjardins' very good suggestion was for us to turn around and take one step up every time we sing 'I'll climb My Stairway To Stardom'.

"I'll do whatever it takes
'Til my Big Break comes along.
I'll climb My Stairway To Stardom
(STEP UP)
And I'll keep singing this song."

Verse #3 was supposed to be just me singing while Diddy and I did a Couples Dance in front of the stairs. But the Box-Step is so tricky that Miss Talbot got the others to sing along with me. At least David shone his spotlight on only Diddy and me the whole time.

"Up my stairway, step by step, song by song,
When I'm best, in all the West, I'll mosey along,
'Cause I won't stop, 'til I'm on top, and I can say
Hey look at me, HOO-HOO-HOORAAYYY, I'm on BROADWAY."

Then I ran back to my step, David handed Diddy his flat hat, Diddy snapped it and it turned into a Top Hat which he put on. David handed him his cane which Diddy twirled three times careful not to hit anyone and then did two slow Pivot Turns while tap-tap-

tapping his cane on the floor and then he stood still in his Fred Astaire show-off pose and all us girls yelled:

"OOH-LA-LA!"

Then came the CHORUS again. This time we all just did step-touches on the spot and sang while Rosy did The Lindy Hop going both ways on her step as a solo because nobody else could do it.

"I'll do whatever it takes
'Til my Big Break comes along.
I'll climb My Stairway To Stardom
     (ALL STEP UP)
And keep on singing this song."

Then the music STOPPED. Us Dancers did a FREEZE. And David shone his spotlight on the Saloon's swinging doors.

BUCKY BURST THROUGH THEM with cap-guns blazing. He pretend-galloped around the whole Saloon shooting up a storm while Chuck The Buck yelled "WATCH OUT GUYS 'N' GALS! IT'S ROPIN', RIDIN', SHARP-SHOOTIN' BUCKY BEDDOES!"

Then Bucky stopped fast, holstered his guns and Mr. Alvarez lifted him up on top of the Bar and handed him a Lassoo already wound up and ready to go. Bucky took it and started spinning it 'round and 'round over his head while all us girls and Diddy ran and got into a straight line below him along the front of the Bar with our arms linked together. Then Daddy quick brought his arm down, the band started playing at their loudest so far, Rosy said "AND!" and UP went all eleven Left legs.

We'd been practising and practising our Kick Line which is the trickiest part of the whole routine because everybody has to kick up the very same leg at the very same time and Madame Desjardins says nobody's leg goes higher than anybody else's even if you can. Right kick, Left kick, Right kick, Left kick, up-down, up-down, up-down, up-down, while we yelled out in perfect time to our kicks:

"<u>LOOK</u> at those <u>PALM</u> trees,
 <u>LOOK</u> at those <u>CARS</u>,
 <u>LOOK</u> at the <u>DI</u>amonds on those
 <u>MOOO</u>vie… <u>STARS</u>.
 <u>LOOK</u> at those <u>LETT</u>ers,
 <u>LOOK</u> at them <u>SHINE</u>,
 <u>WHAT</u> do they <u>SAY</u>? It's the
 <u>HOLL</u>ywood <u>SIGN</u>."

The music STOPPED. We quick turned to face the bar and did a Bump-Your-Bum at the audience. The rest of them stayed with their bums stuck out while I turned around to the audience and yelled:

"HA-HA WILLIAM MORRIS, YOU MADE A MISTAKE, I FOUND ANOTHER AGENT, YOU MISSED YOUR BIG BREAK."

And I did three very good Forward Hip Thrusts.

Mr. Alvarez lifted Bucky down off the Bar and he galloped over to sit with his parents and the rest of us ran back to our steps for THE BIG FINALE. We got our fringes going on the downbeat and started SHIMMY-SHIMMY-ING as fast as we could go and still be able to sing at the same time and we did the CHORUS again, but this time with exciting new words.

"I did whatever it took,
I shimmied and shook all along.
I climbed My Stairway To Stardom
    (STEP UP)
Now the WHOLE WORLD'S SINGING MY SONG."

The girls' shiny red shimmy-shimmy fringes and my gold ones were shaking and Diddy was Paddle-Turning on the spot with his cane rat-a-tat-tatting on the floor. It was all very RIVETING. Then as a surprise for the audience we started up the CHORUS again with even more different words while all of us including Diddy SHIMMY-SHIMMY-SHIMMY-SHIMMIED like crazy!

"They know my name in Montana
I'll be famous before very long."

Then we stopped shimmy-shimmy-ing and quick Jazz-Stamped all the way up every step and spread out along the balcony with me in the middle right at the top of the stairs and we all posed with our hands straight up over our heads and sang:

"NOW I'M ON TOP OF MY STAIRWAY
AND STARDOM IS WHERE I BELO-O-O-O-O-O-NG."

The second we finished our *"NG"* in *"BELONG"*, Daddy whipped his hand sideways to stop the band. Nobody made another peep.

I dropped down into a Splits and quick whispered "KILL THE LIGHTS."

I got back up fast and when the lights came on we were all standing perfectly still in show-off poses and we stayed like that in order to be wildly effective. It worked. We got given a Standing Ovation that lasted so long Chuck The Buck said into the microphone "YOU KIDS ARE GONNA HAVE TO BOW SOONER OR LATER OR THE CROWD'LL GO NUTS!" So we did but the crowd went nuts anyway.

It was perfect.

Then the Band took a break, Old Curly put some Western Music on the P.A. and turned the ordinary lights back up. Us dancers plus Bucky and David spent the next two hours signing our autographs on all two hundred of our very excellent Programs.

The INTERNATIONAL Lucky Jazz Dance Club
Presents
MY STAIRWAY TO STARDOM

CHOREOGRAPHER	Bonbon Beagelle
MUSIC WRITER	Mr. Gilliland
WORDS WRITERS	Rosalind & Paulette Kohler

The Children Of The Chorus

HEADLINER	Paulette Kohler
DANCE CAPTAIN	Rosalind Kohler
DANCERS	Bernice Alvarez,
	Esther Cohen
	Rebecca Cappelletto
	Eleanor Privett
	Darlene Privett
	Margaret Upright
	Joy Upright
	Marjorie Gilroy
	Didier Desjardins

| TRICK ROPER | Wilbur Beddoes |
| USHER/LIGHTS/PROPS | David Cohen |

Fort Lively House Band

Lead Singer/Guitar	Charlie Buckler
Fiddle/Vocals	Buddy Vickers
Mandolin/Slide Guitar	Marty Wannell

Guest Musicians

Bandleader/Saxophone	Max Kohler
Piano	Jeannie Gilroy
Drums	Sticks Kirkpatrick
Trombone	George Privett

Helpful Grown-Ups

Costume Maker	Isobel Kohler
Make-Up Artist	Loretta Beddoes
Hairdresser	Pearly Pitt
Stage Manager	Helen Talbot
Roping Expert	Alberto Alvarez
Creative Suggester	Delphine Desjardins
Program Editor	Liddy Frisch
Program Flunky	Connie Alvarez

Uncle Cyril and Auntie Nurse Beryl told Rosy and me one more time how talented we are and then they hugged us goodbye because they were leaving to drive to The Grand Union Hotel in Fort Benton for the last night of their honeymoon but then right after they left the Saloon Albi Alvarez told everyone over the microphone be sure to stick around because he'd brought Fireworks for later so I quick ran out to the parking lot to warn them what they'd be missing but too bad for them they'd already left.

It didn't get dark enough for Fireworks until after ten o'clock so us kids got to stay up late eating desserts and drinking Pop-Over-Ice and Jazz Walking and Shimmy-Shimmy-ing to whatever the band was playing until it was time to watch them get lit and go off in the empty lot next door which was very loud and exciting and when some cars out on The 91 stopped to watch and honked their horns it was even louder and more exciting.

51. The Party's Over

I was standing at the window of the room they put all us kids to bed on quilts on the floor in because they needed the mattresses for grown-ups. Every one of my best friends and Rosy were asleep behind me with their costumes still on and nobody told us to wash our makeup off so none of us did. I was leaning out with my elbows on the window sill so I could see what was going on with the grown-ups down below who were all outside because it was too hot in the Saloon but nothing interesting was happening.

Somebody had rolled the piano out into the yard and Mrs. Gilroy was playing Home-Home On The Range with Buddy Vickers singing, Marty Wannell playing slide guitar and Sticks Kirkpatrick on drums. Mr. Gilroy was shaking his maracas very slowly with his eyes closed.

Mr. Beddoes' black jacket was off and I don't know why but his tie was wound around his head and Loretta was sitting on his lap talking in his ear.

Madame Delphine Desjardins was holding a fancy glass and box-stepping with Old Curly in the parking lot.

You could tell that Mr. and Mrs. Privett were trying to do the Shimmy-Shimmy but it wasn't working out because they wouldn't be serious and stop themselves laughing.

Pearly was drinking something pink right out of a pitcher and cutting Miss Alma Nielsen the Mormon Librarian's hair very-very short.

Mr. Cohen was dancing on top of the outdoors bar with a bottle on his head and Mrs. Cohen was clapping and laughing like crazy but he could have easily fallen off and broken his neck or the bottle if he wasn't careful.

Nonna Cappelletto was playing with little Nico and Nina who Becca says are allowed to stay up late because they're European so that her son Manny could dance with his wife Carlotta for the first time since she got T.B.

Mr. Alvarez was riding a neighbour's horse bareback up and down the road out front with Mrs. Alvarez holding on to him for dear life even though she didn't have to they were going so slow.

Mr. and Mrs. Upright had fallen asleep under the Fort Lively Hotel & Saloon sign with their empty bottle of Communion Wine on the ground beside them.

Daddy was way at the other end of the yard playing a whole different song to Isobel on his sax that might have been It Only Happens When I Dance With You.

Miss Talbot was still holding her bouquet and slow dancing with Nigel Oswald.

Miss Paisley and Chuck The Buck had disappeared again.

THE END

ABOUT THE AUTHOR

Val Brandt has written plays, opera librettos, musicals, cantatas, documentaries, speeches, poems, short stories, song lyrics, commercials, international marketing campaigns and wide-ranging Web content – while based in Edmonton, Toronto, London UK, Vancouver and countless sublets and hotel rooms around the world. So it's no surprise that her debut novel, *A Bag of Lucky Teeth*, is peopled with quirky characters doing extraordinary things under serendipitous circumstances.

Manufactured by Amazon.ca
Bolton, ON